family
pieces

misa rush

ISBN: 0615391583
ISBN-13: 9780615391588
ThINK Write Publications, LLC

For Maeli & Graden

∾ *Dream Big* ∾

acknowledgments

Thank you first to my wonderful husband who watched as I stayed up in the wee-wee hours, night after night, never really knowing if anyone would ever read my work; to my neighbor and friend Anita Westlake who read and reread early versions not to mention her patience at having to listen to me rant on our nightly runs; to Shannon DeGrado and Brian Fisher at Go Fish Promotions in Scottsdale, Arizona for my incredibly perfect front cover. Thanks to Bellamonte Women's book club for giving brutally honest feedback on a first draft. Thank you to Tara Lehr, Amanda Scott, Emily Dille, Michelle Richards, Andy Shaw, Dawn Weiss and Kari Dean for giving early feedback and unending support. Thanks to Kristin Lindstrom at Flying Pig Media for your guidance. Finally, thank you to Mom and Dad for being my cheerleaders at anything I do.

preface

One Choice. One Secret.

Choices are made every day. Some bear no consequence. Others have life-altering results. I should know. My mother made a choice. She kept a secret. Her intentions were pure. With every beat of my heart, I believe she thought keeping her secret was in everyone's best interest. She thought the secret would be buried with her, never to be revealed. She thought wrong.

~ 1 ~

Karsen woke before the sound of her alarm and prepared herself for the first day of the new semester. A nervous energy brewed in the pit of her stomach. In her junior year at Arizona State University, she didn't remember ever feeling anxious over a few new classes; nonetheless, it was an uncomfortable sensation that she simply couldn't shake. It burrowed deep down inside like the tickle one gets in their throat just before a full-blown cold.

She pulled her burgundy cashmere sweater over her head, attempting to bury the uneasiness with the giddiness of wearing a new outfit. The sweater had been a Christmas present from her mother, and she loved the soft feel against her skin. Maybe her discomfort stemmed from the strained conversation she had had with her mother the day before. *Maybe she should call and apologize*, she thought.

She dialed her mom's cell number, which went straight to voice mail.

"Hey, Mom, sorry I missed you. I'm headed out to class, but I just wanted to say sorry for our fight. I'll try you back tonight. I love you." She hung up promising herself that she'd call again in the evening.

Karsen reached beneath her sweater and pulled out her necklace. Closing her eyes, she tenderly pressed the end of the silver charm against her lips. She took a deep breath and exhaled slowly, trying to release her tension. "Today is going to be a great day." She smiled and repeated this mantra to herself.

Looking back, Karsen couldn't remember a time when she hadn't worn her necklace. She found herself fiddling with it often particularly when she felt worried or homesick, just as she did now.

"Some people may think it's silly," Karsen remarked once while explaining the meaning of her necklace's puzzle-shaped charm to her boyfriend James near the beginning of their relationship. "Somehow it makes me feel connected when I'm away. Like part of a bigger plan – my family is always with me no matter where they are." James had listened half-heartedly, more interested in unbuttoning her shirt than learning about her family history.

Karsen opened her eyes and glanced in the mirror one last time. Her dark hair fell just past her shoulders in a sleek-straight style that was both elegant and trendy. Even though she'd heard how pretty she was over the years, a twinge of insecurity always nestled itself in the back of her mind. She felt average at best compared to the flawless beauties flocking the campus and still wondered often how she'd landed a guy like James.

She dabbed one last coat of gloss across her lips and then, satisfied with her appearance, gathered her book bag and headed to campus where she'd arranged to meet Hanna outside the physical science building.

ᕲᕳ

Arriving at their meeting spot, Karsen waited for Hanna. Hanna and Karsen had been paired as roommates the first day of their freshman year and had been inseparable ever since. Karsen glanced down at her watch. Their chemistry class was about to begin and the perfectionist in her hated to be tardy.

"Hurry up! We're going to be late," Karsen yelled, waving Hanna on when she finally spotted her. Hanna scurried toward her, immaculately dressed in a cream-colored sweater, brown hounds-tooth skirt with coordinating chocolate-brown knee high boots. Hanna's knack for finding designer clothing on clearance, mixed with her natural beauty and perfect blond hair, made her the spitting image of a model out of the girl's favorite fashion magazine, *Urbane*.

"Sorry. Sophia was talking my ear off. I couldn't get away," Hanna muttered, catching her breath as she reached Karsen's side. Her cheeks were flushed even though the temperature barely topped sixty degrees on the mild January morning.

"What's going on now?" Karsen asked, adding, "cute outfit by the way."

"Thanks. Sale-rack, Macy's," Hanna said. The two girls set off toward class, walking at a brisk pace. "Anyway I would've been here on time, but you know my sorority sister. Just the usual 'my boyfriend broke up with me over break' saga."

"What else is new?" Karsen laughed at the 'on-again off-again' relationship of their mutual friend, thinking to herself again how lucky she was to have found James. Certainly, they'd had a few quarrels, but they had never ventured anywhere near break-up territory. "They break up every holiday. I'm beginning to think he does it so he can welch out on buying her a gift."

"You could be right," Hanna smirked. "Anyway, how was your break?"

"Good. My parents flew back to Indiana yesterday. I always look forward to seeing them, and I hate to admit it, but I was kind of ready for them to go. My mom couldn't stop grumbling about James."

"What about now?" Hanna opened the door to the lecture hall, holding it open for Karsen.

"She still doesn't think he's right for me. We've always been so close. I just don't get it. Sheesh, I don't do drugs. I don't smoke. I get straight A's and I'm her daughter. Don't you think she should trust my judgment?"

Hanna wrinkled her cute button nose. "You'd think. But, maybe she's just worried about you. He did have quite the reputation before you two hooked up."

Karsen shrugged. "Maybe, but she doesn't know that. Plus we've been together now for two years. Anyway, who are you to judge? You're the one who introduced us in the first place." Had it not been for Hanna's prodding, she doubted she would have ever had the courage to even speak to him. But thank goodness she had.

"Yes, I know. But only because I was tired of hearing how perfect he was. And you took it from there by spilling coffee all over him. How was I to know that he'd find your klutziness attractive?" Hanna said with a laugh. "Anyway, has your mom liked any of your boyfriends?"

"Not really," Karsen said, still cringing from the memory of the coffee caper, maybe one of her most embarrassing moments ever.

"See? I'm sure it's just a "mom" thing," Hanna reassured her friend.

Karsen hoped she was right. She still couldn't imagine why her mother didn't like James. He was three years older than her, but what was three years in the scope of forever? He had already graduated and was even taking masters classes while launching the start of a more than promising sales career. The more she thought about him, the more perfect he seemed, which didn't matter since she was unmistakably in love with him already.

The lecture hall buzzed with chatter as the eighty-some students settled in. The girls secured two spots together mid-way up the center. The seats were red cloth, slightly faded and worn from overuse, each with an old-style writing desk that swiveled up and across to write on.

"So, what did James get you for Christmas?" Hanna asked, settling into her seat.

"Not a ring." Karsen's voice bled disappointment. Even though she and James had never specifically discussed their future, Karsen couldn't help but think that surely he'd propose soon. Their relationship had progressed like clockwork. The natural next step was to live together, but Karsen knew that would never fly with her mother unless there was a ring promising a commitment.

"Maybe he wants to wait until you graduate."

"But that's another year or more. We could at least get engaged." Karsen bent over and shuffled through her bag, then pulled out a magazine page she'd torn out of *Brides*. "Look."

"Wow! That's an amazing dress!" Hanna grabbed the page from Karsen and examined it in detail. "It must cost a small fortune."

"Only half a small fortune and James is making good money. I figure I can splurge. After all, you only get married once, right?"

"Yeah, usually, I guess," Hanna murmured sarcastically in agreement as she handed the page back to Karsen. "Why are you in such a rush to get married anyway? You're only twenty-one."

"Seriously, have you met my boyfriend? It's like I've landed in my very own fairy tale. He's everything I could've ever imagined for a husband and more. Why would I let him get away?" Karsen met James when she was a freshman. As cliché as she knew it sounded, for her, it was love at first sight. His dark hair and muscular build made her knees buckle, but it was his dark espresso eyes that she couldn't peel her own from.

"I'm sure your mom will come around soon. At least she cares. My mom's too busy with her own drama to care about mine. I'm sure she just wants you to be happy."

"You're probably right. Guess I'm lucky to have a mom that cares *too* much," Karsen smiled. "I'll talk it out with her tonight. I can't stand it when we argue."

Before Hanna could segue into another topic, the professor bellowed over a small shirt-clipped microphone, bringing the class to order. "Good morning class. Welcome to Chemistry 351. If you're not supposed to be here, this is the best time to exit." Karsen tucked the picture back into her bag then focused her attention toward the front.

∽

An hour later, Karsen and Hanna exited the science building and were welcomed by a crisp blue, cloudless sky. The sun beamed down, making Karsen wish her sweater had been a cardigan that she could shed. She felt a vibration through the front pocket of her bag and scrambled to free her pink-and-clear Swarovski crystal-encrusted phone before it went to voice mail.

"Hi, Daddy!" Karsen answered in an upbeat voice. The three-hour time difference made it three in the afternoon in Indiana, an odd time, she thought, for her dad to be calling.

"New Blackberry?" Hanna asked.

"Shhh," Karsen said turning away and plugging her open ear. "Sorry, Dad. I couldn't hear you. Hanna was talking. We're just leaving chem class. What's up?"

"It's your mother," he started, his voice sounding much further away than the two thousand miles between them. "Honey, I'm afraid she's been in a car accident..."

"What?" Karsen's face drew white as she listened.

"What's wrong?" mouthed Hanna, her face immediately conveying her worry.

"Is she okay?"

"I'm sorry, honey," Carl Woods continued on the other end of the phone. His voice shook as he struggled to form the words. "There's no easy way to tell you this, but she's gone. Your mom is gone."

"No, No, NO!" Karsen gasped, slowly shaking her head in disbelief. Her eyes filled with tears, as a crippling constriction overtook her chest, causing her to a make a hiccup sound. "Oh God, oh my God, NO!"

The next morning, Karsen lay on the bed covers, knees curled up in a fetal position. Her tears had come and gone throughout the night; she hadn't slept more than a mere ten or twenty minutes. Karsen held the charm of her necklace tightly against her heart, her eyes fixed on the family photo on her dresser, the last family photo that would include her mother.

For the most part, Karsen's life to date had been picture-perfect. Against the odds, her parents were still happily married, and she'd been raised with her older brother in a typical middle-class home. She and her brother Brad, two years her senior and an aspiring stand-up comedian, had always been close. She had even followed him to the same college.

"Hey, sis," Brad said as he ran his hand soothingly over the top of her head. She had heard him enter the room but did not turn to look. Her eyes gazed into space as she continued to hold tight to the necklace. She couldn't move. She couldn't breathe. All she could do was let the tears stream down her cheeks.

"We've got to get going or we'll miss our flight," he coaxed, his voice deep and somber. Dark circles surrounded his usually vibrant brown eyes. His black hair looked disheveled and she could tell he hadn't slept either.

"I know." Her reply was barely audible. She had no recollection of how the airline tickets had been arranged or any other detail of their trip back home. Brad had taken care of everything.

"Are you packed?" He asked noticing the suitcase still open on the floor.

"Yeah," she said, unsure. She had haphazardly packed and couldn't recall if she put in enough clothes for the week. Her mind wandered, unable to focus on anything. Had she told her mother she loved her? She couldn't remember. She never imagined her mother would not be there for her. Who would help pick out her wedding dress? Who would share in the joy of her first child? *This can't be happening*, she thought. *This just can't be happening.*

Brad zipped her suitcase and placed it by the door. He pried apart the sticky, white paper tags still marking the flight information from Karsen's last trip, and placed the wad in the garbage. "Come on, sis. Hanna's waiting outside."

Karsen sniffled and dragged her unwilling shell of a body off of the bed. Every inch of her body felt numb. She felt like a zombie, a foreigner in her own body. Brad watched as she wiped her tears. He had shed his own in private. He knew more would come, but right now he needed to be strong. Someone had to be. He propped the door open with his foot as he waited for her to turn off the light, then they both left together.

Hanna waited by the car and watched as Karsen locked the front door. At a loss for the right words to say, she helped load their luggage into the cramped trunk of her less than glamorous 1998 Honda Civic. Unable to afford to fly back to Indiana with them, driving her friends to the airport seemed the least she could do.

"You know I'd come if I could," she finally said, interlinking her arm with Karsen.

"I know." Karsen gave Hanna's hand a slight squeeze before freeing herself and climbing into the back seat. She offered no elaboration. She didn't want to talk to anyone, not even her best friend. She just wanted someone to wake her up and tell her this was all a bad dream.

Hanna glanced at Brad. "You ready?" Hanna had known Brad since the first day she met Karsen and considered him handsome in a quirky sort of way, but she never thought of him too much beyond being her best friend's brother.

"Yeah." He nodded and climbed into the car.

༄

"Where is James anyway?" Brad asked Karsen as Hanna merged onto the exit toward the airport. He peered over the headrest from the passenger seat, waiting for Karsen's response. Karsen stared blankly out the window.

"Isn't he going to the funeral with you?" Hanna asked.

"Well...uh...no. He wanted to," Karsen fibbed. Her voice struggled not to crack. "It's just that...he just started his graduate classes and with his work, it's hard for him to get away right now."

"Right," Brad said sarcastically. The word escaped his mouth before he could stop it. He didn't intend to cause Karsen more grief under the circumstances. He just didn't understand what his sister saw in him.

"Brad, give him a break. He's under a lot of stress right now," Karsen fired back defensively. Her insides twisted into a knot as the words passed her lips. For the first time, Karsen had to admit her own disappointment in James.

Just as he did most nights, James had arrived at her apartment after work the night before. Letting himself in, he barely noticed that she didn't get up to greet him. "You won't believe the day I've had," he said heading straight to her fridge to grab a beer.

She sniffled.

"What's wrong with you?" His tone was less than sympathetic.

She didn't speak.

"Karsen," he set his beer down and sat beside her. "Really, what...did you get a B on a test or something? It can't be that bad."

"My mother..." She couldn't bring herself to say the words.

"What?"

She sat silent. Realizing how upset she was, he put his arms around her and pulled her closer. "What, hun?"

"My mother's dead."

"Oh God, K. I'm so sorry." She rested her head against his strong chest.

"She was in a car accident. How could this happen?"

"I'm sorry. I just don't know what to say." He held her, shocked himself at the news.

"Why? Why now?"

"Oh, K. I wish I could say something that would help. I just don't know." He was, for once, at a loss for words. "I'm so sorry."

"We're flying back tomorrow. Brad booked tickets for us, but I need you there. Please come."

"Karsen, I can't."

"James, please. I need you. I can't get through this alone."

"You're not alone. Brad and your dad will be with you."

"But I want you there. Please. The funeral isn't until Saturday. You won't have to miss much work; you can fly out Friday afternoon."

"I just…I just can't ask for time off. I'm sorry. I was going to tell you when I came in, but I'm just about to land a client that will almost guarantee me a promotion to district sales manager. I can't leave right now."

Karsen pulled back and glared directly into his deep brown eyes. "I'm sorry my mother's death didn't come at a more convenient time for you."

"Karsen, truly, you're being emotional."

"Of course I'm being emotional. My mother was not supposed to die." She couldn't believe during this period of greatest need he would not even ask for the time off work to be with her.

"You know I would go. I just can't leave town. Not this weekend."

Rather than force the issue, Karsen bit her tongue, telling herself that his focus and determination would be the driving force to secure their not-too distant future together.

The fact that Brad was upset about James didn't surprise her. He never hesitated to show his disapproval of his sister's relationships. It was no secret he didn't care for James. In her mind, this would have to change if he was going to be his brother-in-law someday. She once welcomed her ever-protective big brother's concern. Now she wished he'd simply give James a chance.

The car fell uncomfortably silent as they drove. Karsen and Brad were both lost in grief, a pain Hanna couldn't even imagine and didn't want to.

For the remainder of the drive, Karsen watched without seeing as the familiar Arizona landscape passed by through the window. She held her necklace tight as she searched to make sense of it all. Nothing could have prepared her to lose her mother. She felt as if a piece of her was missing.

~ **2** ~

Addison Reynolds's blood pressure rose as she scanned the ad on page thirty-two. As CEO of *Urbane*, one of the world's top fashion magazines, she had walked into her Manhattan office this Friday morning to an urgent – and angry – message from one of her largest and long-time advertisers, George Montague. "This is unacceptable! Pull all my ads, NOW!"

She scanned the advertisement apprehensively. At first glance everything appeared accurate. Then she saw it. There, in the services list, in black, bold letters: "Brow, Lip and Chip Waxing."

Addison cringed at the now obvious typo that would be seen in this month's issue by over a million avid readers. "What the hell is a 'chip'? It's chin!" she muttered to herself in exasperation. Not the most popular service by any means, but still – 'chip' waxing? How many staff members had missed it in proofing the ad of one of her most important clients?

She hit the all-page button.

"Jacob! My office." Her tone meant pronto.

Addison's new junior assistant, Jacob, appeared in a flash. She didn't even give him time to shut the door behind him.

"One letter. Do you realize one letter could cost me millions?" Addison snapped.

His perplexed facial expression told her he didn't.

"How did this happen?" she demanded, pushing the magazine across her desk toward Jacob, her highly polished nail pointing to the word 'chip' on the page.

Like a deer in the headlights, Jacob stuttered, knowing the question was strictly rhetorical. He had been thrown into the fire when Addison's senior publishing assistant went on maternity leave prematurely,

11

and had not yet gotten a clear read on Addison's opinion of his capabili-
ties. Although his credentials out of college were glowing, he lacked the
practical experience one obtains on the job. He consistently felt as if he
should be updating his resume. The one positive characteristic he had
going for him was he was willing to work long hours to get the job done.
But no matter how many hours he worked, no matter if terrorists had
held the staff hostage, or aliens abducted them before proofing, there
was no acceptable explanation to make the terrible typo tolerable.

Impatiently, Addison held her hand up for him to stop before Jacob
uttered an entire sentence.

"Never mind. Never mind. I don't want to hear an excuse. Just come
to me with a solution. One hour," she ordered, waving him out of her
office. Jacob did not delay. Shaking, he was out the door as quickly as he
had appeared.

Sitting back, her head resting against the chair, Addison stared at the
ceiling. She didn't mean to belittle Jacob. But mistakes at this level are
catastrophic. Like your husband getting caught in the shower with the
nanny, the trust between two parties completely ruined. Work was her
marriage. If she failed, she had nothing. Or so she believed.

Breathe. She inhaled deeply, closing her eyes. Exhale – hoo. Inhale –
exhale - hoo. All too often, she felt the stress within her boil to where she
thought she would explode. She knew it was unhealthy yet she couldn't
seem to curb her behavior. By definition, she was a classic workaholic.
She spent thirteen-, sometimes fourteen-hour days at the office, then
ventured to evening press outings and charity events. She didn't consider it a sacrifice. This was her identity. Her choice since she had taken
over the magazine's day-to-day operations upon her father's retirement
four years ago. On the outside, her life looked like the picture of success.
But lately, on the inside she felt as though something was missing. She
wondered if she were having an early mid-life crisis or if she were truly
in over her head.

Her thoughts were interrupted by the voice of her administra-
tive assistant on the speakerphone. "I have Mr. Montague on line one,"
reported Marjorie.

Addison thanked her and inhaled one last, deep cleansing breath.
She visualized a peaceful conversation. In her most professional but sincere voice she picked up the line.

"Mr. Montague. I received your message and before we begin, let me apologize profusely. The mistake is unacceptable. We are working on a solution to rectify this immediately..."

"Mistakes did not happen when your father was in charge," interjected the voice on the other end of the line. "I was afraid of this." Montague's thick, Italian accent dripped with disdain. Addison inwardly boiled at the insult. It had been four uneventful years since she took over the reigns of *Urbane* from her father, and now one mistake and she's suddenly incompetent? *How easily clients forget*, she thought. She pushed her own irritation into the pit of her stomach and buried it there.

"Please understand, Mr. Montague. This was a one-time oversight. Obviously, we will make all necessary strides to see that it does not happen again..."

"My reputation cannot allow that chance," Montague interrupted. "You do realize there are competitor magazines vying for my business every day. 'Chip waxing.' What the hell is a chip? I'll be the laughing stock of the industry!" His voice rose again.

Remaining calm, Addison said empathetically, "Mr. Montague. I understand your frustration. I've been there, too. But from my experience, if you allow us the opportunity to resolve the issue, we can move forward with a clean slate. You have a history here. Trust me, I will not allow the reputation of my father's magazine to be tarnished."

Silence.

"Mr. Montague?"

"Fine. I'll expect a phone call tomorrow."

She heard the phone disconnect. She'd bought a little time, but found no comfort in his tone. They needed a solution. Fast.

ᏅᏉ

"Addison," Jacob barged through the door to her office unannounced.

"Shit, Jacob!" She was pulling her shirt overhead. The photographer for her new editorial photo would be there momentarily. Jacob turned, averting his eyes. "Don't you knock?" she asked.

"I'm sorry, but we have an idea," he replied excitedly, his hand shielding his eyes.

"Great. Let's have it. You can uncover your eyes now."

He looked directly at her, trying to portray a renewed sense of confidence. "A two page, comp advertorial. One side describing the spa's latest treatment, the other page, in bold print, "If you can tell us what your 'chip' is, we'll wax it for FREE."

Jacob waited, trying to control his belabored breathing. His palms trickled with sweat.

Addison's response was not immediate. She hated giving anything away, but circumstances warranted it. The concept itself was unique, she thought, using humor to diffuse the error. While there was always the risk that acknowledging the mistake would bring more attention to it, she figured it was one worth taking. She could sell it to Montague because it would double the exposure for the spa in the magazine and build a new clientele for a lesser-known service.

"Work up an article and print a mock-up. I want it on my desk by 2 p.m. Not a minute later." She shooed him out so she could finish changing.

᏶

David, Addison's photographer, arrived promptly for their nine o'clock shoot. She updated her photo for the inside editorial page every three months to keep it fresh. In reality, she'd rather be behind the scenes than in the magazine at all, even though her looks could easily rival any cover model. Much to her chagrin, in addition to *Urbane*, her flawless beauty and sporadic love life kept her dabbled across the news and, of course, the occasional tabloid.

"Addy, darling! How are you?" David flared his arms to grant her a welcoming embrace. "You look stunning as always," he added admiringly. David had photographed her for the last four years. She liked how his photos perfectly captured her professional image.

"You always make me out to look a zillion times better than I really do, my friend. How have you been?" Addison kissed him on both cheeks in greeting.

"Good. Extremely busy. I just shot the fashion show for Givenchy yesterday. It was unbelievable. Gerdie had a baby six weeks ago and commandeered the runway with her taut little belly. Had I not seen the baby myself, I'd think it was a hoax."

Smirking, Addison thought to herself, *she probably doesn't eat,* and focused on the task at hand. "So where do you want me today, David? By the window? In the chair?"

Bored with shooting the standard, stifling corporate headshot, he made his usual plea to try something new.

"Oh, Addy. Let's make it real today, shall we? You aren't the stuffy broad you portray. Let's let the rest of the world in on the secret," he said mischievously.

Addison started to say no, but stopped mid-sentence. "You know what? With the morning I've had, I don't have the energy to argue with you. What do you have in mind?"

"Yes!" David exclaimed like he'd just won the lottery. He pulled his camera bag over his shoulder and tossed her the coat hanging by the door. He then grabbed her hand and hurried her toward the elevator before she could change her mind.

Taking the elevator to the lobby, he quickly led her through the exit to the outside curb. Addison followed willingly, but still felt a bit less than her usual take charge, alpha-dog self.

Climbing into a cab, David directed the driver to Central Park.

"You want to shoot in Central Park? Should I find a bench with a bum to pose with?" Addison asked sarcastically.

David shot her a piercing look, surprised to hear a comment like that come from her. "Addy, I can't believe..."

"Sorry. That came out wrong," she cut him off mid-sentence, realizing she didn't like the person she'd become over the last few weeks. She was behaving like a bitch and she knew it, yet she couldn't seem to get herself under control. She had to get a grip.

After a short ride, the cab driver pulled to the curb where David indicated. David paid the fare and led Addison to a large, quiet area within the park.

"Stand over there. We're going to shoot a soft, natural side of you." He pointed to the base of a large tree trunk, the branches above still dusted with a light layer of snow. He quickly unpacked his camera and flipped through his bag to choose the appropriate lens.

"You do realize that it's winter, right?" Addison shivered as she shed her coat and walked to the tree.

He held his finger to his lips, ignoring her remark and instructed her further. "Foot up. Hands crossed behind you. Chin down."

"You mean my chip?" she asked. He looked at her funny, not getting the joke. She laughed nervously, which broke her gloomy mood. "Read next month's issue."

"Okay, eyes up at me."

As she glanced up, she felt like a trained monkey. How models did this for a living was beyond her.

David walked over to her. "Fabulous. Now dear, take down your hair." Her fingers trembled from the cold as she pulled the bobby pins out, allowing her warm chestnut hair to fall in soft waves around her shoulders. David paced backwards.

"Hmmm." He squinted, face perplexed. "Still too stiff. Off with the scarf," he demanded.

Addison pulled it off and threw it aside.

"Better. Now, unbutton the top few buttons."

"Why, David. I never...," she teased, knowing it was all for the image.

"Sorry dear, you know you're not my type. All right, you look sexy, girl! Come on, give me sexy. Grrrr!" David raised his brows suggestively.

Addison couldn't help but giggle and began to relax. "What did I agree to?" She shook her head as she undid two buttons. Her necklace peeked out above the opening.

"Perfect," he said, lifting the viewfinder to his eye. The shutter clicked repetitively as he snapped what seemed to Addison to be a hundred photos.

"I can't feel my fingertips, David," she said, blowing into her fists to warm them.

"All right, we're done. Here." He handed her her coat.

"Thanks. You're going to owe me for this one." She pulled on her coat and wrapped her scarf snuggly around her neck.

"Not once you see the prints. They're going to be magical!" he said excitedly, making a starburst gesture with his fingers.

"You mean marvelous?" she corrected.

"No, magical. I just have a feeling these photos are going to bring you happiness."

~ 3 ~

Flying into Chicago was predictably unpredictable. In the summer, the winds or lightning storms could close down the airport without warning. In the winter, the snow often grounded more planes than not. But Karsen and Brad managed to make their connecting flight.

When they arrived in South Bend, their dad stood waiting just beyond the secured area. Under his jacket, Karsen could see the faded blue of an old Colts t-shirt that she could tell hadn't been washed. His eyes looked more tired and aged than she remembered from just a few days before. He hugged them one at a time, holding each embrace longer than his usual welcome hug.

"Hi, Daddy," Karsen muttered. For a brief moment, she felt as though her mother would appear, having popped into the one novelty store in the tiny municipal airport while she awaited their arrival. The feeling passed and she held back tears as only the three of them trudged toward baggage claim. Life as she once knew it would never be the same.

Outside, the rain poured down. The car was parked in the economy lot and by the time she climbed into her father's car, Karsen's dark hair hung soaked around her face.

"Are all the arrangements set?" Brad asked his father.

"I wish I could say yes, but your mom always took care of these sorts of things. The viewing is scheduled for Friday evening and the funeral services on Saturday."

"Karsen and I can help finish the planning tomorrow. Try not to stress about it, Dad. It will come together."

Karsen kept quiet. She couldn't help but think of how frivolous people were taking a year to plan a wedding, yet they had only a day to plan her mom's final farewell. It didn't seem right.

◠◡

They arrived at the Woods's home and conversation eased slightly as they made small talk over where to set the suitcases and whether or not they were hungry. Karsen scanned the room as her mother's favorite companion, her fluffy, five-pound Maltese, pounced at Karsen's feet.

"Hey, Belle, ol' girl," Karsen bent down to pet her. The dog looked as though she appreciated the attention. "Yeah, I miss her too." Karsen couldn't help but understand. She also sensed her mother's absence. Although her mother's belongings filled the house like she'd return any moment, Karsen felt an indescribable void deep inside.

Mr. Woods and Brad finished moving the luggage to the bedrooms before returning to the kitchen.

"I've got deli meat for sandwiches, if that's okay with the two of you. Sorry it's not anything fancier," Carl said.

"Sure, Dad. That's fine." Brad answered.

Karsen couldn't fathom eating, but at her father's insistence she prepared a plate. The three sat down at the kitchen table.

"Dad?" Brad began. "You didn't really tell us what happened."

Carl finished chewing, more to delay than out of manners. "I'm sorry. I guess I didn't want to burden you. It doesn't matter anyway. Nothing does."

"I understand. But, I guess I just need to know how." Brad said.

Karsen sat silently. She picked a tiny bite from the corner of her sandwich and tried to force it down.

Mr. Woods looked down. He knew this conversation was inevitable. Just like the phone calls he had to make. "She was just running up to the market." He paused to clear the lump in his throat. "She headed down County Road 17 like she always did. Another car was heading in the opposite direction and crossed over the line. He didn't hit her, but your mother swerved. The roads were still wet from the thunderstorm we'd had the night before. Apparently, she lost control and veered head-on into a tree."

"Oh, Mom, no," Brad said softly as Karsen sat numb, unable to process anything more.

"The police said she died instantly."

"Was the guy drunk?" Brad felt his blood start to boil.

"No, he even stopped to call for help. In his statement, he admitted that he glanced down to check a text message. Damn cell phones. Worse than drinking if you ask me."

Karsen couldn't listen any longer. Instead, she excused herself and set her plate of untouched food in the sink. On the counter, she noticed a plastic bag still housing her mother's possessions collected from her vehicle. Her mom's keys, lipstick and a photo of the family were among other items. Seeking comfort, she cocooned on the floor in the living room and bundled herself under a blanket by the fireplace. Belle snuggled around her feet. She turned the television on to deafen the silence, but had no interest in watching. Just as she felt more tears begin to emerge, she heard her father and Brad enter the room.

"Dad?" she asked, biting back the tears.

He looked up from the television. "Yes?"

"I was just wondering what you were planning to do with Mom's necklace."

He paused awkwardly.

"Well?"

"I want her to have it," he mumbled.

"You're going to bury her with it?" Karsen asked, hoping that was not his intention. The last thing she wanted to do was upset him, but to her the piece meant everything - the connection to her family and now the only connection left to her mother.

"It was one of her favorite possessions. I want her to have it." Her father turned back to the program as if to indicate the decision had been made.

"But it's also a part of us, part of our family tradition. I'd like to keep it. Maybe hand it down to my own kids someday." Karsen had heard the story from her mother, Katherine, numerous times. How, when Katherine was born, her father, Karsen's grandfather, wanted to give her mother a special gift. He handmade three interlocking charms, each in the shape of a puzzle piece that fit together perfectly - one for him, one for Grandma and one for the new addition, Katherine. Growing up, Karsen's mother continued the tradition by having a jeweler make pieces for her own husband and two children.

Brad hesitated to interfere, but finally chimed in to support his sister. He saw no point in leaving a necklace where it would never be seen again. His voice was softer than usual. "Dad, I see your point, but Karsen's right. I think Mom would have wanted to keep the pieces together."

Their father wanted to avoid the conversation entirely.

"I'll think about it," he muttered, sounding somewhat defensive and on the brink of tears.

"Please, Dad?" Karsen pleaded one last time.

"I said I'd think about it. It's just a damn piece of jewelry."

"No it's not!" Karsen argued, "Maybe to you it is, but it's not to me. I get why you'd want her to have her wedding ring, but why the necklace? They're meant to be passed down."

"Karsen, let it go."

"Why are you getting so mad? I really don't understand, Dad?"

He stood and looked down at her. "Your mother is gone, Karsen. It was her tradition. Not yours!" Frustrated, and not knowing the right thing to do, he clicked off the television, bid them both goodnight and retired to his bedroom.

"He's being unreasonable," Karsen said, lowering her voice. The last thing she wanted to do was fight.

"Sis, he's grieving. Give it time."

"But the funeral is Saturday. If he resists, it'll be too late."

"I won't let that happen," Brad promised. He knew how much the tradition meant to his mother. There was no doubt in his mind she would rather keep it going than have the necklace herself. "I'm going to make some hot chocolate. Do you want one?"

"Sure."

Brad stood up and went to the kitchen. He heated up two cups of cocoa with a hint of Baileys mixed in each. Returning, he handed a mug to Karsen and took up residence again in the old lounge chair where he had been sitting before.

"Thanks," she said taking a sip. The hot liquid finally warmed her from the inside and momentarily calmed her lingering frustration. She still couldn't fathom why her father was so angry over the necklace. He was normally so easy-going. Then again, under the circumstances, how could she expect anything to be normal?

∽

Karsen woke in the morning and stumbled groggily into the kitchen. There was a loud thud as her big toe slammed against the kitchen island's baseboard. "Oooouch!" she screamed. She looked over at Brad who was still in the recliner where he'd fallen asleep the night before. He didn't budge. From his position, she doubted he had moved the entire night. Through the back window, she could see her dad smoking on the patio, a nasty habit he refused to break. She had always feared he would be the first to go. Never had she imagined her mom would be first. Her mom had been the picture of perfect health.

Noticing the brewed coffee steaming in the pot, Karsen quietly thanked her dad. The aroma held a hint of cinnamon, just like her mother always made it. The now familiar twinge of regret and remorse passed through her as she reflected again on the last visit with her mom.

"I know he's attractive, Karsen, but I just don't get why you want to tie yourself down," her mother had said.

"Because I love him, Mom. What's not to like? He's the whole package."

"I don't know, Karsen…I think you're limiting your options and you're focusing on having a family instead of a career. What you think you want now may be different than what you want in say…five years. You're so young and you have plenty of time."

"Urgh! You just don't get it." Karsen snapped, giving her mother a half-hearted hug goodbye. The scene replayed over and over again in her mind. Not "I love you, Mom," not even "Goodbye." Had she known it was the last time she'd see her, certainly she would have controlled the meaningless bickering. Her heart longed for one more chance. One chance to rewind life just long enough to end things with her mother on a loving memory instead of with a strained, petty disagreement over her choice of men. She wondered if the feeling of regret would ever go away.

She opened the cupboard to grab a mug and broke into a slight grin. "Unbelievable," she whispered to herself, cherry picking the Tweety Bird mug she'd received on her tenth birthday from among a mishmash of others.

She filled her cup, then parked herself on one of the bar stools lining the counter of the island. Nursing her sore toe as she held the mug close to her chin, she closed her eyes and allowed the steam from the coffee to penetrate her face before taking a sip. As she opened her eyes, she noticed Brad's keychain lying on the counter. She ran her finger over the link – a silver charm in the shape of a puzzle piece. She pulled the chain from beneath her sweatshirt and held the two pieces together. They slid together perfectly.

"Hey," muttered Brad, finally stirring back to the land of the living.

Startled by her brother's voice, Karsen quickly placed the keychain back on the counter and stuffed her necklace back under her shirt. She didn't feel up to revisiting last night's drama.

"Morning, sunshine," Karsen replied. Sliding off her perch, she walked back over to the cabinet for another mug and poured Brad some coffee.

"Thanks," he muttered, and then groaned as he stretched and managed to lift his stiff body out of the chair. "Man, was I beat." He smoothed back his black, wavy hair from his face and joined her at the counter. "Not the best chair to sleep in overnight."

"No kidding." She laughed and pushed the mug toward him.

Brad poured a dollop of vanilla-flavored creamer into his cup and swirled it with a spoon. He added a sizeable amount more and watched as the dark, black liquid molted into a smooth, creamy blend of more creamer than coffee.

"Do you think he's okay out there?" Karsen asked, looking out to the patio.

Brad's gaze followed hers and saw their dad sitting alone on the porch. "I don't know. It'll probably take awhile. I hear it's after the funeral that's the hardest, when the house is silent. He hasn't been alone in thirty years."

"The viewing isn't until four. I was thinking we probably need to help clean up the house. Not that I want to spend today cleaning, but we've only got two days before we leave."

"You read my mind. I was thinking the same thing," agreed Brad. "I'm sure he'll be pissed if we touch any of her personal things, but straightening up a bit couldn't hurt. There is more stuff in this house than I've ever seen. We probably need to make sure this month's bills are paid, too. One less task for him to worry about."

"Mom really took care of everything, huh?"

"She also kept everything, the pack rat."

Brad grinned, finally noticing the mug Karsen chose for him. He looked funny – a little too manly perhaps – as he lifted the Spider Man mug he was drinking from and clinked it against Karsen's Tweety Bird mug as if in a toast.

That afternoon, they sorted through what seemed to be their entire childhood histories. Moments they had forgotten flooded back through piles of dusty birthday cards, photographs and outdated articles of clothing. At times, Karsen began to understand why her mom had held onto so many things. Karsen had been the one recommending her mother clear out the clutter for years. Intellectually, she knew that they were only things – material items with little to no value. Emotionally, she couldn't fathom letting any of her history go.

❧ 4 ❧

Returning from the funeral service, their father excused himself and retreated straight to bed. Following Brad into the family room, Karsen slipped out of her shoes and sat down on the sofa. She rubbed her feet, which still ached from standing in high heels for three long hours. Between the viewing the day before and now the funeral, she felt completely exhausted.

"You think he's down for the night?" Karsen asked. It was only eight o'clock.

Brad popped the top off the bottle of Amber Boch he had retrieved from the fridge and settled back in the recliner. His tie hung awkwardly, partly untied around his neck. "Probably. I'm sure he's beat. I know I am. Could you believe how many people came? The entire town showed up, I think."

"Did you happen to see that one guy in the back during the service?"

"Didn't notice anyone in particular. Why?"

"It just seemed odd that he was standing back by the door instead of coming in, almost like he didn't want anyone to know he was there."

"Do you think he knew Mom? Or knows us? Maybe from growing up?"

"Maybe. There were so many people I didn't know, but most people introduced themselves and gave their condolences. I don't remember seeing him afterwards at all."

"Huh. Who knows?" Brad didn't think it worth pondering over. "I'm sure it was nothing. Maybe he was a funeral crasher looking for free food." He smiled broadly.

"Not funny, Brad."

She flung a couch pillow at him, which he caught mid-air with one hand. He shook his head at her then sipped his beer and grabbed the remote to turn on the television. He searched through the channels, finding an old, overplayed sitcom that he could probably recite by memory. It was mindless but neither of them had the energy to care. They sat and watched in silence.

ᏻ

The next morning was Sunday. Opening her semi-blurred eyes, from not having removed her contacts the night before, Karsen glanced out the bedroom window, which looked out to the front street. She saw a worn red, four-door sedan sitting across the way. The car seemed out of place, but she shook it off. After all, she didn't live here anymore and it was probably just the neighbors.

She wobbled to the bathroom. Photos from her childhood adorned the otherwise bare white walls along the way. Karsen had lived in the house for eighteen years and had never paid much attention to the décor or her mother's style. It was just simply home. Now, though, every detail seemed to jump out at her. The house had an old-fashioned, *Brady Bunch* feel about it. Certainly different from what you see in the latest edition of *Trend Home* magazine. Elementary school photos from every year filled the edges around an oval frame with her high school senior picture highlighted in the center. She was just three years older now, but this morning, it felt like thirty.

She found her saline solution on the bathroom counter and placed a drop into each eye. After several blinks, her contacts resumed their moisture and she could once again see clearly.

"Shit," she groaned, wishing now she couldn't. Looking at herself in the mirror, she looked shabby, no, *more like pathetic*, she thought. Her eyes were red and swollen both from incessant crying and lack of proper sleep. "If James could see me now," she mumbled, as she turned on the water to rinse the remnants from the prior day's eyeliner that still rimmed her eyes in a raccoon-like circle.

When she got back to her room, she checked her cell phone for what seemed like the hundredth time. There were no missed calls. No messages. James had not even called yesterday, the day of her mother's funeral. *Perhaps he had called the house instead of her cell and chose not to leave a message.* She tried to justify his actions, but deep down all she longed for was to hear his voice.

Karsen joined Brad in the kitchen. She opened the kitchen pantry, remembering precisely where every dish, plate and food could be found. For over twenty years, her mother had maintained the same organization. The pantry was stocked full and looked as though it could easily feed a family of ten through a year of famine.

Brad pulled out the pancake mix and one of several bottles of syrup while Karsen started the coffee. "I actually think I'm hungry," Karsen said, realizing she hadn't eaten a full meal since they left Arizona.

"Did I say I was making any for you?" Brad held the box of mix over her head as if to pour the complete contents out. Physically he was stronger than her, as most men naturally were, but he was barely taller in height. She grabbed the box and tugged it from his hands, dusting them both in white powder.

"Nice try, Big Brother." She extended her right leg in a roundhouse kick, coming inches from his privates. He instinctively covered his unit with both hands. "Hey, watch it!"

"At least my hours of kick-boxing classes come in handy for something." She stuck her tongue out at him like they were children. As Brad cleaned up their mess, Karsen set down the box of mix on the counter and proceeded to pull out the griddle and a mixing bowl. They then worked together to make the pancakes.

"Mmmm…I smell coffee." Their father groggily rounded the corner.

"Nice of you to join us, Sleeping Beauty," teased Karsen.

"No wait, he'd have to be the Beast," Brad said with a chuckle.

"No, that's a different story, idiot."

"Oh, whatever. What the hell do I know about fairy tales?"

"Bickering banter. Your mom always laughed at it," Carl said wistfully, shaking his head with a smile. "But you both drive me bonkers."

Karsen blew him a kiss like she did as a child. His hand grasped the air to catch it, then motioned as if to put it in his pocket. "For later," he said with a wink. Karsen returned what she always deemed her dad's greatest gesture of affection with a perfect, gleaming white smile.

"You slept over twelve hours," Karsen said in amazement, as his usual allotment hardly surpassed five or six.

"It's the first real sleep I've gotten since…well, since the accident. Guess it caught up with me," he replied.

"Probably the anxiety over all the arrangements didn't help," Brad said.

"You guys did more than I did. I don't know what I'd do without you two."

"Starve." Karsen smirked and handed him a plate stacked with pancakes warm from the griddle.

"Thanks." He poured a mound of warm maple syrup overtop, the sweet aroma making his mouth water before he took the first bite.

"What did you want to do today, Dad?" Karsen asked.

"I thought I'd go to the cemetery and then out to the boat. Sitting here has too many reminders of her." He paused realizing he'd planned to be alone. "That is, if you guys don't mind."

"I don't mind. I'm fine just relaxing," Karsen said.

"Whatever you want, Dad." Brad patted his back. "I need to work on some new material for my next show anyway." He'd given his first performance at the Improv a year prior and his growing interest in stand-up had blossomed into a flourishing hobby. His last act created such a buzz, he wanted to make sure his next performance surpassed it.

"And I've got homework I should do." Karsen added to make her dad feel less guilty about leaving them.

After their father headed out, Brad settled into his favorite chair.

Feeling less than enthusiastic about tackling her homework, Karsen felt the need to explore, although she wasn't sure what she was looking for or why. She entered her parents' bedroom. The room looked eerily unchanged from what she remembered growing up.

Moving to the closet, she felt the different textures as she guided her fingers across her mother's clothes. The closet would need to be cleared out at some point, but for now she knew her dad would not allow it. She held her mother's navy blue cardigan up to her face and inhaled the few traces of her mom's lingering scent. The previous day's emotions hastily tore at her heart. She sank to her knees on the floor as the tears spontaneously flowed once again.

"I'm so sorry, Mom!" she wailed. "I'm sorry for not listening to you when I was a teenager. I'm sorry for all the times I intentionally disobeyed your wishes. I'm sorry for not eating my vegetables and for telling you that you were an awful cook when you weren't. I'm sorry I pushed you away like all teenagers do. I'm sorry I pushed your buttons to make you mad just because I knew I could. I'm sorry I didn't tell you I loved you more. I need you, Mom. Why, God? Why now? Oh, God I need my Mom!"

Her impromptu outpouring of emotion was unintentional. She had tried to be strong, but how could she face going back to school knowing her life would never be the same?

She didn't know when but Brad's arms had cradled around her. They huddled inside the closet and he rocked her gently, soothing her until her sobs eased into sniffles. She had cried before, but this meltdown took Brad by surprise. He hated seeing her hurt.

"Shush, K." He held her.

"I need her, Brad. I still need her here."

"I know."

"I didn't tell her I loved her. The last time I saw her, I didn't tell her."

"Mom knew you loved her. Here," he said reaching into his pant's pocket. His fist transferred the contents into her hand.

Karsen's eyes strained to focus on the necklace with its delicate charm now lying in her hand.

"Mom's?"

"Uh huh. I took it off her before they closed the casket. She'd have wanted you to have it, K."

Her eyes blurred with tears once more. "Does Dad know?"

"Yes, I told him."

"Was he pissed?"

"Let's just say he wasn't happy, but he'll get over it. Like I said, Mom would've wanted you to have it."

"Thanks."

"Are you going to be okay?" he asked, as he helped her stand and walk over to the bed.

"Yeah." At least momentarily, she did feel a little better after her cathartic episode. Karsen wiped her tears and blotted her nose with the back of her hand as Brad kissed her tenderly on the forehead before returning to the living room.

Clenching the necklace in her hand, Karsen's eyes focused on her mother's brown, oak dresser. The dresser had been part of the family as long as she could remember, with a traditional look that remained timeless.

Karsen opened the top-middle drawer, the one her mom kept her jewelry in. Her eyes were quickly drawn to the reason for her search - two familiar charms – puzzle pieces like the one she wore around her neck and the one she still held in the palm of her hand. An upside down wallet-sized photo had gotten wedged into the corner of the drawer. Karsen slid the picture out of the crevice it was lodged in and turned it over. She couldn't place the photo, but recognized it as a baby girl; it looked old and she wondered if it was her mother.

Placing her mother's necklace on top of the dresser, she removed her grandparents' charms and laid them alongside it. She grabbed her dad's off the top corner of the mirror where it hung, then instinctively reached behind her neck, grasping the small latch of her own necklace. A strand of her hair intertwined around the clasp and pulled as she removed the chain. She unwound the dark Karo-colored thread and flicked it aside.

"Hey, Brad. Bring me your keychain," she yelled, anxious now to complete the puzzle.

"In a minute," he yelled back.

"Never mind. I'll get it myself." She had no patience to wait for him and, her mood brightening, jogged to the kitchen to retrieve her brother's keys.

Back in her mother's room, she laid the pieces in a row – first Grandpa's, then Grandma's, her mom's, Dad's, then Brad's and finally her own. Her eyes starred blankly as her fingers adjusted the pieces. Something wasn't right. *Huh?* She thought quizzically. She bit at her fingernail. *That's odd.*

"Hey, Brad. Come here," she yelled again.

"I told you I would bring it in a minute. Hold your horses."

"No, come here. It's missing."

"What's missing?"

"A piece."

"A piece of what?"

"There's a piece missing. It doesn't fit," Karsen said with some irritation. "Just come here!"

Brad sauntered back to his parents' room. "What?" He sounded exasperated at the interruption.

"Look. Mom's charm and Dad's charm. I tried to put them together, but they don't link. They're all supposed to fit together. That's why we have them."

"Are you sure that's Dad's piece?"

"Of course I'm sure. It was right here where he always leaves it."

"Huh." Brad wasn't sure what to think.

"What does this mean?"

"I'm sure it's nothing, Karsen." He shrugged it off. "They're just charms. The pieces were symbolic - a simple, silly tradition."

"You don't think it's anything then?"

"Nah, maybe they never did really link."

"Well, I still find it peculiar that every piece fits except these two." She pushed the pieces closer together with her index finger.

"I'm sure there's a logical explanation. What, I don't know, but I'm sure it's nothing."

Brad didn't admit it, but the goose bumps on his arms validated that his sister just might be right. He moved the pieces together with his finger. There was a piece missing. The lingering question was why?

❧ 5 ❧

Even bundled in her favorite DKNY pea coat, Addison still felt chilled from standing in the cold earlier without a jacket. She had headed straight to her lunch appointment as soon as David had wrapped up. Especially today, the thought of her next meeting brought a smile to her face. Flakes of snow had dotted her coat's dark navy wool while she waited in front of the bistro for her friend Emily and her daughter, Adelaide. Friday lunch dates had become an almost guaranteed tradition since the day her goddaughter was born. Her eyes smiled as her arms flew open wide in welcome as they approached.

"I LOVE the shoes, Adelaide. They're fabulous!"

"Tank ou," sing-songed the two-foot-tall munchkin. Her pigtails, neatly accented with glittery star barrettes, swung as she looked down to admire the white dress shoes adorned with rhinestone butterflies on her feet. Addison knelt down to her level. "You think I could borrow them?"

"No. Yur too big!" Adelaide said and added, "They're my shoes!"

Addison chuckled and kissed the top of Adelaide's head as she straightened up again.

"She gets more adorable every time I see her," she said to Emily as she kissed the side of her friend's cheek. "She's growing up so fast!"

"With your influence, Addy, she'll be wearing high heels and power suits before she's ten," Emily shook her head in mocked disbelief.

"At least she'll look great conquering the world, except you're going to have to teach her about not wearing white after Labor Day."

"Very funny, Addy. I'm sure you'll teach her that. You'll probably have her editing your magazine with her crayons by the time she can read."

"What's wrong with that, Emily? You want her to be a strong, independent woman, don't you?"

"Of course. Just like you. Addy and Adie. I can see it now. Just make sure you don't forget about little ole me."

"Never." Addison winked at Adelaide who was turning in circles to entertain herself. "At any rate, let's get inside. It's freezing out here."

Addison opened the door, unwound the cashmere scarf from her neck and motioned the hostess that there would be two for lunch. "Oh, and a highchair please," she added, pointing to Adelaide.

"Right this way." The hostess grabbed two menus from a dark wood stand behind which water trickled over a cascade of stacked stone. She guided them through a maze of tables to a corner booth nestled in the back.

"Guess they didn't hear you say 'Nobody puts Baby in a corner,'" Addison joked.

"Apparently, you're showing your age with that movie line," Emily grinned.

"You got the joke, so I guess that means you're old, too."

"Old!" Adelaide repeated.

"Hey! Who are you calling old, little one?" Addison tickled Adelaide under her arm. Adie giggled and repeated the word "Old!" Addison wrinkled her forehead and pursed her lips in an exaggerated pout as Adelaide continued to laugh.

The restaurant bustled with activity. The man and woman at the table adjacent to theirs appeared to be bickering. *Married couple*, Addison thought. She noticed an elderly couple in another booth. They were saying little but appeared to be enjoying their time together. They ate slowly and meticulously. Addison wondered how long they'd been together. She, at the ripe old age of thirty-nine, had never married. Not that she hadn't had relationships that could have easily led down that path. "Two paths diverged in a yellow wood," Robert Frost once wrote. Addison chose the path allowing her to keep her emotions unexposed. She'd been burned one too many times. That and no man stood a chance against her work.

"How's your mom doing?" Emily inquired while fumbling to find the safety belt on the high chair. She peered under the chair then glanced back at Addison, clearly frustrated. "This thing is crap. Apparently, they don't expect many two-year olds at their posh café."

"*Beyond McDonalds* - A look into one woman's impossible journey to find toddler-friendly and wildly upscale dining." Addison's hands flared emphasizing the headline.

"Are you always on?"

"Sorry." Addison was always on though. She had practically grown up at *Urbane* magazine. Her mind was a constant machine, churning out ideas to keep her ahead of the competition.

"So, back to your mom. How's she doing?" Emily gave up buckling the belt and set a pile of fruit snacks in front of Adie to occupy her.

"Initially good. The doctors are optimistic." Addison paused. "She's scheduled for surgery next week and chemo will follow, depending on the results."

"And how are you holding up?" Emily grimaced over the kid's menu, noting the grilled cheese sandwich was made with Brie.

"You know me. I'm a rock."

"Come on, Addison. It's your mother, for heaven's sake. You're allowed to show some emotion once in awhile."

"Funny. Ha. Ha," Addison said mockingly. "It's not that I don't care, of course I do. I just don't think worrying does any good."

Emily looked up from the menu. "Addy, it's just Adelaide and me here and Adie doesn't care how strong you are. Trust me, she cries all the time."

"I'm fine, Emily." She closed her menu and crossed her arms.

Emily huffed and shook her head. "You internalize your feelings too much. It's not healthy, Addison."

"Maybe so, but are you my shrink now, too?" Addison asked in a cutting tone. She wasn't sure why, but Emily's persistence was striking a nerve. Addison knew she had a knack for blocking her feelings to where she felt completely emotionless. That's how she'd learned to deal with numerous life situations. But to intentionally block her emotions over her own mother's illness made even Addison question how detached she could really be.

"Good afternoon, ladies." A perky blond dressed in a white, button-down shirt and black dress pants disrupted their conversation. A single strand of pearls around her neck added a classy touch to the simplistic outfit. Had it not been for the white apron tied at her waist, she would have blended in with the rest of the executives out to lunch. "To let you know, today's special is a seared Ahi tuna, laid on a bed of mixed greens with pomegranate vinaigrette dressing and jicama spears."

"Great, thanks." Emily wrinkled her nose at Addison.

The server retreated with a simple, "I'll give you a few more minutes."

Emily couldn't contain herself. "Seriously, whatever happened to a tuna salad sandwich on rye?"

"Give it a try, Ems."

"Sorry. I used to love new places. It's just frustrating with Adie. There is nothing here she'll eat."

"I understand. If you don't like it, we'll go back to Carnegie Deli next week. The reviews here were great. They say it's the best new bistro in New York City. I just thought it would be worth checking out at least once."

The server returned and took their order, freeing Emily to steer the conversation back to Addison's mom.

"So, are you going to get a mammogram?"

"Hadn't thought about it, why?"

"Because it's hereditary. You're at a higher risk for breast cancer if it has been found in your family."

"No, I think I'll be fine." Addison stirred a packet of sugar into her passion-flavored tea and then took a sip to test whether one was enough.

"Addy, you're my friend. You need to take this seriously. You are not invincible. You might think you are, but you're not."

Addison exhaled, trying to suppress the wave of irritation rising within her. She did not want to discuss this. After a short silence, she finally responded, sounding as if she were presiding over a boardroom rather than speaking to her closest friend.

"I understand your reasoning, Ems; I do. But my mother's illness won't be indicative of my own future. You have nothing to worry about. I promise."

The server returned and set down each of their entrees. Emily instinctively swiped hers away from the tiny little hand reaching for her hot plate. She shot the server a callous glare as if to ask whether she had ever served a table with a toddler before.

"Anything else?" the server asked politely.

"We're fine," Addison answered before Emily could wage a full-scale war against the bistro.

Emily doled out a smug smile.

"The waitress can't help the menu, Em."

"No, but she can be more careful about the dish of scalding food she just swung over my daughter's head. Anyway, don't change the subject. I want to talk about you. I wish you'd reconsider being checked. You're getting older too, you know."

"I understand your concern, but really stop pressing. I'm fine."

"I won't stop. I think it's important, and I think you're being unreasonably stubborn. It's a simple test. What are you afraid of? I've done it myself."

"I'm not afraid." Addison looked away.

"Then why are you so defensive?"

"I'm not."

"Then just go get checked, to appease your BFF if for nothing else." Emily grinned to lighten the tone then took a bite of the grilled Brie sandwich. "Hey, this is not bad."

"Ems, really, my mother's condition has nothing to do with me. Can we just drop it?" Addison's voice softened in an effort to set Emily's mind to rest. She speared a bite of spinach from her salad and placed it in her mouth. The conversation hadn't left her with much of an appetite.

"No, we can't." Emily struggled to understand why this had become an issue. She simply was trying to impress the importance of early detection. She couldn't fathom her friend not taking what she considered to be reasonable precautionary measures. "Addy. Come on…be reasonable. I'm just worried about you."

Before she could finish Addison stood abruptly, her anger taking over. Typically controlled and even-keeled, the rage that rose inside surprised her. She looked down at Emily with an undeserved contempt and blared, "I am being reasonable! She's not my biological mother, EM-IL-Y. I'm adopted, damn it!"

Twenty-five years of bottling up her secret poured out in an instant. Her voice bordered between upset and pure resentment. Maybe she needed to finally purge the truth. Maybe Emily had pushed too far. She didn't really know. Without another word, or an explanation, she grabbed her purse and stormed out of the restaurant.

Emily's jaw dropped in shock as she tried to digest Addison's outburst. *Adopted?* They'd been friends for years, decades actually, and Addison had never said anything about it before, or gave any inkling that her parents weren't her biological mother and father. Emily sat back against the booth and slid down, noticing the multitude of eyes now directed at her. She furrowed her brow in disgust and the snooping onlookers quickly returned to their own conversations as Adelaide began to cry.

∽ **6** ∽

Back at the office, Addison again pressed the all-page button on her desk phone. "Jacob! My office, now!"

Three lines rang simultaneously. "Is anyone working today?" Addison's voice blared over the loud speaker. "We are a people business; we talk to people, not machines!" One of her many pet peeves was the phone going to voice mail. Still aggravated from her meltdown at lunch, she felt like a shaken-up bottle of pop ready to blow. She was typically a fair, level-headed boss, but lately it seemed like every little occurrence unnerved her.

Jacob scurried through the door. He was dressed flawlessly in a grassy-colored button down shirt that made his jade eyes glimmer. He had a boyish, just out-of-college look with lean muscles and honey-colored hair.

"What's the status of next month's issue? A mock-up should have been on my desk days ago! First Montague's mishap and now I don't even know what the next issue will look like? Are we amateurs or what?" Addison demanded.

Jacob's voice cracked as he replied, "We're working on it."

"Do you realize it goes to press in three days and I haven't even seen the initial proof?" She paused as he gazed blankly back at her. "I want it on my desk by five sharp, not a minute later! I can't afford another mistake."

"Yes, ma'am."

"And it's Addison, not 'ma'am.' What am I, fifty?"

"Of course not." Jacob retreated toward the door.

"Jacob," Addison said catching him before he left. Knowing another order would follow, he obediently stopped and turned toward her like an enlisted soldier attending an officer.

"Can you also have Marjorie get me a coffee? A non-fat, decaf, one-pump peppermint mocha, hold the whip... venti, no grande. Ah, hell. Venti – with whip."

"Certainly," he replied, hoping to God as he made his escape that she ordered the same drink consistently and that Marjorie would know the details.

෨ഌ

The page button beeped through the rings on Addison's phone.

"It's Emily Blaker. Line two," announced Marjorie.

"Urgh...Tell her I'm on the other line. Better yet, tell her I'm in a meeting and won't be available for the rest of today...and I'm flying to London until next week."

"With all due respect, she's called every hour on the hour all afternoon. Can you just talk to her?"

"No."

"Just know this is affecting my productivity." Marjorie's voice bordered between serious and utterly sarcastic. She had been Addison's father's assistant for thirty-five years prior to Addison taking charge, an unheard of feat in today's world of takeovers and layoffs. Now she worked more to occupy herself versus needing an income, which gave her the confidence to push the boss's buttons without fear of getting canned.

"I'll take it if she calls again. Now go, Marjorie. Line one is ringing."

"Fine. She's only the closest friend you've got." Click.

Addison leaned back in her sleek, black Herman Miller chair. Marjorie certainly had no right to comment on her personal friendship, but she knew she was right. She stared at her office. Unquestionably a change from the traditional style her father had maintained. She'd revamped the entire area after his retirement. A magazine diva must not have a plain Jane office, she'd commented to Marjorie who questioned the turquoise accent wall. The office had a retro flare that Addison had successfully pulled off to look modern. A swirled silver rod positioned five hand-

40

blown glass spotlights overtop of her extra-large desk. The glass swirled shades of blues and greens coordinating with the wall. She'd imported the two modular chairs sitting in front of her desk from Italy and accented them with sequined throw pillows to add a little extra sparkle.

She thought it a wonder the magazine was successful under her dad's less than creative ways. Even so, she had learned her business acumen from watching him. He was disciplined. On the rare occasion she attended work with him as a child, she'd mimic his every move. There were days when she would pretend it was her magazine. She would gesture as he did, repeat orders she'd heard him command. Sometimes even now she felt like it was all pretend.

The phone beeped again. "Yes?" Addison said, agitated.

"It's your father. Are you taking *his* calls today?"

"Funny, Marjorie." Addison picked up the line. "Hi, Daddy," her voice sweetened. She'd maintained 'Daddy' throughout years when most would have transitioned to 'Dad.' There was something about it that made her feel more connected to him – a connection she longed for that, too, seemed all pretend.

She was thankful for everything her adoptive parents had provided during her childhood. She knew they loved her as much as she did them, but parenthood had not come easily to them. Most envied her – the family's money, the status, the success. But no one knew the truth, or at least no one had until she blurted it out in the middle of the bistro. She half expected to see her name and her highly public disclosure on the cover of every tabloid magazine in the morning.

"Hello, Addison. I just wanted to call and make sure you were planning on visiting your mother at the hospital," her father said. "She'll be admitted Sunday."

Hearing his voice so soon after her lunch fiasco, made her feel like she wanted to shut out the world again. "I'll try." Addison realized their roles had flipped in recent years. She was now the career-obsessed, no-time-for-anyone executive, and her parents wanted *her* time. She couldn't help but remember all the times she needed them and they weren't there for her. Not the way she needed them to be. Especially the day she found out that she had been adopted. There was no personal touch, no intimate conversation. Her parents, in the process of enrolling her in boarding school, were filling out emergency medical forms. Her blood type was O, matching neither her mother's nor father's type. Without any emotion, like a business transaction, she'd been told very matter-of-factly that she was not their biological daughter. She was only twelve. Not nearly mature enough to handle the immensity of such a discovery with no support. Her eyes welled up at the memory.

"Addison? Helloooo?" Her father's voice brought her back to the present.

"Sorry. I'm a bit distracted today…deadlines. You remember, right, Daddy? Next month's issue is going to press in three days and I haven't seen the proof, let alone approved it."

"Your mother," he avoided her excuse and returned to the topic at hand. "You do remember she is having surgery Monday?"

A double mastectomy, Addison cringed at the thought. "Yes, I didn't forget. I'll stop by to visit. I promise, okay?" Addison did a quick calculation in her head. Her schedule was tight. She'd have to take the proof home to review, which meant another working weekend.

"I expect that you will."

"I said I promise."

"Very well then."

Addison placed the receiver down and closed her eyes. She was no stranger to busy schedules or stressful situations, but lately even she thought enough was enough.

∾ 7 ∾

The long flight to the Phoenix airport left Karsen lethargic. She couldn't get the missing link out of her mind. She knew there had to be an explanation, but the perfectly obvious person to ask was unavailable, at least without the help of a medium. Her mother and she had been close. Why would she have told her all the pieces fit if they didn't?

She felt shabby as she waited for her bags. Her make-up had long worn off and her hair was flat. The gray velour sweat suit she wore provided comfort but did little on the attractiveness scale.

"Let me help you with that."

A strong arm reached over her shoulder, lifting the suitcase from her hands. Startled, she looked behind her.

"James!" she cried, wrapping her arms around his neck, causing him to stumble from the weight of the suitcase.

"Hey, K." His deep voice was a long-awaited comfort.

"You must have gotten my text. I wasn't sure if you'd be here. I missed you." She went to kiss his lips. His head turned and she grazed his cheek instead.

"Me, too," he said turning to Brad. "Hey." He tipped his head in a masculine acknowledgment.

"Wasn't expecting to see you here, your busy schedule and all," Brad commented, his voice dripping with sarcasm. James may have welcomed her home, but his lack of attentiveness over the last six days scored no points in Brad's eyes. As far as he was aware, Karsen had spoken to him only twice during their trip.

"Give it a rest, Brad," Karsen said. She did not have the energy or the patience to moderate their petty squabbling in the middle of baggage claim.

Karsen grabbed her purse and magazine. She'd bought the new issue of *Urbane* during their layover in Chicago, although she'd fallen asleep on the flight before she'd even read the first page.

Brad hoisted his bag over his shoulder and pulled Karsen's suitcase behind him. James offered no assistance.

"I can drive you home." James pressed against Karsen from behind. Brad bit his lip and drew in a deep breath attempting to mitigate his contempt.

"I'll see you later, okay bro?" Karsen said.

"Fine with me. I'll call you tomorrow." There was no doubt in Brad's mind that Karsen deserved better. He had tried several times to talk sense into her to no avail. Women always think they can change a man.

No sooner had they entered Karsen's apartment, than James's hands began groping at her. "I missed you," he said.

"Really?"

"Of course." He kissed her neck from behind and wasted no time beginning to undress her.

"But, you didn't even call Saturday. I wanted to hear your voice." She'd still felt hurt that he had not made the trip back to Indiana. Yet his attention now was on her and she needed him. Or, more appropriately, she wanted him.

"Karsen," He sounded frustrated. "I told you, honey, I had to work."

"On Saturday?"

"Yes. Clients don't care whether it's the weekend or not." He kissed her neck again. "Now, do you want to talk or can we just make up for lost time?"

Forgetting the past week, she abandoned her disappointment with him. They recklessly tore at each other's clothes. He kissed her aggressively. She could feel him hard against her. He was here now and that was the only thing that mattered. She needed to feel protected, like everything would be okay.

The bed bounced as they fell onto it in unison. The weight of his body made her feel safe. She needed him to want her, to love her. Her mind cleared and his rhythmic motion soothed her until she felt his body collapse beside her. Afterwards she lay still, his arm draped across her chest, and felt the rise and fall of his chest as he panted.

James rolled to the side of the bed and reached for his boxers. "I should get going," he said, beginning to dress.

"You're leaving?" Karsen sprang up in disbelief. He had always stayed before.

"I've got an early meeting with another potential client tomorrow." He sat at the side of the bed to put on his shoes.

"Honey, can't you just stay with me tonight? I don't want to be alone." She put her arms around his waist and linked her fingers. She felt like a child trying to keep her mommy close for just one last goodnight kiss.

"I'm sorry, K." He separated her hands and stood up, walking toward the kitchen counter to grab his keys.

"PLEEASE!" She gave him her best puppy-dog look. The look that once made him bend over backwards for her.

"It's work. You'll understand someday." He kissed her forehead as he finished tucking in his shirt. His voice patronized her as if a college student couldn't possibly understand the pressures of an actual real job.

"We barely talked while I was gone. I miss you. Are you sure you can't stay? I do have an alarm clock, you know?"

"I'm sorry, Karsen. I'll call you tomorrow." He turned and shut the door behind him. Karsen's heart sank as she blankly processed what had just occurred. The dimly lit room around her was dead silent and she suddenly felt an overwhelming awareness that she was completely alone. She lifted her body heavily out of bed and secured the deadbolt on the front door. The floor creaked as she crept back into bed. She lifted the covers over her head and curled up into a tight ball. As she fought back tears, she tried to put her lonely thoughts out of her mind.

෴

Monday morning started early. At five o'clock, Addison's alarm blared. She felt in the dark for the snooze button. Her eyes squinted into small slits trying to see the numbers. *Five more minutes*, she moaned as she dropped her head heavily back onto her satin-cased down pillow. Even her, a self-proclaimed type A-driven career woman had a hard time getting up in the morning.

Beep. Beep. Beep. The annoying sound blared again. This time, Addison took a deep cleansing breath. She pushed herself up in a single sweeping motion, stretched her arms overhead then dropped them toward the clock, turning it off.

Her mother's surgery was the first of the day. Addison promised her dad she would come by beforehand, even though she had managed to squeeze in a visit the night before. She figured it was also an excuse to get to the office early, not that she ever needed one. She typically arrived before everyone else, setting the precedent that long hours drove success.

Addison arrived at the hospital and quietly entered her mother's suite. Her mother's eyes were closed as she rested. The room had a sterile, smell of bleach and, although better than your typical hospital room, still seemed bleak. Believing in the power of the self-healing mind, Addison often wondered how anyone recovered in such a depressing environment.

She placed one hand over her mother's and the other gently on her forehead. "Mom," she said in a soft voice, "You awake?" Her mom's eyes struggled to open. For the first time Addison could recall, she looked vulnerable.

"Hi, honey. Glad you came by. Doctor says I'll be out of here in two to three days."

"You'll be fine, Mom. This cancer doesn't know whom it's up against."

"I'm not worried about the surgery as much as I am the chemo afterwards." She closed her eyes again.

"Just rest. One day at a time, Mom. Let's get through today. Tomorrow we'll deal with later." She kissed her forehead where her hand had just been.

"How's she holding up?" A deep male voice startled Addison.

"Hi, Daddy," Addison said, turning toward the door as her father came in.

"I'm doing fine, dear," her mother mumbled.

Bryce Reynolds looked over-dressed for the hospital in black dress pants and a stiffly pressed collared-golf shirt. His hair had turned gray years ago, but he still looked younger than his age.

"Good morning, Addy. I brought you some coffee. Thought it would jump-start your day." He handed Addison a Styrofoam cup with a plastic lid from the hospital's cafeteria. Undoubtedly not her first choice, but she couldn't turn down the caffeine. "How's that company of mine holding up, anyway?"

46

"You mean my company, right?" Addison smiled, giving her father a wink. She knew the one thing he was most proud of her for was taking over the magazine. One would think he handed her the throne of England. Or maybe that was just her perception. He'd spent all his time and energy building the company for so many years, leaving only remnants of time for her. She sometimes wondered if he would be as proud of her if she'd chosen a different career path.

Addison waited with her dad until a nurse rolled her mother into the hallway to ready her for pre-op. "I love you, Mom. You're going to be fine." Addison reassured her as she kissed her on the cheek goodbye.

"I'll call you when she's out," her dad promised as he stood alongside the gurney, holding her mother's hand.

"Thanks," she said. She knew her stomach would be in her throat until he did.

⁀

Upon her arrival at the office, Addison busied herself to keep her mind occupied. She started by tackling the flashing red light notifying her there were messages. Most of the messages were the usual business associates; Emily had called three more times.

Addison learned early to only touch each message once. Effective, productive individuals always act. You return the call, delegate to a subordinate, or toss it into the circular file. She'd been tossing Emily's messages for days. Avoidance was another technique she had perfected as a way to handle her personal affairs. Addison wondered at what point she'd lose Emily. There certainly would be a limit to how much abuse she would take. They'd been friends for nineteen years and she'd never told her she was adopted. How she slipped now escaped her.

Addison clicked the speakerphone button and reviewed the voice mails one by one:

Emily Blaker – DELETE
Emily Blaker - DELETE

Josh Crawford – wants to schedule meeting to talk about charity fundraiser (Forward to Marjorie to schedule lunch appointment.)
Linda Clayton – following up on query for article submission – DELETE (Learn to follow procedure. Don't send query letters to the owner. *Writer Lesson #1,* **she thought.)**
Emily Blaker - DELETE
Russell Masters – enjoyed talking to you at the fundraiser last week. Would like to pick up from where we left off? – DELE...

Hhmmm...Russell might be fun for a while. Addison caught herself and stopped one button press shy of losing his number. Russell was the CEO of one of New York City's largest real estate development companies. A self-made multimillionaire, Addison had always been impressed by his generosity at her mother's charitable functions and he seemed to keep his relationships out of the public eye. Success aside, he was handsome, sexy even. Although they had met briefly a few scattered times in the past, it wasn't until their most recent meeting at her mother's latest charity ball that she felt he was attending to her a bit more blatantly. They'd talked most of the evening. She knew he was one of the most intriguing businessmen she'd ever met and still she couldn't help but wonder like a schoolgirl how it would feel to have his strong arms wrapped around her. She pended a reminder to call him in two days. Whether she called him or not, a successful career woman can't look too desperate.

ॐ

"Good morning, Marjorie," Addison called out, seeing her arrive.
"Good morning. The usual today?" Marjorie poked her head through Addison's doorway.
"No, thank you, I've already sent Jacob." Jacob had been arriving early and staying late, working hours that challenged even Addison's.
"Just thought you might need a double shot today," Marjorie joked knowing that sending Jacob had been the norm the last couple days.

Marjorie returned to her desk and Addison returned to her e-mail. They both anxiously awaited her father's call.

⁓

"How'd the surgery go?" Marjorie beeped in to Addison as soon as she hung up with her Dad.

"Well. He said the doctors are still determining what treatment plan will follow, but it looks like they were able to get everything before it spread."

"Good news."

"Great news!" Addison said for both confirmation and her own reassurance. Relieved, Marjorie grinned and returned to her desk.

A few minutes later, Marjorie's head poked through the solid oak door again. "Addison? It's Emily."

"Yes. I got her message. I'll call her today. I promise."

"No, she's here. What should I tell her now? That you're off riding elephants in Asia?"

"What the hell?" Addison's hands clenched and her eyes widened. "Tell her I'm not here," she hissed, visibly flustered.

"Um…she can see we're talking. How about you're teleporting to the Enterprise as we speak? Or perhaps base jumping from the window?"

"Shit! Shit! Shit!"

"Addison, she's your friend. What's the problem? You can't avoid everyone every time you have an issue. Seriously – grow up!" she said in a forced, hushed voice.

"Fine," Addison said out of pure frustration. She should have known Emily would show up sooner or later. "She has five minutes. You can let her in."

Emily's sandy-blond hair was pulled tidily into a sleek ponytail. The days of butterscotch highlights had been lost to diapers and formula. Her make-up, a simple palate of natural browns, gave her an innocent girl next-door appeal, different from the polished, executive look of her friend. As she entered, her face was expressionless.

"I've called at least ten times. What the hell, Addison?"

"I'm sorry. I've been incredibly busy. You know, Mom's surgery, the magazine. I hardly have time to eat let alone socialize."

"Oh, baloney! You've handled more than that and juggled dating three men simultaneously. You're avoiding me. Better yet – you're pushing me away. I won't have it, Addy. You're my closest friend, and I won't let you do this."

"Em, really. I'm busy. I'll call you later." Addison looked at Marjorie who was pulling the door shut.

"No. You'll talk to me now. Good thing you're the boss so no one can fire you." She smirked smugly and straightened her light blue hoodie, noticing a dribble of oatmeal lingering from Adelaide's breakfast. "Fudge!" she muttered, automatically licking a finger and rubbing it over the spot in an attempt to remove it.

The spontaneous, unconscious act of her friend made Addison smile and she paused before responding in her calm, professional tone.

"I'm sorry I didn't return your calls. With all due respect, I just don't want to talk about it. Forget I said anything. It was a mistake. I am who I am. End of story."

"Not end of story. Beginning. Why did you hide this from me for almost twenty years? Don't you trust me?"

"Emily, it's no big deal. Can't you freaking let it go?"

"No! You push everyone away. I've seen you do it before and I'm starting to realize there might be a reason why, but you won't let me in. Addy, I'm on your side. I chose you as Adie's godmother, for crying out loud. Do you think I care who the heck your parents are?"

Addison stared blankly.

"No! I care about you. Why can't you see that?" Emily stared at her, waiting for a response.

Addison rested her head in her hands. She pressed her palms firmly against her eyes to think. Actually, to stop any tears. Emily was right. Of course she was right. She didn't let anyone in. Period. She had been there, done that all throughout college. Superficial friends were only interested in her money and her one serious boyfriend had cheated on her with a sorority sister. Emily had been different. She didn't care about Addison's status. She had emerged as her only sincere, true friend. One that in her heart, Addison didn't want to lose.

The silence of the room was unbearable. Emily grasped Addison's hands and pulled them down with hers.

"Addy," she said softly, "I don't care about your parents. If you don't want people to know, I certainly won't tell anyone. But don't shut me out. It's not fair to me. It's not fair to Adie. She misses you."

Addison continued to sit without saying anything. Thoughts raced through her mind, but no words passed her lips. Emily gave her friend's hands an affectionate squeeze, then picked up her keys off the desk. She had to get back to Adelaide who she had left coloring with Marjorie. "When you want to talk, call me." She shut the door quietly behind her.

For several minutes Addison sat with her head down on her desk. She didn't want to talk about it. She didn't want to think about it. What good would it do anyway? Maybe she did have a chip on her shoulder, but the only person it was hurting was herself. Why couldn't everyone just let her be?

～ 8 ～

"Karsen," Hanna panted as they ran. "Karsen!"

Typically, their conversation flowed continuously, making their usual three-mile loop seem less daunting. Today, Karsen seemed distracted and quiet. Almost three weeks had passed since she returned home from Indiana.

"What is with you today?" Hanna pressed. "I need a story or I'm going to keel over. You're pushing my pace."

"Sorry. I just have a lot on my mind, I guess." Karsen's voice lacked its usual energy.

"Talk to me. Pleeeaase – talk, sing, say anything. I can't run any further without something to pass the time." Hanna wished she had charged her iPod's battery, then it wouldn't have crapped out halfway through their run.

"I found something at my house. Or rather, I didn't find something," Karsen began.

"Speak English, girl. You've lost me already."

"You know my necklace. Well, when I was home for the funeral, I put all the pieces together and they all fit. That is, all the pieces except two. Brad says it's nothing, but if all the pieces were specifically made to fit together, why would there be a gap, like one is missing?"

Hanna knew the history of the Woods's family tradition. *What a cute idea,* she had thought when Karsen explained it to her. Her family barely tolerated each other even on holidays.

"Which two didn't fit?" Hanna gasped, struggling to breathe and pumping her arms harder as Karsen continued to pick up the pace.

"My mom's and my dad's. It looks like one piece should go in between the two."

"That doesn't make sense."

"Precisely my point. And what's weirder, is that my dad wanted to bury the charm with my mom. When I told him I wanted it, we ended up in a fight."

"That's not like your dad. Why didn't you say anything when you got back? And, Lord K, can you pleeeaaase slow down? You're killing me!"

"Sorry." Karsen noticeably eased up. "I don't know. I guess I've just blocked everything out. Things have felt a little off with James lately, Brad has his comedy act he's working on, and you've been busy, too." Her voice trailed off. "Brad thinks it's nothing. Maybe he's right…"

"It is a bit strange. Maybe your mom had a hot, steamy affair," Hanna said jokingly.

"Right," Karsen shot her a piercing glance. She knew her mom too well for that. Then again, lately everything in her life seemed to be falling apart.

"I'm sure Brad is right, K."

Karsen desperately tried to clear her mind as they continued their run. The loop ended in front of the student recreation complex. Already the afternoon temperatures reached well over seventy degrees and it was only late January. Karsen stripped off her fleece-lined running jacket, revealing a pink, spaghetti-strapped tank top. Her broad shoulders gave her a v-shaped, streamlined appearance most guys would be jealous of. She paced, hands on her hips trying to catch her breath.

"Here." Hanna handed her a crisp, cold bottle of water. Karsen thanked her before she guzzled half the bottle in one long swig.

Wiping her mouth, her gaze fell on the large glass wall of windows fronting the gym. Karsen thought she spotted James inside. She waved but he turned away. *Maybe he couldn't see me through the window*, she thought.

"Who were you waving at?" Hanna asked.

"Nobody." *Or maybe it wasn't him?* She was certain it was, though.

"You just wave for the heck of it now?" Hanna joked.

Karsen shook her head. "No, of course not. I thought I saw James in the gym. But, he's usually in class at this time." *Macro-economics at the W. P. Carey School of Business building to be exact.* She knew his schedule as if it were her own. She remembered partly because she was a woman and women remember every miniscule detail when it comes to their boyfriends, and partly perhaps, due to the fact that he droned on and on about the lectures every time they were together.

"Maybe it just looked like him. Anyway, I've got to get home to shower or I'll be late for Brad's show tonight." Hanna discarded her empty bottle into the recycle receptacle. "Seven o'clock, right?"

"Yeah. Brad left the tickets at will call. We'll meet you out front. I think he goes on third after the girl with the nail salon act. Have you heard her yet? She's hilarious," Karsen said.

"Cool." Hanna nodded and headed toward her sorority house.

Karsen walked through campus toward her apartment. Across from the School of Business building, she realized this was the spot. The exact place when she had received the call from her dad about her mother's accident. She could picture the scene like an out-of-body experience: The tears recklessly falling down her cheeks. Her books dropping to the ground as Hanna had embraced her. Panic constricted her chest and she exhaled with a gasp. Even two thousand miles away from home, there was nowhere she could go to escape the realization that her mother was gone and would never be back. Clenching her jacket in her hand, she sprinted the rest of the way home.

ᘐ

"Were you at the gym earlier?" Karsen asked James as she climbed into his car that night. She inhaled the fresh, new car scent. James had wasted no time purchasing the BMW – whether or not he realistically could afford it. It was only a three series - the least expensive model – but nonetheless, it was still a BMW. A BMW intended to scream, "I've arrived."

"Nah, why would you ask that? You know my schedule. I had econ." He started the engine and fiddled with the navigation system even though there was no need for directions to where they were going. They both knew the streets of Tempe inside and out, yet the pride he felt for his extravagant purchase trumped common sense and he mapped the address anyway.

"No reason really... It's just that Hanna and I finished our run through campus and I thought I saw you. It obviously wasn't, but from far away, the guy really looked like you though."

"Well, it wasn't me," James said dismissively.

"So, where do you want to eat?" Karsen asked, knowing they would get dinner before the show.

"How about Caffé Boa? You liked it before." James adjusted the rear view mirror more to admire himself than for driving safety. Karsen didn't recall noticing his displays of vanity until recently. *Stop being critical,* she told herself.

"Café what?"

"Caffé Boa."

"I've never been there," Karsen said quizzically.

"Sure you have. It's right there on the corner of Fourth and Mill."

"Still don't remember."

"We sat on the patio. Don't you remember how quaint it was with the vines and lights? You hogged the fresh buffalo mozzarella appetizer, remember? I can still taste the fettuccine bianca. Mmmm. I think I'll order it again tonight. That recipe has to come straight from heaven." James's voice sounded so convincing that even Karsen questioned her own memory.

"Hun, I know I've never been there. I remember everything we do. Mind of an elephant." She pointed to her forehead. "You must have gone there with your other girlfriend," she joked.

"No, K." James took her hand. It had been so long since he'd held her hand in the car that her mind relaxed. "You were there," he reiterated. "I can't believe you don't remember, but regardless you'll love it." He squeezed her hand tighter.

Karsen closed her eyes. Two years. Over two years they'd been dating. Every bone in her body told her he was the one, no matter how much her mother had questioned her relationship. She pictured their future together and in her dreams it felt real. She always thought she'd have the time to prove her mother wrong.

They covered the short distance to the restaurant quickly and James maneuvered the BMW into a rare street-side parking spot. Karsen smoothed her dress – a fitted, brown-striped halter that hugged her waist – as she climbed out of the car. The strappy brown sandals tied at her ankles drew attention to her sleek, striated calves.

"Come on." James, who had once opened her door for her, had jumped out on his side and now stood impatiently at the curb.

"What's your rush? We have an hour and a half before the Improv's doors open." Karsen folded her sweater over her arm and closed the car door. She always felt funny having a sweater at hand, but even in the peak of Arizona's summer the air conditioning in most restaurants chilled her. She watched as James pushed the button on the black key fob then heard the locks click twice behind her.

༄

The two ate politely but Karsen noticed an awkward disconnect in their conversation. She wondered if they were simply maturing, or if their relationship was growing stale. Their conversation used to be playful, a continual mix of flirting and serendipitous getting-to-know-you banter. No matter how hard she tried this evening, they just couldn't seem to connect.

"Hanna and I have Chemistry together this term. Our lab instructor gave us a quiz…"

"That's nice." He cut her off before she could continue. "Did I tell you about the telecom account I landed? My boss had been trying to close them for over six months. I was able to meet with the director of purchasing today, and he signed the contract right then and there."

"Wow." Karsen replied. "That's great, honey."

James droned on about his work and finance classes. Karsen tried to seem interested, but being a communications major, net present value and balance sheets really weren't her thing.

"You want to split a tiramisu?" Karsen asked.

"Really?" James balked at her suggestion for dessert with his 'you don't need to be eating that' tone. Instead, he signaled the waiter for their bill.

"Guess not." Her spirits dampened, Karsen excused herself and made her way to freshen up in the ladies' room. A few minutes later, she returned to the table where she once again joined James. She grabbed her purse from beside her chair and then they headed out to the car together.

༄

Cars moved like snails down Mill Avenue. Saturday nights were known to draw a crowd and traffic was always slow. She sensed James's frustration and wondered whether it was her or the chocked-full street of vehicles and jaywalking pedestrians that was irritating him. They turned down University Boulevard and pulled into the parking lot behind the Improv.

"Are you all right, honey?" Karsen asked. What she really wanted to ask was "are we all right?" but couldn't. Her insecurity wouldn't let her.

"Yeah. I'm sorry. I'm just stressed out."

"Is it work?"

"Yeah, of course. What else would it be?" He grabbed her hand again.

"Hey, there's Brad's truck. Let's park over there," Karsen suggested, thinking they could all leave together that way. James didn't argue. He pulled into an open spot in the next row that had enough room so as not to scratch the doors when they opened them. They both got out of the car and headed toward the club.

"Hanna!" Karsen shouted, spotting her friend in front of the entrance. "Wait up!" Hanna turned and allowed James and Karsen to join her.

"Hi, James. Nice ride." Hanna played into his already pompous ego.

"Thanks. I'd let you drive it, but you know what they say about women drivers?"

Hanna rolled her eyes. "Danica Patrick could run circles around your sorry ass."

"How about we leave the comedy routine to the comics inside, shall we?" Karsen could see the conversation roller-coastering downhill fast. Hanna loved pushing James's buttons.

James led the way to will call and they picked up the tickets that Brad had arranged for them. Inside, the lights were dim. The group stopped at the bar for drinks. An usher then led them to a four-top at the front left of the stage. The show appeared to have a full house; the balcony seats were even filled. *Not bad for amateur night,* Karsen thought. She filled with pride knowing Brad had a real shot at pursuing his dream career.

Looking toward the stage, Karsen spotted Brad waiting in the corner wing. She waved and she saw him smile back at her, clearly trying to maintain his concentration. His quirky smile filled Karsen with a welcome familiarity. Karsen grew up at the butt of his jokes. She certainly appreciated that his new material excluded her. His skits were tame compared to those of most comedians, focusing in mostly on childhood mishaps. Clean, relatively speaking. Karsen beamed with delight every time she watched him perform. She wondered if their mom could see him, too.

Karsen sipped her apple martini, which was usually her drink of choice. Tonight her stomach felt unsettled and while the others were well into their second drink, her first one sat barely touched.

At eight o'clock, Brad took the stage. Even though she'd heard him rehearse, Karsen's belly hurt from laughing. She thought about their childhood joke after joke.

"Dad had a phrase, no matter what the injury. Sympathetic, he was not. Stub a toe – 'It'll feel better when it quits hurting.' Break a leg – 'It'll feel better when it quits hurting.' Cut your arm off with a chainsaw – 'It'll feel better when it quits hurting.'"

Karsen wiped the inside corner of her eye. She laughed so hard that she was crying. Hanna leaned into her and whispered in her ear, "Hey, K, I think I might have a thing for your brother." Before she could respond, Hanna's attention veered back to Brad's act.

For a moment, the thought caught Karsen off guard. Hanna's flawless looks with Brad? Not that he was bad looking; he was related to her so their features were similar. His nose had a slight bump and he wasn't built like the guys she'd seen Hanna date. Looks aside, though, *this might not be a bad thing*, Karsen thought. At least she knew Hanna liked her, which was more than she could say for Brad's last girlfriend.

Karsen poked Hanna in the ribs. "You think what?"

"You heard me right. I think I'm interested in Brad." Hanna's cheeks turned a pinkish-red.

"You've known him for years…what prompted this?"

"I don't know. He's funny, amazingly nice and handsome in his own way. What's not to like?"

"Seriously, Hanna. This is Brad we're talking about. My brother Brad." Karsen still was somewhat taken aback by the thought.

"Yes. Seriously. Now, hush. I'm missing the best part." She gazed back at Brad up on the stage.

Following Brad's performance, the lights lifted to a soft glow as the intermission began.

"Stupendous!" Hanna, a bit tipsy, threw her arms around Brad's neck as he joined them at the table. *She certainly goes after what she wants,* Karsen thought. Brad looked startled by Hanna's sudden affection.

James handed Brad a beer. "Thought you might want this."

"Thanks," Brad said, wiping sweat from his brow. "It's so damn hot up there." He drew a long swig from the bottle.

The four of them watched, laughed and applauded the remaining three acts. Hanna flirted relentlessly, touching Brad's arm, smiling coyly, her approach boldly increasing over her third martini. James became more touchy-feely toward Karsen as well. With several beers down, his hand crept up the length of her thigh. She stopped him mid-leg.

"Stop it!" she whispered sternly, giving him a perturbed glance. He persisted. "Stop. I mean it." Her irritation grew by the moment. She never had been a fan of inappropriate displays of affection in public.

After the show, the crowd poured through the exit like cattle. A tipsy Hanna let out a jestful "Moooo!" Karsen walked in slow, baby steps beside Brad. She nudged him with her elbow. "Hanna needs a ride home. She's in no shape to drive."

Brad nodded. "Yeah, I noticed."

"Can you take her?"

"Sure."

They encountered no resistance from Hanna at the idea of Brad driving her home. "I can drive you back here tomorrow to pick up your car," Karsen promised as they loaded Hanna into Brad's pick-up. Hanna nodded like a bobble-headed doll as her eyes closed and she drifted immediately to sleep.

"Nice date," James joked. Brad replied with a wry smile as he circled around to the driver's side.

"Give me the keys," Karsen demanded, grabbing James's hand.

"I'm fine," he said sternly, holding them out of her reach.

"I mean it. Give them here. I'll drive." He didn't budge.

"Unless you want ten days in tent city and a pair of pink boxers, you'd better let her," Brad shouted, knowing James would be more likely to save face in front of him than give in to Karsen.

"Whatever. Here." James forcefully pressed the keys into Karsen's hand and headed toward the passenger side door. Karsen mouthed the words 'thank you' to Brad before easing into the driver's seat. She took her time adjusting the seat and mirrors to fit her. She looked over at James reclining back in his seat with his eyes closed and felt a mix of disappointment and anxiety. She'd looked forward to their date night all day and the evening hadn't lived up to her expectations.

No one got lucky that night. Brad dropped Hanna off to the guardianship of her sorority sisters. He had never thought of her as more than Karsen's friend before and certainly would not take advantage of her altered state. Yet a flicker of interest stirred inside him. He wondered whether he had misinterpreted her signals all together. Or perhaps, the alcohol simply made her overly friendly. He wasn't sure if she would still be interested once she sobered up.

Karsen drove carefully up the Loop 101 to Indian School Road where she signaled to exit. James had moved from Tempe to south Scottsdale to be closer to work. His apartment was older, but clean. It was in walking distance to Oregano's, Karsen's favorite pizza joint. Her mouth watered just thinking that a pizza cookie would hit the spot. Unfortunately, James's inebriated state made him more suited for home than a public venue at the moment.

Entering his apartment, James lay down on the bed. "Come here, babe."

"In a minute."

By the time she'd gone to the bathroom, he'd fallen asleep. His arms and legs sprawled out, spanning the width of the bed like the murder victim on a crime show. She removed his shoes and turned him on the bed.

"Come're, Nik." He said groggily.

"What?" Karsen questioned, but he had already rolled over and was sound asleep.

She glanced through his closet and pulled out one of his white oxford button down shirts to sleep in. She had seen women in the movies dress this way and rather hoped he'd think she looked sexy when he awoke. After she turned out the light, she crawled under the covers and snuggled in beside him for the night.

꩜

Karsen woke the next morning before James. In the kitchen, she scoured the cupboards. Typical bachelor. There was hardly any edible food. Thank God there was coffee. She loaded the coffee pot and hit brew. The strong aroma of dark roasted coffee beans made her feel refreshed.

A few leftover holiday cards and miscellaneous mail sprawled across the counter. She picked several pieces up, intending only to help straighten up a bit. A photo crept out of one. Curiosity getting the better of her, she opened the card. Inside, inscribed in notably feminine handwriting, was a note.

> *Dear James,*
> *Thank you for a wonderful weekend. Can't wait to visit again.*
> *Love, Nikki*
> *P.S. I've enclosed a reminder for you while I'm away.*

Karsen stood, momentarily shocked. She looked at the photo again. A voluptuous young lady, probably a few years older than herself, posed in a pink-polka dot string bikini.

Karsen viewed the second card, apparently a Christmas card from his grandparents. There was nothing out of the norm that popped out at her there. The third, also from the holidays, stopped her point blank. Her whole body felt numb as she read the words.

> *Dear James,*
> *Have a splendid holiday. Hope you are well and give our best to Nikki.*
> *Love, Jackson and Stephanie*

Jackson was James's brother. Stephanie was his wife. But Nikki? Who the hell was Nikki and why were they asking about her?

Karsen dropped the cards, scattering them across the table.

"Come' re, Nik," rung in her ears and her stomach wrenched into a knot. No. She ran to the bathroom shutting the door behind her. *No. No. No.* As she struggled to catch her breath, her mind rambled in thought… *if the thank you card was dated in January that meant she visited here. Not only was she here, but she was here while I was burying my mother.*

"Not this weekend," he had said.

Karsen lost her senses. She frantically opened drawers in search of something. What she wasn't sure. Evidence that another woman had been in his apartment. That was it. She opened the first cabinet. Bath towels. Next, wash clothes. Off to the side a zip lock baggie leaned against the wood. She pulled it out. Make-up. She WAS here. As nausea rose in her throat, Karsen dropped the bag and stumbled back against the wall, sinking slowly to the floor. She sat, hands over her face, and wept.

"Hey, K. Karsen, honey, what are you doing in there?" James called through the door. She didn't answer. "Come out, K. Come out and let's play." He said meaning play in the seductive sense. "You've been in there forever." He seemed oblivious to her sniffles. Her eyes felt like two swollen cotton balls.

Fury spread through her, making her skin flush as she staggered to her feet.

"Play?" She threw open the door. "Play? PLAY! Apparently, you've been PLAYING enough, ASSHOLE!" she screamed, lunging at him, fists flailing against his chest, tears streaming down her cheeks. "You jerk!"

James overpowered her. He grabbed her arms and secured them tightly against his chest. She fell into him, sobbing uncontrollably. He froze, perplexed by her actions.

Realizing she was submitting, she pushed him away.

"You cheater! I trusted you!"

"K, what are you talking about?" He tried to corral her in a bear hug. She resisted. "Come on! You're being crazy! What has gotten into you?"

"You cheater! You lying jerk!"

"Karsen, stop!" His voice was stern and he tightened his grip on her wrists to keep her from hitting him again. She struggled against him until he finally released her.

"I found the make-up!"

"What make-up?" His eyes glanced and he saw the bag on the counter. *Shit*, he cringed silently.

"The cards! The make-up! Nikki! Who the hell is Nikki?"

"Nikki?"

"Yes, Nikki?" she hissed.

"An old friend."

"We've been together for two years. I've never heard you mention a Nikki."

"Karsen, honey, you're freaking out over nothing." Karsen knew he was lying. He continued, "She's just a friend."

"She was here!"

"No."

"She met your brother and sister-in-law. I haven't even met them!" Had he known Nikki longer than her, maybe longer than they'd been dating? She felt bile churn in her stomach.

"Karsen, don't be so immature."

"Immature? IMMATURE? You cheat on me and I'm supposed to be mature? How does one react to the crushing news that her boyfriend is sleeping around? Brad was right all along! My mother was right all along! I'm so stupid!" she wailed.

"Enough, Karsen. I didn't cheat. You know that."

"Do you think I'm that naive? That you can sweet talk and rationalize your way out of this? What I know is that this is not my make-up. What I know is that single men don't keep make-up in their apartments. What I know is that I've never eaten at Caffé Boa before last night!"

"You shouldn't have been looking through my cabinets," James countered, his stance and tone becoming defensive.

"Don't turn this around on me. This is not my fault! This is your fault and right now this is over!"

She couldn't believe the words were coming out of her mouth. She was standing in front of the man she'd dreamed of marrying. She had clipped the photo of her dream dress out of *Brides* magazine just weeks before, the perfect off-white strapless gown. She gathered her clothes and returned to the bathroom slamming the door. Within minutes, she exited wearing her crumpled dress from the night before. Her tussled hair and make-up made her look like she'd had an unexpected one-night stand.

James made one last attempt to plead his case as she headed toward the front door.

"Karsen, please! You're being ridiculous. Let's talk about this!" he shouted.

She slammed the door behind her and ran down to the sidewalk in front of the building. Pulling out her cell phone, she called for a cab and didn't look back.

∾ **9** ∾

The "chin" debacle with Mr. Montague was settled. Crisis averted. Her mother's surgery had gone well and next month's issue was almost complete. Addison should have been relieved. Unfortunately, the stress had not released from her body. Her shoulders felt tense and her back was in knots that had taken up permanent residence. Her next massage wasn't scheduled until next Friday and her massage therapist booked out weeks in advance, so there was no chance of moving it forward.

Addison craved a distraction. She needed a release. She wanted someone to talk to and she knew what that meant. She sucked up her pride and called Emily. There was no answer so she left her a voice mail, apologizing for her recent behavior. She still didn't want to talk about her adoption, but at least she would make the effort to resolve the friendship.

Unable to reach Emily, her mind then turned to Russell. She hadn't returned his message yet either and still wasn't sure if she wanted to. It was late, however, and she figured he wouldn't be home so she dialed his number. The phone rang three, four times. Expecting voice mail, she flinched when he answered immediately feeling a twinge of regret.

"Hello?" His masculine voice penetrated the line. He had a slight accent she couldn't quite place, but it added to his appeal.

"Helloooo...?" his voice queried again.

"Russell?" Addison caught him, her momentary pause lingering so long he almost hung up.

"Yes, this is Russell."

"Addison Reynolds. I'm returning your call."

"Ah, yes. Hello, Addison." The background noise drowned out his voice.

"Perhaps this is a bad time." Addison apologized, certain she had caught him out.

"No, no. Hold on a moment." She could hear shuffling. When he came back, the racket of the background had dissipated. "That better?"

"Yes, much. I was... I was returning your call."

"Yes, you said that," he teased. "The two-day calling rule, huh?"

"Guilty."

"I was going to invite you to dinner." He waited for a response. "So?"

"Soooo?" Addison repeated.

"What are your dinner plans tonight?"

Addison looked at the clock. "It's after seven."

"Yes, but you're calling me now. I'll bet you haven't left the office."

"Guilty again."

He continued, "If I had to guess, you'll probably pick-up Chinese on the corner and eat at your loft while watching prerecorded episodes of *Lost*. And, anyway, if not tonight you'll make me wait another two days."

"Actually, *Lost* is a rerun. The series finale was last month. I planned to stop by the hospital then finish a book I've been reading."

"Everything okay?" His tone changed at the mention of her hospital visit.

"Yes. My mother had surgery. She's doing fine now."

"Then you are free for dinner," he said, as if 'no' would be an unacceptable answer.

"How about I meet you at," she paused as she calculated the time she needed in her head, "say eight-thirty?"

"Works for me. Have you been to the new seafood place on Fifth?"

"No, I haven't, but it sounds perfect. I've wanted to try it anyway."

"Shall I pick you up at your place then?"

"Um, actually, how about I meet you in front of the restaurant? That will give me time to wrap up a few things here and run by the hospital beforehand."

"Great. Then it's a date."

"Yes, Russell, I suppose it's a date." She hung up the phone trying hard to minimize the smile spanning across her lips.

After finishing outlining the layout changes for next month's cover, Addison logged off her computer and headed down the elevator.

"Good night, Ms. Reynolds," the security guard said as Addison walked by. Even with the guards, the building at night, with its dim lighting and utter silence, felt uncomfortable.

"Good night, Ed," she replied, smiling back while unconsciously quickening her step.

 ⌒◦

Her visit at the hospital was brief. Her dad had already returned home for the night and her mother slumbered peacefully. Addison pulled a chair beside the bed and sat in the dark. Her mother looked frail. Not the perfectly manicured, upscale wife and mother she'd always portrayed. Lying in bed, she looked powerless. Her face showed her age without the layers of moisturizer and make-up.

Addison's heartstrings had wavered ever since the day she had learned of her adoption. She reached across the bedrail and held her mother's hand as she slept.

"I know you love me, Mom." She paused to see if she would wake. "I just can't help but wonder if you ever regretted me. You and Dad were always so wrapped up in work and events. I spent more time with Nanny Marie than you sometimes. If my 'real' mother could give me away, maybe you wanted to, as well?" There were moments Addison felt her parents adopted her only to complete the family portrait – mother - father – baby – not because they longed to be parents.

Her mom stirred, but did not open her eyes.

"I know I should be thankful, and I am. You've given me a life most people can only dream of. But, is it wrong that I still wonder how my life could've been different?"

Addison closed her eyes and thought back for a brief moment to the one time she attempted to reconnect with her biological mother. As a teenager, she had even taken a bus across several states. "I went to find her once, Mom. I never told you and Dad." The twelve-hour trip proved pointless. On the ride there she kept imagining the reunion in her mind. Her real mother opening her arms to embrace her, tears falling as she admitted her grueling guilt over letting her go. Lucky for Addison, the school was too afraid of a scandal. Since she was already back safe and sound by the time they figured out she was gone, they punished her but didn't tell her parents.

"I thought if she could only see me, that she'd take me in. I was so young, so naive." The loving reunion never occurred. As Addison approached the house number she'd written down on a scrap of pink paper, she witnessed a scene she hadn't imagined - a mother in her mid-thirties playing lovingly with her two children. With Addison's limited exposure to young children, she roughly estimated them to be around the ages of one and three. What was clear to her was that her mother – the mother who gave up one child – had moved on. Addison obviously represented the past, a mistake long forgotten.

"I love you and Dad more than I can express." Addison held her mother's hand firmly.

Her head fell forward and her neck responded by snapping it up with a sharp jerk. Realizing she must have dozed off, Addison looked at the time. She was late. She kissed her mother goodnight and silently promised herself she'd visit again tomorrow.

Addison hailed a taxi outside the hospital, an easier feat than on Madison Avenue. As the driver attempted small talk, Addison primped. A dab of berry-stained lip color and a fresh pat of powder refreshed her face. A quick spritz of cucumber melon body spray and she felt awake again.

Her cell phone rang and Emily's name appeared on the screen. Having initiated the contact, she had to answer.

"Hello?"

"Addy?"

"Hi, Emily. You got my message?"

"Yes. I'm glad you called. I've missed you. Adelaide missed you."

"I'm sorry I pushed you away. But, Em, I still don't want to talk about it, okay?" Addison waited.

"Okay. Just remember that I'm here if you change your mind."

"Thanks." She saw the sign for the restaurant. "Ems, I hate to cut this short but I'm meeting someone for dinner and the taxi just pulled up."

"No worries, I understand. Is it a date?"

"Actually, yes. It's with Russell from the charity fundraiser."

"Well, good luck. Don't do anything I wouldn't do," joked Emily. Addison laughed.

"Hey, Saturday is your birthday right? How about I take Adie and you have a mommy day? I'll buy you a trip to the spa for your birthday. What do you think?"

Emily typically hated when Addy offered expensive gifts, but she couldn't help but beam over the thought of a day of pampering. "Sounds perfect!"

"See you then." Addison hung up the phone. She felt better knowing she and Emily were back on the right track.

She could see Russell waiting as the taxi pulled toward the curb. Recognizing him was easy. His black hair was buzzed into a clean military cut. If there were any hints of gray, she had not noticed it. He was tall and well built. She remembered gazing up at him even when she was wearing five-inch heels the day they met.

She climbed out of the cab and adjusted her skirt, being careful not to over-expose her legs through its slit. Before she could turn to pay her fare, the cabbie drove away. Russell had paid the tab. *A nice gesture*, she thought.

"Hello, Russell. You didn't need to take care of that, but thank you anyway."

"My pleasure, Addison. Now shall we?" His hand gently found the curve of her lower back as he guided her through the door of the restaurant.

Typically, Addison felt at ease creating casual conversation, but Russell made her nervous. Her stomach churned with butterflies like a child before a first recital. The giddy feeling was a welcome change.

Luckily, Russell led the conversation throughout dinner. It was exactly the distraction Addison desired. His voice mesmerized her and she could have listened to him for hours. She'd been out with her share of men - actors, doctors, and lawyers - somehow Russell was different. His stories held her interest, far from the mundane resumes and self-indulgent conversations other dates had offered.

Time passed quickly. The restaurant cleared as they lingered over after-dinner coffee. Both seemed content to remain in each other's company. Realizing tomorrow's work pace would be relentless whether Addison's love life sparked or not, she reluctantly started to say goodbye.

"I should probably get going," she said, reaching in a sharing gesture toward her purse.

"Oh no, you don't. Tonight is on me. You can't seriously think I'd let you split the bill." Russell motioned to the waiter for the check.

"Next time then," she said, thanking him.

"Next time. I like that." He smiled. Addison noticed his lips parted slightly crooked and wondered what other small details she would discover about him.

"Saturday?" he questioned, offering date number two.

"Can't. I already have a date." She could see his expression tighten. "A play-date." She corrected. "My goddaughter. She's awfully cute. I'd invite you, but she might smother you in kisses and I'd be jealous."

"Really?"

"Don't get too excited. She's two. Her taste in men has not yet developed. She's especially drawn to the four men who play the Wiggles." They both laughed at the thought of four grown adults prancing around gaily in primary colored shirts.

The staff attacked their table like vultures the moment they stood up.

"Guess they want to go home." Russell winked as he helped her on with her coat.

"Me, too. I'm exhausted."

"In that case, let's get you to bed."

Awfully forward, Addison heard her own voice in her head.

Noticing her caught-off-guard expression, he added, "I didn't mean with me." Her lips pursed in an embarrassed smile, showing a glimpse of her softer side. At the same time a warmth rose within her as she imagined what he'd be like in bed.

He assisted her into the next available cab. As she settled in, he leaned in and brushed her lips with the lightest kiss. She longed for more. He slipped his business card into her hand.

"Text my cell when you're home so I know you're safe. It's on the card." She nodded in agreement.

"Goodnight and thank you."

"The pleasure was all mine, Addison. I'll call you," he said, shutting the door. She rather hoped he would.

❀

Karsen didn't know where to turn when she arrived back at her apartment. She tried Hanna's cell. No answer. Her mom was gone. Her dad would sympathize, but not really understand and he had enough on his shoulders anyway. Brad. She'd dialed his cell then hung up. She didn't want to hear I told you so. He'd never really expressed that before but she was certain he felt like it. Especially the time in high school when she'd found herself in a precarious situation at a party involving too much alcohol and a less than reputable male classmate. She and Brad had attended the party together. Yes, she had flirted with the guy and, yes, she shouldn't have been drinking but he was forcing himself on her. She felt helpless, at least until Brad burst through the door and pulled the guy off. That moment she remembered vividly. The moment Brad saved her. And he had always been there to save her ever since.

Brad was driving when he saw her missed call. He immediately pressed her speed dial number.

"It's over," he heard through a muffled wheeze. He knew what she meant without any further explanation.

"I'm on my way."

Brad flipped his phone closed. *Never mind the audition.* Irritation rose within him and he was uncertain whether the source derived from James or Karsen. *Family first.* There would be other auditions. He only had one sister and she needed him. At the next available opportunity, he made a U-turn and drove away from his dream.

Karsen had left the door unlocked. Brad entered, speaking soothingly.

"K, are you okay?" There was no reply. He could hear her sniffles from the bathroom. He moved quietly, trying to side-step the balled up tissues that covered the floor like a layer of fresh fallen snow.

"I'm sick. Physically sick." Karsen's knees were curled underneath her while her head hung over the toilet. She held her hair back with one hand, steadying herself against the rim with the other.

"It's just your emotions taking over. You'll be okay, sis."

Brad grabbed a towel and wiped his sister's face. He stumbled through tying her hair back like a father trying to put up ponytails for the first time.

"I thought he was the one."

"I know."

"I picked out a dress. I mean, not that he proposed. But two years we've dated. We've talked about it. He's such a liar!" Her sobs rose again.

"I know you don't think so now, but this will all work out. It always works out for the best."

"I wanted to call Mom. She knew, too. Why did everyone know he was wrong but me?"

"Because you loved him. He just wasn't smart enough to know what he had."

Brad helped her up and tucked her into bed still in her jeans and tank top. He pulled a chair from the kitchen table and sat watching over her until she finally drifted to sleep.

A light knock tapped against the front door and Hanna peeked through. "Karsen?" she whispered.

"In here," Brad called softly. "She fell asleep."

"Oh." She kept her voice hushed. "I can take it from here." She said in an effort to relieve him.

"It's okay. I mean… I was on my way to an audition when she called, but she needed someone. I couldn't not come."

"Audition? What audition?"

"Nothing really."

"Brad, what audition?" Hanna pressed.

"Well, there's a new show coming out. A reality competition for stand-up comedians."

"What? What are you doing here – go!" He looked perplexed. "I'll handle this. We all knew it would happen sooner or later." She quieted her voice even further to assure Karsen couldn't hear. "I mean not in the beginning, but with his history and behavior lately… I just had a feeling."

"I know. Me, too."

"So, then what are you waiting for? Go!"

Hanna pushed Brad toward the door. He turned and spontaneously kissed her slightly, hitting the corner of her lips. Her eyes danced and her cheekbones lifted into a smile. "Go!"

✺ 10 ✺

Monday, Karsen drug herself out of bed and unenthusiastically faced the day. She'd missed too many classes already. She couldn't afford to be absent again or she'd need to drop the semester entirely. Nor did she want her grades to suffer. Her 3.9 GPA qualified her for a supplemental grant that paid her out-of-state tuition. Without it, she'd find herself back in Indiana.

She pulled on a baseball cap, jeans and a t-shirt, grabbed her lime-green, down-filled jacket and headed out the door.

Her eyes remained puffy and sore. She felt as though there were no more tears left in her. *Time to buck-up*, she told herself. She'd lost her mom and her boyfriend. She felt alone. Nevertheless, she had to be strong or she'd lose herself.

✺

She skipped her usual coffee, the campus Starbuck's now serving as a painful reminder of how she met James. Besides, her stomach was too uneasy. Usually, she tended to gain weight under stress. This time was different. The thought of him being intimate with another girl made her physically ill, and over the last couple of days she'd dropped at least three pounds. James had attempted to call. He left several messages with insufficient apologies and even worse attempts at explanations. It didn't matter. Karsen knew she could never trust him again.

Hanna joined her in chemistry lab.

"How you holding up?" she asked, setting her backpack on the table beside her.

"Getting by I guess. I don't really have any other way to be."

"I'm sorry. Is there anything I can do?

"No. You've been a great friend. I appreciate everything." Karsen opened her lab notebook to the experiment they were about to attempt.

"Hey, how'd Brad's audition go?" Hanna was anxious to hear. After his quick kiss – just a peck, really, she'd told herself – she'd still hoped he'd call her himself, but he hadn't.

"What audition?" Karsen had no idea what she was referring to.

"Oh, he didn't mention it?"

"No."

"Oops. Maybe I shouldn't have said anything. Well…apparently, he was on his way to a try-out for a new reality show. It's supposedly a contest like the singing ones, but for comedians. He was going to skip out on the audition to take care of you when I showed up and made him go."

"Seriously?" Karsen asked, perplexed, although she was not at all surprised by the fact he would drop everything for her. It was typical Brad.

"Yeah."

"It probably wasn't that important if he was willing to pass it up," she said, even as she felt pangs of guilt in her already unsettled gut.

"Doubt it. That brother of yours is something else. Mine hardly ever calls me. He'd never come to my rescue."

Hanna paused then, deliberating over whether to tell Karsen about the kiss.

"K?" she started. "He kissed me. Well, really it was just a peck. He was probably just excited to get to the audition. But, well, I know under the present circumstances the timing is not so good, but do you think he's interested?"

Karsen sat quiet, staring blankly. For a moment, Hanna regretted her comments, but before she could apologize for being insensitive to her situation, Karsen all but burst out laughing. Dear, confident, breathtaking Hanna doubted whether a boy liked her - and not just any boy, her own brother, with his skinny little butt, quirky looks and knack for constantly poking fun.

"Hanna, I don't think you have anything to worry about," she assured her friend. Hanna felt a wave of relief flow through her.

The girls stopped gabbing as the professor approached to check their progress on the assignment. Karsen's bag vibrated at her feet. Her hand reached down discretely, feeling for her phone. She glanced down at the text message.

OMG. I made it 2 round 2! Call me. I'll explain. B

She tipped the phone so Hanna could read the text. Her eyebrows rose and her eyes widened in excitement. Karsen texted him back, trying not to alert the professor who would call her out for disturbing class.

In Chem. Call U L8R.

Karsen tried to focus on the experiment, but the two-hour class felt like an eternity. Finally, class was dismissed and she called Brad back.

"Hey!" he answered.

"Hey! Hanna told me about the audition. Why didn't you tell me?"

"I'm sorry. I don't know why really, but I guess I didn't want to get too excited about it. Thousands audition. I was trying to keep my hopes in check. The chances of being chosen for the show are so small."

"But you said you made it to the next round."

"Yes. I got a call back. The producers want me to audition again. They selected forty to audition in Hollywood and then they'll narrow it down to ten for the show. So, it's still a long shot. But, I made the first cut. I never dreamed I'd make it past round one. I still can't believe it!"

"So, what is the show exactly?" Karsen asked.

"It's called *The Funniest Comic*. Original name, I know. Anyway, it's a new reality show where comics compete. Kind of like *American Idol*, but trust me, if I sang people would laugh."

"I can't believe you didn't say anything before."

"I know. I just figured I'd go, get eliminated and not have to be embarrassed that I wasn't good enough."

"You don't give yourself enough credit then." Karsen paused, contemplating whether to bring up Hanna who was standing beside her. "Uhmm. Hanna was disappointed you didn't call her."

He paused a moment. "Oh…. So she told you. I wanted to call her, but I wanted to tell you first."

"So you wanted to call her?" Karsen repeated so Hanna could hear, hoping he would elaborate further.

"Let's change the subject," Brad said. He wondered again if he had misread Hanna's signs. She seemed interested. But him? He wasn't the type of guy she usually dated – the handsome, built-like-a-quarterback type. He couldn't imagine why she'd be interested in him.

"Heeelllooo? Brad, you still there?" Karsen broke the long silence.

"Sorry."

"Anyway, Hanna's headed home to change. She's going to meet me to run. I'm sure you could catch her if you call her now." Karsen still had some doubts about her best friend dating her brother, but she loved them both and if they could be happy together, then she was willing to share.

"Thanks for the information. Talk to you later?"

"Of course. Oh, congrats again on your call back. I'm so proud of you!"

"Thanks. Bye, sis."

"Bye." She pushed the "End" key on her phone.

∽

"Here's her diapers, wipes, pack-n-play, a change of clothes, sippy cup..." Emily unpacked the arsenal of baby supplies.

"Is she moving in?" Addison said facetiously.

Emily ignored the comment, continuing to unload and explain Adie's routine. "She's been going on the potty some, but keep a diaper on her anyway. I don't want her to have an accident on your new designer couch. I don't know what you paid for it, but I'm sure it was more than I could afford to repay if she ruins it. And... she can climb out of the pack-n-play. If she's really tired she won't, at least not until she wakes up, so get to her quickly."

Emily was about to begin another sentence when Addison interrupted, trying to reassure her.

"We'll be fine."

"I'll be back around four. If Greg can pick her up earlier..."

Addison interrupted Emily again. "No need. Now go. Relax. Adelaide and I have playing to do."

"You're the best!" Emily sincerely meant it. Not only had Addy agreed to take Adelaide for the day as a birthday present, but she had arranged a full day for Emily at the spa just as she promised. Massage, pedicure, hair, even lunch was included - a full day without diapers and that sometimes sassy child of hers. No matter how much she loved Adie, mommies need a break, too.

"I know," Addison agreed. "Only teasing."

"Bye, sweetie. Mommy loves you."

"Bye-bye, Mommy!" Adie waved and blew a kiss. Emily blew her a kiss back, waved and ventured out the door before Adie realized Mommy was leaving without her.

Addison thought about what it would feel like to have a child. At her age, she knew the chances of having her own were slim. Her biological ticker was running its last race. It wasn't that she never desired children, she'd just never found the right guy or at least never allowed herself to keep one around long enough. But she had Adelaide in her life, and it was the next best thing.

"Adie. What do you say we go to Barneys?"

"Barney!" Adie clapped. "I luv u. U luv me..."

"No baby. Not Barney. Shopping. Want to go to the store?"

"Yea! I go to store!" Adie exclaimed with delight. She would've agreed to anything.

⁓

"You're a shopping pro, Miss Adelaide." Addison held up two Prada bags. "Which one do you like?" A lady browsing through the handbag section stared at her. By the look on her face, Addison could tell she wondered if she were really going to let a two-year-old pick out a bag – and such a pricey one at that.

Adie pointed at the new spring line's woven shopper bag in pink, white and taupe. Addison held it up higher. "This one? That's what I was thinking, too. You have wonderful taste, my dear."

Addison placed the more subdued tan bag back on the shelf. "How about we go check out the baby girl clothes for you?" she asked Adie as if speaking to an adult.

"OOO-kaaaay," Adie chimed, drawing out both syllables. Addison loved listening to her voice. She sounded like she was the lead in a musical, singing every word.

In the toddler girl's section, they gave Addison's gold card a workout.

"You'll be the envy of all the girls at preschool. Little Suri Cruise and Violet Affleck will have nothing on you." But Adelaide no longer seemed interested in her godmother's banter. Her thumb was deeply planted in her mouth and her eyes began to grow heavy.

Addison figured she could nap in the car. She wanted to visit her mother who had been released the day before from the hospital. She was now resting at their home in Bedford, roughly fifty miles outside of the city.

"Uh-oh!" Adie's eyes got big again. Her thumb popped out of her mouth. "Poopy! Poopy-stinky. Yuck!"

Addison grimaced. "You didn't."

"Poopy," Adelaide repeated. The recognizable stench crept into Addison's nose.

"You did." Addison's shoulders and upper body hunched forward in dismay. "You're supposed to tell me when you have to go potty, Adie."

Addison finished paying for their purchases then fumbled to quickly cram the numerous bags beneath the already over-packed stroller. "Where's the ladies' room?" She asked the sales associate.

"Take the escalator," she paused noting the stroller, "Actually, take the elevator behind men's coats down to the first floor, then take a left. Look right and you'll see it from there."

"Thanks." Addison hurried, trying not to inhale. "Lord, Adie, what did your mother feed you this morning?" Thumb planted firmly back in her mouth, Adie simply stared up at her.

They arrived at the bathroom and Addison surveyed her options. The stroller wouldn't fit in a stall. The lounge area was immaculately furnished, but a lady sat there nursing her baby. She didn't want to change a stinky diaper in front of her. "Ah-ha. The changing table!" Addison said, not realizing she was thinking aloud. She unbuckled Adie and lifted her out of the stroller. Addison locked her elbows, keeping her arms straight out in front of her as if to keep the smell as far away as possible. She laid Adie on the marble slab, hitting the back of her head slightly.

"Whhaaa!" Adelaide cried.

"Sorry, honey," Addison said, rubbing the back of the little girl's head. Adie fussed and wiggled her body uncomfortably. "It'll just take a moment, sweetheart. Now where are the wipes?" Adie squirmed restlessly as Addison dug through to the bottom of the stroller. "Voila!" she exclaimed holding up the diaper wipes that were buried behind the mass of shopping bags.

"All done." Addison lifted Adie off the rock-hard table and secured her back into the stroller. Adie seemed relieved. She waved both hands, repeating the sign language symbol for all done after Addison.

"You're happy about that, huh? Let's get out of here, shall we?" They rolled past the nursing mom whose look suggested that Addison had no mothering skills whatsoever.

❧ 11 ❧

After class, Karsen returned to her apartment. Now that James wasn't making his nightly visits, the apartment felt deserted. She felt alone, more alone than ever. The ceiling fan hummed against the silence as it circled on high. She made a cup of tea and turned on the television. Other than a rerun of "Oprah," nothing interested her. The episode was about a recent book on the law of attraction. Karsen speculated about what she could have possibly done to attract the recent events of her life. In two months, her picket-fence existence had been kicked in, trampled over and all but destroyed.

She was desperate for something to do – anything that would distract her. Karsen remembered from her psychology class that there were stages to grief. She made her way to the couch, opened her laptop and Googled the word. Several links appeared. She clicked on the one detailing each stage. It showed five. She had sailed past the first – denial. Her mom was gone. James had cheated. There was no denying either. Anger. Yes, she was undoubtedly angry. God, was she angry. Bargaining, depression and acceptance. Acceptance seemed distant, she couldn't fathom accepting the amount of loss she'd experienced in such a short time.

She sipped her tea. The hot liquid burned her tongue, leaving a rough, coated feeling. She set the mug back on its coaster and closed her eyes. In the midst of the weekend's commotion, she'd neglected to call her father. Sunday calls home had become routine. So routine that she realized she should have known the mid-week call meant tragedy the instant her dad had called about her mom. She contemplated calling him now, but with the time difference she assumed he was probably already asleep for the night.

She refocused her eyes on the computer screen. The television still played in the background and she could overhear the dialogue. "You bring about what you thank about." Karsen found it hard to feel gratitude. She felt shell-shocked and unsure about the future. She longed to rewind the past two months and erase them altogether. The only feeling she felt in her heart was bitterness.

Her screensaver flashed on and she circled her finger across the touch pad to clear it. She wanted to keep her mind occupied but had limited ability to focus nor the ambition to tackle any schoolwork. As she continued to surf, a "Create Your Family Tree" link appeared in a box above her open window. Pop-up ads – she hated them. Those annoying boxes continually wasted her time and bogged down her processing speed. Out of habit, she moved her mouse to click the corner X to close the ad. Her hand paused. *Family Tree*. She thought about it. There were only three immediate family members left. Dad, Brad and herself. Her grandparents had all passed away and her family never developed a close connection to any of their aunts, uncles or cousins.

Instead of closing the box, she clicked on the hyperlink. Within seconds, she was launched into ancestry.com, a homepage for a genealogy website. There were several links spanning across the top. Create your family tree, name search, blog, about us. She clicked on the name search and typed "Woods" into the open box and 5,190 records appeared. "Wow, I didn't realize we had such a popular name," she said aloud. She narrowed the search "Katherine Woods," reducing the hits to less than 800, but she didn't have the patience to ruffle through that many records.

She clicked the blog site and marveled at the number of posts. There were suggestions about how to research ancestors, links to other recommended sites, and stories and interesting family discoveries. One family linked their ancestors back to the Lincoln family. Karsen was intrigued. There were also stories about finding missing family members.

Karsen returned to the family tree link. Maybe it would be fun to learn more about her extended family. At least it would provide temporary entertainment and the service was free so it fit her budget.

Karsen called her dad the next afternoon.

"Hey, Daddy."

"Hi, sweetheart. Is it Sunday already?" he teased, knowing she missed the weekend's call. Her mother would have tried to call her, but he just figured he'd talk with her later.

"Funny. How are you? I just thought I'd check in since I was a bad daughter and didn't call you yesterday."

"Too busy for your old man. I get it," he laughed.

"No, of course not. I had a really bad day. Did Brad tell you?"

"Tell me what?"

"That James and I broke up over the weekend."

"Oh, no. I'm sorry, honey. Are you doing okay?"

"I suppose." She knew her dad didn't know how to handle emotional situations, so she held back the details. She also knew he'd fly out with a shotgun if she told him why they broke up.

"What are you up to?" she asked, changing the subject.

"Oh, the usual. Work, eat and sleep. I've been taking the dog for a walk every night. It's been good for us both to get out."

"That's good. Say, Dad, did you ever realize that your necklace charm and Mom's didn't match up?"

He paused, contemplating his reply. He didn't want to draw any more attention to the charms than there already had been. He knew if Brad gave Karsen Katherine's charm, she'd try to fit them together. He wasn't surprised the topic had resurfaced again, but rather hoped after their argument Karsen would have let it go already. "Oh, I never paid much attention to those things, sweetheart. It was your mom's family tradition. I told you before, I just went along with it."

"So, you never tried to fit them together? Mom always said all the pieces fit. That was the purpose of them being puzzle pieces," Karsen pressed. "I can't believe I never tried to put them together before. I just believed her, I guess."

"Hun, your mom loved Grandpa's idea. You know she was a sentimental junkie. That woman never missed a chick flick. But, I don't know the logistics of it all. Grandpa made the first three pieces. Maybe the pieces were too hard to match up. All the rest were made by a jeweler." He didn't elaborate further. "Well, I should get back to work, I suppose. Good to hear your voice, honey," he said, anxious to end the conversation.

"Ok, Dad. Talk to you Sunday."

Karsen hung up the phone. Her frustration grew. She didn't know if she was frustrated not knowing the truth, or with herself for not letting it go.

༦ᦗ

"You did what?" Emily's eyes ballooned open as she looked at the shopping bags sitting on Addison's floor. She couldn't even guess the amount of money it took to fill them.

"I said I bought a few things for Adie."

"Mommy, look at me!" Adelaide waddled out in a pair of Addison's high heels. She giggled at herself as she tottered around the living room.

"Good job, Peanut." Emily smiled down at her daughter then turned to address Addison. "Seriously. Barneys? We can't accept this. You'll have to return it - all of it. Her clothes are from Target, maybe Carters, but not BARNEYS!"

"They're gifts, Em. It's okay."

"It is not okay. Do you realize that kid's clothes get pooped on, peed on, and puked on? Or if not one of the three P's, they outgrow them before you get the tags off. You can't pay that for baby clothes."

"Yes I can. I did and I will again." Addison wouldn't budge. "Adie loves them. Anyway, if she's going to model for my next edition, she's going to need something to wear. I mean other than her 'Tax Deduction' t-shirt. It's cute and all, but not exactly classy."

Emily looked perplexed. "You're joking, right?"

"About what?"

"You don't really plan to use her for a shoot?"

"Well, yes. I mean, with your permission, of course. She's adorable. I was thinking about an article on working moms – you know, the complexities of juggling both a high-powered career and a family. Adie would be perfect, and we'll compensate her appropriately."

"Pay Adie?" Emily tried to get her head around the thought of not only her two-year-old daughter earning an income, but an income larger than her own as she was now a stay-at-home mommy. What would Greg think?

84

"Yes, I'm sure you can put the money in a trust fund or education account, right? Or, Adie could throw one big shindig for her third birthday party. Ice cream and cake for all the toddlers in Manhattan."

"Up! Up!" Adie held both arms toward Addison. Addy leaned over, grabbed her up under her armpits and propped her naturally against her hip.

"You want to model, don't you Adie?"

"No!" Adie replied.

"She says 'no' to everything," Addison said, shaking her head. The word had to be the most common one among Adie's age group. No meant "no," no meant "yes," and no meant "maybe," or simply "I don't know any other word to say."

Addison grabbed Adie's hand as the little girl giggled and tugged on her necklace. "Don't pull that, sweetie."

"Is that new?" Emily asked. The necklace didn't look typical of something her friend would wear. The simple silver chain and charm looked almost rustic. There was no gold, diamonds or other precious gems adorning the piece.

"No," replied Addison, nonchalantly stuffing it back into her blouse.

"Oh, I just never noticed it before."

"So what about the shoot?" Addison asked again.

"I don't know. I'll talk to Greg and let you know. If he's okay with it, well then, I guess I will be, too." Emily smiled and lifted Adie out of Addison's arms and into her own. "Thank you again for today. It was just what I needed."

᠗

"Ready to go?"

Hanna jogged up to Karsen. Her hair was looped into a loose ponytail and her pink shoelaces were tied in double knots. "How about the five-mile loop today? I almost ate an entire pan of brownies by myself last night."

"Stewing over anything in particular?" Karsen asked.

"Not really. Well. Maybe? That schmuck you call a brother hasn't called me."

Karsen laughed. "It's been like one day, Hanna. You crack me up. Since when are you insecure about a guy? Sheesh!"

"I know. I know." She covered her face with both hands. "I don't know what my deal is lately. I'm so used to the guy pursuing me. What's with your brother?"

"Hanna, he likes you. He's probably just in shock that you like him. Give it time." Karsen placed her hands against the wall and pushed back to stretch her Achilles, first one leg and then the other. She kneeled down and tightened her shoelaces, reset the timer on her watch and was ready to go. Their loop headed up Mill Avenue to University then weaved through campus, ending back where they began.

Not five minutes into their run, Karsen tentatively broached the topic of her necklace with Hanna again. She was not sure what she was seeking. Perhaps she was hoping for confirmation that she should let it all go, or perhaps reassurance that she should not. "So…I asked my dad about the necklace pieces last night."

"And?"

"And nothing. He was unconcerned or at least uninterested. He implied maybe the jeweler that made ours never matched my mom's in the first place."

"And do you buy that?"

Karsen reflected momentarily as she looked both ways before stepping off the curb to cross the street. "I guess. I mean my parents were happy. It wasn't like they hid anything from each other."

They ran a few more minutes without chatting. "What if he doesn't know?" Hanna suggested.

"Know what?"

"Or, what if he knows something and doesn't want to tell you?" Hanna took a sip from her water bottle and checked her watch. The conversation slowed them off their usual pace, but since she was feeling on the sluggish side, she didn't mind.

"He wouldn't lie to me."

"I didn't say lie. More like fib or withhold information is what I was implying."

Karsen shook her head. "I still don't think so." She paused. "Why can't I just let this go? I feel like I'm torturing myself over something trivial. Brad's probably right. They probably never fit."

"Does it really matter anyway?"

"Who knows? Maybe I'm just trying to get back at my dad for the fight we had. I still have no idea why he blew up that night."

"I wish I was more help." Hanna racked her brain trying to think of something to help her friend find some rhyme or reason. "You said a jeweler made yours, right?"

"Yeah. My grandpa made the original three, but he passed away. My mom had ours made at a jewelry shop in town." She paused. "Why? What are you thinking?"

"Call around and find the jewelry store," Hanna said.

"Why?" The thought hadn't occurred to Karsen.

"It's a long shot, but maybe the store would know if they fit. There have to be some kind of sales records for a custom piece, don't you think?"

Karsen pondered the suggestion. Hanna might be right. She contemplated the logistics of tracking down the store. There were several possibilities.

"So, has James called any more?" Hanna redirected the conversation. She was hoping the answer was no. She didn't want to see Karsen hurt any more.

"Just once. He left another voice mail, late at night as usual. He really needs to give up on the make-up booty call. Fat chance."

"Are you sure you're still doing okay?" Hanna knew Karsen put on a strong front, but she continued to worry about her.

"Up and down, I guess. The busier I keep, the better. One thing is for certain. You don't have to worry about me going back down that path. Once a cheater, always a cheater, right?"

Hanna smiled. "My thought exactly."

Rounding the corner, Karsen slowed and began walking a few steps before they reached their usual finishing mark.

"Slacker!" Hanna jabbed.

"Whoaa!" Karsen blinked, trying to adjust her eyes. Her hands reached out to balance herself as she staggered. Her sight blurred into a sheet of black, spotted by an array of flashing stars.

"Are you okay, K?" Hanna instinctively grabbed Karsen's arm to steady her.

"Just dizzy. Overdid it, maybe?" She blinked as her vision cleared. "I think I'm okay."

"It seemed like our usual pace. Weird. Maybe you just need to eat?"

"Maybe. My appetite has been a bit out of whack lately...instant diet. I'm even fitting into my skinny jeans." Karsen tried to run down her food intake over the past several weeks. All the stress she'd been under had taken its toll, and she had all but lost her taste for food. Hardly anything sounded appetizing and what she did eat rarely settled in her stomach.

"Why don't we grab a bite at the student center? Maybe getting something into your system will help."

Karsen nodded in agreement and they headed toward the food court.

∾ **12** ∾

Russell called Addison persistently from the moment they ended their initial date. She secretly enjoyed his attention, but still didn't want to let her emotions take control. She'd pursue dating him as long as she commanded the ship.

Both of their schedules were tight, yet their relationship bloomed via text messages and voice mails. Other than a few brief late night conversations, they'd had little time to connect without the aid of electronic devices. With the swing of emotions she'd experienced recently, Addison was looking forward to relaxing Sunday when they'd arranged a second date.

Russell arrived at Addison's loft promptly, his arms adorned with an elaborate bouquet. The flowers were not your typical flower arrangement but a spray of orchids direct from the Big Island. The birds of paradise gleamed in hues of red, yellow and orange, accented by sprigs of lavender dendrobrium throughout.

"These flowers are unbelievable, Russell! Where did you find them?" Addison exclaimed.

He grinned, content that he pleased her. "Sorry, I can't divulge my secrets. Gives other men a fighting chance." He kissed her cheek. "May I come in?"

"Yes, of course. Let me find a vase for these." She led him into the kitchen. As she searched for the right sized vase, he gently laid the flowers across the black granite countertop. Her spacious 4,000 square-foot condominium lacked no creative restraint. The décor could easily adorn the cover of *Modern Living* magazine. The walls were a soft shade of taupe, with one deep eggplant accent wall drawing interest to a series of three large sepia tone photos. The photos were abstract, artistic photos, nothing like your traditional family portraits.

"Nice place, Ms. Reynolds," he said, using her surname to both emphasize his sincerity and amuse her with formality. Although he lacked nothing in the financial arena himself, her voguish perfection impressed him.

"Thanks. I have a secret calling to be an interior designer," Addison smiled as she continued to arrange the flowers. "What will it take for you to give up this florist?" She realized she was being uncharacteristically flirtatious.

"Hhhhmmmm. Well, let's see… We're only on the second date. If I told you my thoughts on that, you'd probably kick me out." He walked up behind her. His hands gently landed on the curve of her waist while his lips lightly brushed her neck. He inhaled subtly, absorbing a sweet, delicate scent. "You smell wonderful."

Her body welcomed his touch. "Cucumber melon body spray. It's my favorite. It has that crisp, clean but still sweet scent, not flowery like an old lady." She wondered if he thought her explanation ridiculous. She turned slightly, moving away from him. She certainly wasn't a prude. She'd even had the occasional one-night stand, but she held back from him. "There. That may be the most beautiful bouquet anyone has ever given me."

She stepped back, admiring her handiwork. "Shall we get going?" she suggested, knowing that if they lingered much longer they may not make it to dinner at all.

"Sure. I made reservations at the new sushi place just across the street from the park. I hope that's okay?"

"Sushi sounds great." She grabbed her long black, wool coat from the hall closet and wrapped a shaggy, multi-colored scarf around her neck for an accent more than warmth. As she locked the door behind them, she felt a giddy, girlish excitement for what the evening might bring.

◌⌇◌

Three weeks had passed since the breakup. James's calls had finally ceased, allowing Karsen to refocus. She continued plugging through her classes, trying to catch up from her extended absence. Alone in her apartment, she dabbled with the family tree website well into the night. Not knowing where to begin, she spent most of her time engrossed in other people's stories. Stories of hurt, fear, joy and hope, stories that allowed her to feel emotions vicariously instead of having to feel her own.

She hadn't been herself lately, which she chalked up to stress and perhaps a touch of mild depression. She felt unusually fatigued and still harbored a bit of queasiness at times. She'd even contemplated scheduling an appointment with a counselor at the student health center. Hanna's idea really, not her own. However, she couldn't bring herself to do it, figuring she'd been through a lot and anyone in her shoes would be feeling the same.

Another week went by, and Karsen's subconscious nudged her on. She just wanted to feel normal again. Maybe Hanna was right. Maybe talking to someone would help. *I'll make an appointment tomorrow,* she thought, finally acknowledging that she had to do something. Normally, this would be a time she'd call her mom. Hanna listened empathetically but had little experience to draw advice from. Brad had finally initiated a first date with her. Between his classes, auditions and now Hanna, the time he allocated to Karsen was limited. She needed someone who could focus on her.

෨෧

"Sign in here."

The receptionist handed Karsen a clipboard with several pages of forms.

"Fill this out and bring it up when you're done. We'll also need a copy of your insurance card."

Karsen nodded and looked around for a pen. The receptionist plucked a large, artificial yellow daisy out of a small terracotta pot filled with coffee beans. Taped to the flower was a pen. "We make sure people return them this way." Karsen gave her an uncomfortable grin.

She sat down in a corner chair, trying to be as inconspicuous as possible. The last thing she needed was to run into someone she knew. She didn't want to admit she was there to see a therapist. She filled in her contact information, insurance and health history. When she finished, she handed it back to the attendant.

"Will this appointment show as a therapy session?" she asked in a hushed voice. "I don't want my father to see it on the insurance. I don't want him to know."

"No need to worry, dear. It will read as an appointment here, but you can just tell him it was an annual well-woman check-up. That will usually scare any dad away."

Karsen smiled wanly and hoped she was right. It took everything in her to sit back down in the waiting room instead of running out the front door.

"Karsen Woods." A nurse called her name. Karsen gathered her bag and met her at the door. The nurse led her to a scale, which Karsen thought oddly unnecessary since she was only there to see a shrink. "Just your vitals. It's routine," the nurse said.

The nurse proceeded to check her blood pressure and temperature. She then left Karsen alone in the doctor's office. The office was furnished with a desk and two chairs upholstered in an earthy green ribbed fabric. Karsen scanned the diplomas and licenses on the wall. A slight medicinal smell lingered from the adjacent exam rooms. Her apprehension intensified as she waited. The familiar queasy feeling from the past several weeks crept up her throat.

"Karsen?" The door opened behind her. She stood and turned to see a woman doctor with her hand extended toward her.

"Hi." Karsen reached out to shake.

"Sorry for the wait." The doctor turned to close the door. "Would you like a bottle of water?"

"No, I'm fine thank you," Karsen said uncomfortably.

"I'm Dr. Warren. Is this your first time talking to a psychiatrist?"

Karsen nodded.

"Nervous?"

Karsen nodded again like a child who has lost her voice.

"Don't be. We can talk as little or as much as you like."

Karsen appreciated her gentleness. Dr. Warren looked to be in her early forties. Her hair was tucked neatly behind her ears and she wore stylish glasses that gave her an intellectual look befitting her profession.

"So, is there anything you wanted to talk specifically about today?" Dr. Warren asked.

Karsen fiddled with her necklace. "I guess." She paused. "I guess… I don't really know where to begin."

"Just start where you feel comfortable. All I'd like to do today is to get an idea of your background first and then we can discuss where we go from there."

"Okay." Karsen tapped the charm of her necklace against her lip. It was a nervous habit she had developed since childhood. "I guess I've been feeling… um…not myself lately. My mother was in an accident just after the holiday break and I found out my boyfriend was cheating on me two weeks after that."

"Those undoubtedly are significant events. And your mom's accident…was it serious?"

"Yes." Karsen tried to retain her composure. "She passed away. Instantly, we think. It was a car accident."

"I'm sorry. You certainly are going through a lot right now. I can understand why you're not feeling like yourself. That is perfectly normal. However, I do think it's good that you're here. Asking for help doesn't undermine your personal strength. It will only help."

Karsen felt her apprehension wane and started to open up about her feelings over the last two months, including her queasiness and fatigue. Dr. Warren listened intently, gently prompting Karsen with additional questions when needed.

"Karsen, I know grief can display itself in many ways. I certainly know there is an emotional component and that talking to me, or another psychologist, is going to benefit you. However, I wanted to ask one more question stemming from your physical symptoms."

Karsen looked up at her.

"Your chart shows the date of your last period as December 31. Are you sexually active?"

Karsen wondered how this was relevant, but answered nonetheless. "I was. That is, until we broke up. My periods have always been irregular. I've been told because of my athletics that it is normal. I swam all through high school and I run about twenty miles per week."

"Well, sometimes that's true, exercise can alter your cycle but," Dr. Warren hesitated, "have you taken a pregnancy test just in case?"

Karsen sat bewildered. *Pregnancy test?* The thought had not even entered her mind. They'd used birth control. The likeliness of one sperm meeting one egg in one 24-hour period was slim. Then again, how many teens get knocked up every year?

"Karsen?"

"No. I can't be...pregnant. We used birth control."

"Even birth control isn't one hundred percent effective."

Karsen's mind raced. The nausea, the lightheadedness, the fatigue. It all made sense now, but not once had she thought that she could be pregnant. She tried to think through every time she'd been with James. The last time was the night she had returned from Indiana. Had they used anything? She couldn't remember. Her emotions had taken over and all she remembered was his leaving afterwards.

"Karsen."

"Yes...?" she replied absently.

"They can do a test for you here if you are concerned. At the very least it will clear the possibility and ease your mind. I think it's a good idea." She reached over and placed her hand on Karsen's to comfort her. Her voice was soothing, like a mother's to a child.

Karsen agreed, not knowing what else to do. A disconnect took hold of her and once again she could hardly believe what was happening.

෴

Karsen thumbed through an old issue of *Urbane* while sitting back in the waiting room. Unable to focus, she glanced only at the pictures. Time inched along. Fifteen minutes felt like hours. "Karsen Woods." The same nurse from earlier called her name again and led her back to the same office. "Dr. Warren will be back in momentarily."

Karsen sat again in the same green chair, this time noticing the tiny frays on its upholstered arms. She nervously picked at the threads.

Dr. Warren returned and leaned against the front of her desk in front of Karsen. Crossing her arms, she looked down at her legs, also crossed at her ankles. She didn't speak right away as if trying to formulate a way to soften the blow.

"Karsen, as I suspected, the test came back positive. You are pregnant."

Karsen gazed blankly past Dr. Warren. Her disbelief immobilized her. She heard the words and tried to process the information. She was just getting back into some kind of normal routine. She wasn't happy, but at least she was taking strides to move on. *Everything that has happened and now this?* She blinked back tears as she took in the news.

"I know this is not what you expected when you scheduled your appointment today; however, it's better to know early. Calculating from the date of your last period, you're probably eight weeks along, or somewhere thereabout."

"What am I going to do?"

"Well, that's a decision only you can make. However, first we need to confirm how far along the pregnancy really is. The reception desk can schedule an appointment for you to come back for an ultrasound. Then, I'd like you to schedule another appointment with me. We can continue our session from today and talk about your options with the pregnancy as well."

"Options?" Karsen never imagined herself facing these choices.

"Yes. I'd like you to get in tomorrow if possible, the sooner the better. In the meantime, I'll have the nurse practitioner write a prescription for prenatal vitamins for you to start."

Karsen fumbled through the motions of thanking Dr. Warren. She felt as though she'd been knocked out in a fight, but her opponent continued to kick her in the gut.

"Is there a friend you can confide in?"

"Yeah." Karsen mustered in reply. She looked down at the appointment card crumpled between her fingers. Tomorrow would confirm the inevitable.

ೂ

The moment Karsen arrived at her apartment, she dialed the phone frantically. The phone rang four or five times before transferring into voice mail. "This is Hanna. Leave a message and I'll call you back.... beeeep."

"Hanna. Pick up the f'in phone!" Karsen hung up and dialed again.

Pick-up. Pick-up. Pick-up…Pleeeaaase, pick-up! Karsen tapped her foot impatiently with each ring. Two rings, three rings…

"Hello?" A sleepy voice crackled on the other end.

"Hanna?"

"Hey, K. I was up until two in the morning studying. I'm exhausted. What time is it anyway?"

"It's nine-thirty."

"Awww…class isn't until eleven. I could have slept at least another thirty minutes. I know you don't understand, Ms. Early Riser, but some of us need our sleep."

"Sorry."

"So, what's up? You called twice. It better be important."

"Actually, it is." Karsen ran down her morning for Hanna.

"Pregnant?" Hanna repeated, uncertain that in her haze she'd heard correctly. "What?" She sat up on her bed, instantly awake.

"Hanna. I don't need lectures right now. I'm not even sure how this happened. But, unless this baby was immaculately conceived, it's James's. What am I going to do?"

"Well, I figured that, unless you've been holding out on me. But weren't you careful?"

"Apparently not careful enough. Hanna, can you do me a favor. Please don't tell Brad. I mean, at least not yet. I need to figure this all out first, okay?"

"Okay. I'll come over tonight after my exam. We can talk then. Say six-ish?"

"Thanks." Karsen clicked off her Blackberry and set it on the table. She stared at it. The cheerful pink crystals seemed so important before. She had begged her dad to buy the phone for her and spent several painstaking hours placing the crystals for decoration. Now the whole thing seemed trivial. She questioned why she ever cared about a stupid piece of electronics. How silly and immature she'd been. She was barely an adult herself. How could she raise a child? How could she afford to raise a child? More importantly, how could she raise a child ALONE?

❧ 13 ❧

As promised, Hanna arrived that evening at Karsen's apartment. "I brought ice cream." Hanna held up a carton of cookies and cream in one hand and two plastic spoons in the other.

"Thanks." Karsen managed a meager grin as she grabbed one of the spoons and welcomed her in. "As long as I'm going to get fat anyway, I might as well dig in."

"You wouldn't be fat, you'd be pregnant. There is a difference." Hanna made her way to the couch and sat down. She popped off the lid and took a bite. "Now come sit down and let's figure this out."

Karsen sat facing her. She scooped out a bite and let the sweetness linger on her tongue.

"I can't believe you're pregnant." Hanna said.

"Trust me. It was the last thing I was thinking. Have you seen those shows where girls show up at the ER and have a baby claiming they never knew they were pregnant? I always thought they must be crazy. How could I not have known? The dizzy spell. The nausea."

"You were under a lot of stress. Those symptoms could easily be stress related. Stop beating yourself up."

"I know. I wish I could."

"Have you thought about what you want to do?"

"Not really. I figure I need to do the ultrasound tomorrow and then I'll decide when to tell James. I'm sure that's going to be fun."

"Maybe he'll surprise you?"

"Right. It's James we're talking about. He puts on a good show...I certainly fell for it. But, he's a conceited asshole. Everyone knew it but me. You think he is going to want a kid right now?"

"Karsen."

"I know. I know. Stop beating myself up, but how? I mean. What happened to my life? Everything always came so easily to me before. My life was practically charmed. Now, everything is going wrong and I don't think I can take any more."

"It's going to be okay, K."

"I keep telling myself that. Then more things keep happening. Maybe it's a mistake. Maybe the test was wrong," Karsen said trying to convince herself.

Hanna couldn't stay late and left. The rest of the night passed slowly, the ongoing stress and fatigue weighing heavily on Karsen. She couldn't sleep. She watched the hours click by, one by one, on her digital alarm clock, until the sun finally shone through her window. She tried to imagine telling her father, and every time her heart started pounding against her chest and her eyes watered until she couldn't stand the thought any longer and buried her face back into her pillow.

In the morning, Hanna landed unannounced on Karsen's doorstep just before eight-thirty. She knocked on the door. Karsen felt a rush of relief knowing she wouldn't have to go to her appointment alone, although she should've expected nothing less from her friend. She cleared the lump in her throat. "Hey."

"Hey." With everything her friend had been through, Hanna couldn't help but worry. She knew Karsen was strong, but she also knew she'd never experienced anything near this magnitude. Just one of the traumatic events she had endured would be hard enough, but it seemed the hits just kept on coming. Hanna was determined not to let her down. "I thought you might want someone to go with you."

"Thanks. You don't know how much so."

A different nurse than the day before escorted Karsen back down the familiar hallway to an examination room. Hanna followed behind. There was a large black and white monitor along with a machine similar to a computer. Karsen took a seat on the long examination table and nervously fidgeted as they waited for the doctor. Hanna sat quietly on a small chair by the wall, not knowing what to do or say.

A woman dressed in light blue scrubs entered and introduced herself as the ultrasound technician. Her nametag read Mary and Karsen estimated she was in her early forties. Mary asked Karsen to pull up her shirt and tucked a towel between her belly and her jeans. She squirted a clear jelly on the area just below Karsen's belly button and then moved a wand-like device over top.

"See that," Mary pointed to a flash on the screen. "That's the heartbeat." Her voice was tender. Karsen concealed her disappointment and simply nodded her head in acknowledgment that she indeed saw the tiny pulse of a heartbeat. She had dreamed of having children, but the scenario in her perfectly planned imaginings differed greatly. She'd envisioned herself experiencing this moment except it was not with Hanna by her side. She pictured her husband holding her hand, both of them laughing and smiling at the first sight of their child. How naive she'd been, ridiculing the mass of teenagers who found themselves pregnant claiming their birth control failed or they only had sex once. It only took once and, birth control or no birth control, there was no denying that a life was growing inside her.

"Dr. Warren estimated about right. The fetus is measuring right around eight weeks. Any earlier and the heartbeat may not be visible." Mary typed a few keystrokes before setting down the device and wiping the excess gel off of Karsen. "Everything looks good at this point. Congratulations."

She handed Karsen a four-by-six piece of slick white paper. Karsen scanned the black and white image that looked like nothing more than a small peanut.

"Thanks," Karsen said out of obligation. How could you tell a stranger this was not what you wanted? How did other girls react? How many unplanned pregnancies had this technician dealt with working at the college health facility? Perhaps she assumed Karsen was just another statistic.

"Go ahead and get dressed. Dr. Warren will be in."

Karsen mustered another thank you.

A few minutes later the door opened and Dr. Warren entered with Karsen's file in hand.

"So everything appears to be normal at this point. Based on your measurements and the date of your last menstrual cycle, your due date calculates to October sixth."

Due date? Karsen had prayed all night that the test was wrong, that she wasn't pregnant, or if she was that she'd miscarry and it would all go away. Then she felt horrible and ashamed at wishing for an unsuccessful pregnancy when so many women couldn't conceive.

"Now, I know your friend is here..." Dr. Warren continued.

"You can say anything in front of her," Karsen interrupted. "It's okay."

"All right then. You do have options and I'd like to help you through them. You should take some time to think. When it comes to an unplanned pregnancy, the last thing you want to do is make a rash decision you may regret. There are repercussions with every path."

"I understand."

"In the mean time, we need you to make sure you are taking care of yourself. The prenatals are a start. No alcohol, no sushi, no smoking, no drugs."

"Not an issue."

"Also, watch your caffeine and drink plenty of water."

"What about running?"

"Exercise is good as long as you don't overdo it and stay hydrated." Dr. Warren closed the file. "Karsen, I'm not an obstetrician. If you decide to keep the baby, we'll need to find you one."

"I understand."

൭

Hanna and Karsen left the health clinic quietly and climbed into Hanna's car. Karsen, armed with a pile of pamphlets on pregnancy, collapsed into the passenger seat. A wave of heat pent up within the car overtook her. She felt both mentally and physically exhausted.

"What do I do now?" Karsen sincerely asked Hanna.

"I can't answer that for you, hun." Hanna placed her hand over top of Karsen's. "You're going to need to tell James soon, though."

"I know."

"And Brad."

"I know." Karsen pulled her sunglasses out of her purse and put them on to hide her bloodshot eyes, wishing she could hide behind them from the world.

∞

That evening Karsen forced herself to eat. She knew if she didn't, the potent vitamins would wrench her stomach. She picked at a left over piece of pizza and managed to finish a glass of milk. Her mind was too tired to search for answers. She knew what she needed to do.

She stared at the names as she scrolled through the addresses logged into her phone. She knew she couldn't tell James over the phone, yet she cringed at the thought of seeing him face-to-face. She inhaled deeply as the blue light highlighted his number and before she could chicken out, she hit send. She listened to the rings across the line as she whispered to herself "Voice mail. Voice mail. Please let me get his voice mail."

"Hello?" The familiar deep voice pierced through her like an arrow and her heart sank.

"James? Hi, it's Karsen."

"Yes. I know." They both sat momentarily lost for words.

"I need to talk to you."

"Ooookaaay." He paused. "So, what do you want to talk about?"

"Not over the phone. Can I come over?"

"When?"

Never, she thought to herself, knowing full well that wasn't an option. "As soon as you're available," she said biting her bottom lip anticipating his response. She couldn't decide if she would rather deal with this sooner and get it over with, or later and avoid knowing his reaction.

"I'm home for the evening."

"Okay. I guess I'll head up now. Are you sure that's okay?" She gave him one last opportunity to postpone.

"I'm sure. See you in a few." He hung up the phone.

The drive from her apartment to his took roughly fifteen minutes. As Murphy's Law would have it, she hit every green light and little to no traffic. Her nerves sent pins and needles up her spine. She couldn't imagine how she was going to tell him. There was no easy way.

"Hi," James greeted her, opening the door and gesturing for her to enter. She felt odd. For so long, she had come and gone freely. Now, it felt like she was entering a stranger's apartment.

"Hi."

"Would you like a beer?" he asked as a formality. She could see his open on the counter.

"No. Better not."

"Okay. Suit yourself. Water?"

"No really, I'm fine. Thanks."

Awkwardly, she suggested they sit down on the couch. She sat on one end, he on the opposite.

"So, what brought you up here? You wouldn't return any of my calls." The tone of his voice sounded like a scolded puppy, surprised that she hadn't forgiven him.

"I didn't want to talk to you."

"So, why are you here?" He sounded flustered.

"I wanted..." she stopped. "I'm not sure..." She gazed vacantly across the room noticing the framed photo of them had been removed from the end table. There was no indication anywhere of them ever having had a relationship.

"Just spit it out."

She fought for the right words to soften the blow, but her mind drew a blank. Before she realized it, her mouth spit out two simple words – "I'm pregnant" – before her brain could stop her.

"What?" James leaned back uneasily against the arm of the couch. His expression callous, he lifted the beer bottle to his lips.

"I'm pregnant." She looked into his eyes trying to analyze his reaction.

"Are you sure?" he asked, expressionless.

"Yes."

"And it's mine?"

"Yes," she snapped indignantly.

"Karsen! How did you let this happen?"

"How did I? How did I let this happen? As if you weren't there?"

"You know what I mean."

Karsen took a deep breath and bit her tongue. She wanted to scream, "This is as much your fault as it is mine," but she held back. Finally, she answered.

"I don't know."

"You don't know?"

"No, I really don't know. This is as much a shock to me as it is to you. We always used condoms. You did that night I got back, right?"

"I don't remember. Anyway, I thought you had started taking the pill."

"No, I was going to, but I hadn't had a chance to go get a prescription."

"Honestly, Karsen! How long have you known?" He stood up and glared down at her.

"Since yesterday. It's not like I've been hiding this from you. Man, you're defensive."

"How am I supposed to be? I didn't know you'd get knocked up like a high school cheerleader?"

"Well, I guess that makes you captain of the football team then, doesn't it?" Karsen's voice began to waver.

James turned away angrily, took a swig from his beer, and then turned back to face her. "Well, what are you going to do?"

"What do you mean, what am I going to do?" She glared up at him, instantly feeling abandoned.

His voice softened as he sat back down beside her. "Well, K, I mean it's not as though either of us are in a position to have a baby right now."

Karsen's heart dropped. Certainly he wasn't suggesting she terminate the pregnancy. And without even the slightest hesitation. Befuddled, her mind searched for some mere resemblance of the man she thought she loved. She hadn't known how he would react. She assumed he'd be shocked, angry even. But his eyes were cold, as if he was a bystander giving advice without an ounce of emotion.

"Karsen." He grabbed her hand. "I'm here for you. You know that." She felt the tension release from her shoulders. "I'll take care of any... any expenses."

She pulled her hand away. There was no fight left in her. She stood up, gathered her purse and walked in silence to the door. She left no closer to deciding on a path, yet she was clear on one thing. Crystal clear. James would not be on it.

∽

Hanna struggled not to tell Brad about Karsen's situation. She contemplated bringing it up hypothetically, like another friend's dilemma, but didn't. She couldn't betray Karsen's trust. Part of her worried Brad would pull away from her, making his sister his priority over her. She questioned her own loyalty, which perplexed her with guilt. On one hand, Karsen and she were like sisters. On the other, withholding information from Brad felt deceitful.

She pulled her car in front of the sidewalk and beeped the horn in a short burst. As she waited, the strident sound of the over-burdened air conditioner competed against the radio. She began to dial Karsen's phone, but before it connected she saw Karsen close her apartment door.

Karsen opened the passenger side door and climbed in.

"Hi," she said, trying to sound alive. She pulled the seat belt across her chest.

"Hey, K. So, how'd it go last night?"

"Horrible." She thumped her head against the seat.

"He was upset?"

"Upset? Ha! More like nonchalant. He actually said he would 'take care of expenses.' And when I say expenses, he wasn't referring to long-term child support."

"No way! I always knew he was a pig." Hanna felt her blood boil. "If I see him…"

"Hanna." Karsen raised her hand signifying enough. "There's no point. Really, I appreciate it, but after everything that's happened I shouldn't have expected anything else."

"Oh, honey, I'm sorry. I, I just hoped… I mean, MEN! It's so much easier for them to cop out."

"I know."

"Are you okay?"

"I think so. I mean something good has to come out of all of this, right?"

"I hope so. Have you thought any more about what you're going to do?"

"A little, but I still feel so confused."

Hanna made a left turn onto Echo Drive and pulled into the line of cars waiting to park at the trailhead. Six or seven vehicles were lined up single file, snatching parking places one at a time as other vehicles pulled out.

"Are you sure you should be doing this?" Hanna asked. They hiked frequently, but the hour-long trek to the top of Camelback Mountain required an ample amount of exertion.

"I'll be fine. Expectant women have run marathons. I can handle this. At any rate, I'm hoping some fresh air will help me get my head on straight."

Hanna didn't argue.

❧ 14 ❧

"A natural, that girl is," commented David as he snapped the last two shots before his memory card read full. "Even her chip is perfect," he teased.

Addison laughed, knowing Mr. Montague's account was secure as ever. The rescind article had been a success and clients were flocking to his spa. "Amazing what people will do when they hear the word FREE," he had said admiringly during their last phone conference.

"She is a beauty, that's for sure." Addison scooped up Adelaide and lifted her overhead.

"Again!" Adie pleaded as soon as her feet touched the floor.

"How about we find some chocolate milk instead?"

"And some lunch," Emily added. "Oh, Addison. She looks like a model."

"Well, that's the point right?" Addison giggled. She knew Adie had that special glimmer to her. With her baby blue eyes and a slight dimple dipping into one of her round cheeks, she had looked like the picture-perfect baby from the moment she'd arrived.

Adie quickly replaced Addison's attention with Jacob's who now held her while fake tango dancing across the hallway. With each turn and dip, she squealed with delight. "More dancing! More dancing!" Jacob, who seemed to be enjoying her as much as she him, obliged.

"Marjorie, can you hold down the fort while I take these ladies to lunch?" Addison asked.

Marjorie nodded as she continued talking into her headset.

"Thanks for entertaining her, Jacob," Emily said as she lifted Adie out of his arms. Adie fussed slightly. The shoot had lingered past her routine eleven-thirty lunchtime.

"Anytime. I love kids. I've got three nieces that love to play with their Uncle J," replied Jacob. He gave Adie a quick farewell peck on the forehead.

"Any preference for food?" Addison asked Emily.

"Anywhere that serves mac and cheese."

"Cheeeese!" Adie repeated, smiling as if back in front of the camera.

The three made their way to a quaint café two blocks from Addison's office where Adelaide blissfully ate her macaroni by placing each piece on her fork with her hand while the two women chatted.

"Any plans for the weekend?" Emily picked up a piece of macaroni Adelaide dropped off the table and set it aside.

"Nothing much. Dinner with Russell on Saturday maybe. We'll see. I need to visit my mom, too. Did I tell you she was home now? I can't remember. I keep telling her to take it easy, but you know my mom."

"Well, at least your mom seems to be heading in the right direction. So, anyway, how was your date with Russell?"

"Which one?"

"Which one? You didn't tell me you saw him again. You've been holding out on me."

"I'm not holding out on you. There isn't that much to tell. The date was good. They were both good." Addison tried to subdue her excitement. They'd only had a couple of dates. Still, even Addison was taken aback by their immediate connection. "We went for sushi and talked."

"Talked. That's it? Nothing juicy?"

"Like I said, there's nothing to tell, really."

"Nothing? Come on. I'm married here. I live vicariously. Give me something."

"Okay. We kissed. Period."

"Details?" Emily pleaded. She cherished her marriage to Greg, but any true romantic misses that fluttering excitement from a first kiss.

"What are we, in high school?"

"Come on..." Emily giggled.

"I'm a grown woman. I don't kiss and tell. How-ev-er," Addison drew out the word, "if a girl was younger and was to kiss and tell, she may add the details of how his strong hands lifted her chin slightly, his lips commenced with the lightest brush before proceeding confidently into a luscious, full-fledged, make your knees weak schoolgirl kiss." Addison suddenly felt like they were in college again.

"Aaaannnddd??"

"And, that's it. It took every ounce of restraint I had to close the door with him on the outside."

Emily looked disappointed. She hoped Addison would finally find someone to settle down with. She hated seeing her alone. Russell seemed perfect, although most of what she knew about him was based on tabloid magazines and television interviews, especially since Addison did not elaborate.

Addison restrained herself from sharing more of her feelings with Emily. A part of her heart had already fallen for Russell, which was bittersweet. It was good, too good. She knew it couldn't last.

༄

Karsen purchased her ticket online and chalked up the expense to one more ding on her credit card. She'd worry about how to pay for it later. She didn't know why, but she knew she needed to think. Not here, not with James so close. At home, she could pretend momentarily that her life was normal. Besides, she reasoned, her dad could probably use some company. She packed a small duffle bag with enough clothes for the weekend: two shirts, a pair of sweats, an extra pair of jeans and her make-up bag. She pulled her hair into a ponytail and poked it through the hole in the back of her ASU ball cap. After calling a taxi, she left a voice mail for Hanna.

"Hey, Han, it's me, K. I've decided to fly home for the weekend. I need to clear my head. I'll have my cell with me if you want to call; otherwise don't worry about me."

The taxi arrived and she directed the driver to Sky Harbor Airport. She called her father from the cab and got his voice mail.

"Hi, Daddy. Surprise! I'm coming to visit. Don't worry about picking me up at the airport. I'll take a cab. See you tonight."

She debated whether or not to call Brad. He'd only try to reason that she'd missed too many classes already and flying home on a whim was completely irrational, so she decided to call him later.

The taxi stopped at the departures in front of terminal three. Karsen climbed out and paid the driver with a meager tip. Embarrassed slightly, she ducked quickly into the building and headed to her gate.

After a turbulent, three hour flight, the captain announced their arrival in Chicago. From there, she took the puddle-jumper to South Bend and a taxi home. As she rode, she figured with the time change, she'd arrive about the time her dad returned home from work. She wondered if he had gotten her message.

∞

Her dad welcomed her with a great big bear hug, lifting her up on her tippy toes. He needed the visit as much as she did, although his pride would never allow him to admit it.

"Hi, sweetheart! Come in. How was your flight?" He took her bag and set it on the entryway bench.

"Fine, Daddy. Bumpy, but we made it. I guess that makes it a good flight." Karsen had recently become a bit skittish about flying. Even though statistically it was safer than driving, she still felt more at ease after touching the ground. Perhaps she was feeling less invincible after the phone call that left her on her knees.

"I thought we'd order pizza. That sound good to you?"

"Sure. I ate in Chicago, so I'm not too hungry." Pizza sounded appealing, but she questioned whether that would change once it arrived. Each day brought new complexities to her ability to eat. One day she loved Chinese; the next, the thought of it made her want to vomit. Then there were the smells. Just the smell of something could send her stomach into a tizzy.

Carl ordered the pizza while Karsen showered and changed into more comfortable clothes. Shortly after she heard the doorbell ring, she returned to the kitchen. The pizza box lay open on the table. Her dad had set out plates and napkins. He opened a beer and offered it to her.

"No thanks, Dad."

He shrugged his shoulders and took a sip himself. Karsen grabbed a Sprite from the cabinet and filled a cup with ice. She pulled a slice of pizza onto her plate and picked a pepperoni off of the top. The cheese stuck to it, creating a long string and she did her best to slip it into her mouth without making a mess.

They made small talk while eating until her dad finally asked what she was really doing home. He sensed there had to be more to it than a friendly visit to poor ole dad even if his intuition was far less keen than any woman's.

"It's just…" Karsen picked at her pizza while contemplating her story. "It's just that I can't face school right now. Losing Mom and then James, I can't concentrate. I needed to get away, and although Jamaica sounded pretty darn good, home is more in line with my budget." She hoped the humor would help squelch his concern. "Anyway, I figured you needed some company. You and the dog can't live on pizza and beer forever. You need a good home-cooked meal."

"Karsen, I appreciate that and hope that's all it really is. But to fly home unannounced for the weekend? You're usually not that…"

"Spontaneous?"

"Irresponsible," he corrected. "You can't afford last minute airfare. Those rates had to be enormous."

"Don't worry, Daddy. I'll be fine. I put the ticket on my credit card, but I'll pay it off right away. I swear."

"I do worry and I will continue to worry about you. Your mother would roll over in her grave if I let anything happen to you." He took another drink. "I'll write a check for the airfare before you leave. When are you leaving, by the way? You are still enrolled in school, right?"

"Yes. I leave Sunday afternoon. I'll be back in class Monday and Hanna will share her notes from today. I've got everything covered. I promise; you don't need to worry."

He hoped she was right, but he still speculated there was more to her spur-of-the-moment visit than she let on.

"Eat." He pushed another slice onto her plate. "You look thin."

Thin, she thought. *Maybe for now…if he only knew.*

∾ 15 ∾

Saturday, Addison spent the morning visiting her mother at her parents' home. As she glanced out the window, the sun peeked through the clouds and a few snowflakes floated down gracefully in the closing stages of winter. While most people with any common sense trudged around winter in clunky brown boots, she sacrificed comfort for style. Her neatly pedicured toes were warmly tucked into her pointed-toe black boots, which she refused to remove even though her feet ached like she had walked a marathon.

Her mom's recovery was proceeding well. The initial scans showed no additional spots of cancer. Her color was back and her spirit lifted.

"You look like you're feeling better." Addison smiled as she entered the living room where her mother was reading.

Her mom earmarked her spot and set the book aside. "Hi, dear. Yes, the doctor said everything is looking good. Still waiting to hear about if and when chemo will start, but otherwise I'm doing fine."

"I'm sure you'll be organizing another charity ball before they can strap on the IV."

"As a matter of fact, I've spoken to Claudia at the Autism Foundation and they have requested I head up their next event in March."

"Mom, you're not thinking..."

"Yes, I am." She cut her off mid-sentence. "And don't worry about me, I'll be fine. No sense moping around here like a wounded puppy."

"This family never stops. Dad will probably be launching a new start-up company before year end," Addison said, shaking her head. "Speaking of Dad, where is he?"

"Hitting balls at the indoor range. No need for him to start a new company. He should be able to join the senior PGA tour as much time as he spends on his golf game lately. Anyway, going back to the fundraiser, I expect March will give you enough time to find a suitable date?" She insinuated Addison's history meant no one would be lined up.

"Yes, Mom."

"Didn't you say you went out with someone recently?"

"Yes." Addison cringed, wanting to avoid any conversation relating to her relationships or lack thereof. Here she was approaching forty and her mother still meddled in her love life.

"Who was that again?"

"Russell Masters. We met at your last charity event."

"Aahhh. I see. Then he will fit in fine. Get me his contact information and I'll make sure he gets a formal invitation."

"Don't get ahead of yourself, Mom." Addison quickly turned the conversation to a far less personal subject. "Can I get you some tea?"

"Tea would be lovely. Thank you."

Addison made her way to the kitchen. She pondered the thought of Russell and her together at a public event. There would be paparazzi and speculation about the two of them together. Certainly, they'd been seen together at the last fundraiser but this would be different. Arriving as a couple would spark interest. She wondered what he'd think about the scenario. Then again, she wondered if he'd even be around by then.

∽

Karsen snuggled deeper under the down comforter on her bed. She felt secure in her old room and for an instant, forgot everything that had happened over the last two months. As her eyes fluttered open, it all flooded back in a horrific wave. She closed them again tightly and sighed. How her life had gone from common, everyday bliss to the plot of a *Lifetime* after-school special escaped her.

She sat up and hung her head forward. Her feet dangled off the bedside. There it was - the now familiar feeling in the pit of her stomach. She grabbed her duffle bag and pulled out a sleeve of Saltine crackers. The wrapper crackled as she opened the package.

"Shit," she muttered to herself, trying to stifle the noise. She didn't know whether or not her dad would question her hidden stash of nausea fighting crackers and she certainly didn't want to find out.

She tiptoed to the bathroom and threw water on her face. She sloshed a bit of mouthwash around in her mouth, spit and then rinsed the sink. Her mission for the day was to search out the jewelry store that may have made the charms, but retail stores didn't open for hours. She figured if she left the house before her father got up, he wouldn't notice her skipping her regular dose of caffeine, which left her with some time to kill.

She slipped the keys to the spare car off the key ring next to the garage door. Luckily, her parents had kept an old beater for Brad and her to drive when they visited home. She scribbled a quick note – *Dad, I forgot I have a paper due Monday. Going to the library to finish it up. Be back later. Love, K* – and placed it beside the coffee pot where he would be sure to find it. Then, she climbed into the car and headed down the dimly lit, tree-lined streets of town. A light mist made the grass glisten. The crisp chill of the morning stimulated her. The streets were familiar, though she could not recall all the names. She subconsciously remembered where each turn led. She hadn't planned where she would go first, but the car seemed to plot the directions for her.

There was no traffic at this early hour. Karsen found herself on the highway and slowed to a stop in the middle of the lane. She turned the car around and parked along the shoulder, staring at a tree in front of her. She could see lacerations in the tree bark and skid marks still striped the edge of the road. Her hands grasped the steering wheel tightly. It was here. In a split second, her life had changed forever. She questioned if the accident hadn't happened, would anything else have changed? Would she have discovered James cheating? Would she, in a moment of emotive longing, have used the same lax judgment leading to her pregnancy? She figured her relationship with James still might have eventually ended, but perhaps not yet and surely not with a life within her.

Karsen got out of the car and walked slowly to the site. She touched the tree, unable to fathom the violent nature of her mother's death. She knew her dad had placed the brown wrought-iron cross at its base as a memorial, but she was puzzled as to who might have left the numerous floral arrangements surrounding the trunk. She couldn't imagine her dad had left them all.

As she stood there, she heard a car approach. Glancing behind her she saw a faded red four-door sedan pull onto the shoulder of the road behind hers and stop. A sense of danger tingled across her skin. She froze momentarily and debated her next action. Her cell phone was in the car. If she ran now she could get it and dial the police.

Panicked, Karsen whirled around and darted toward her car.

"STOP!" she heard a voice bellow as a man stepped out from the intruding vehicle. She didn't. Living in the city, her protective instincts told her to assume the worst as she struggled to open her car door.

"You're her daughter," the man continued to call out as he walked slowly toward her. *Did he know her?* Karsen thought, finally grabbing her phone from the console.

"The girl in the photo. That was you?"

She clutched her phone and turned toward him, her body shielded by the car door. "Don't come any closer!" she sternly shouted. Her thumb felt impulsively for the 9 key. She pressed it.

He stopped.

"Karsen, right?"

"Did you know my mom?" she asked indignantly, not letting her guard down. She moved her finger over the "1" button and pressed down. His face had a familiarity to it she could not place. She traced her memory trying to recollect where she might have seen him as her finger hovered over the "1" button not knowing whether to press it again.

"Not exactly," he said, uncertain how to respond. He didn't want her to leave. Not yet. Not before he could explain.

"What photo? You said you saw me in the photo. What photo?"

"There was a photo in the car."

"How would you know that?" She remembered seeing the Christmas card with their family portrait among her mother's personal effects pulled from the wreckage.

"Can we talk?" he asked, avoiding her question. He softened his tone to help ease her fears, but there was an unsettling desperation in his voice.

She looked at his car again, recognition beginning to register. Could it be the same one she saw parked across the street on the morning of her mother's funeral?

"Were you at my house? Have you been following me?"

"No. Well, not exactly. Please, I just want to talk."

She stared intently until she finally placed his face. He looked different in a hat, his receding hairline hidden. His baby face took ten years off his age.

"You were at the funeral?"

"Yes."

"Who are you?"

"My name is Matt."

Frustrated, she asked again, "How do you know me?"

"I told you, the photo. It was in the car. I recognized you as soon as I saw you at the funeral. I'm so sorry."

"You were there when the accident happened? What are you, a policeman?" She glanced again at the rusting four-door sedan.

"No, I mean…no, I'm not a police officer. But I was there." He paused. "It was my fault."

"What was your fault?" Karsen felt a mix of anger and sadness flood through her, as her heart answered before he could.

"I'm so sorry. The accident. It was my fault."

Karsen stood in stunned silence for a moment, absorbing the shock of his confession. She knew there had been another party involved in the accident. She had read the details on the police report. On paper, the individual had no face, no voice. She couldn't confront this reality, not now. Maybe not ever.

"She's dead and you're here, free?" The thought horrified her.

"Define free? It was an accident. I would never intentionally hurt anyone. You have to believe me!" he pleaded.

She listened disbelievingly, her eyes fixed on his face as he continued.

"I come here almost every day. There's not a moment I don't regret what happened. I'll never be free. I wish I could undo that day. It haunts me. It was an accident. I just want you to know how sorry, how truly sorry I am." His voice cracked. "Can you forgive me?"

He wanted forgiveness? she thought incredulously. His face longed for a response, one she wasn't capable of. She slid into her car without another word, put the key into the ignition and turned the key.

Crestfallen, he stood, feet firmly planted, eyes brimming with tears, and watched as she drove away.

Karsen collected herself as she drove back toward town. Her mind reeled from the encounter with Matt. The man that killed her mother wanted her forgiveness. Her heart hurt. She choked back her emotions and focused on her original purpose.

There were four possible jewelry stores that her mom could have used. Her agenda was tight if she wanted to return home to make dinner for her dad. She couldn't push him too far or he'd begin to question her again on why she came home.

She stopped by the first two. Neither store had records of creating a charm like hers. The third store was part of a retail chain and she doubted they made custom pieces. That left Milton's. Karsen imagined Mr. Milton had to be in his seventies by now. His store had sat among the quaint old shops of Middlebury for the last forty years. The town had a heavy Amish presence and Mr. Milton's old style jewelry fit right in. Karsen wondered why she hadn't thought of his store first. It made sense that her mom would use him as he reminded her of Karsen's grandfather.

She pulled into the parking lot and felt the car rumble over the gravel beneath. She didn't know whether to be nervous. Perhaps she'd find nothing or perhaps he made three pieces and wasn't able to match the original, end of story.

The bells attached at the top of the door jingled, announcing her entry. Mrs. Milton rose from her chair and welcomed her. Her aging hands shook as she waved Karsen in.

"Come in, dear. What brings you here today?" she said, smiling. Her sweet voice reminded Karsen of her grandmother. The soothing sound calmed her.

"Hi, Mrs. Milton. Actually, I'm trying to find out whether my mother bought some jewelry here in the past. She passed away recently so I'm not sure."

"Oh, Mrs. Woods. You're her daughter, Karsen. Look at you all grown up! I'm so sorry about your mom, dear. I'm sure it's been hard."

"Yes, it certainly has been," Karsen answered, a bit bewildered that she recognized her.

"And your dad? Is he well?"

"He's doing all right under the circumstances."

Karsen's eyes scanned the case below. The selection was unique, but the inventory was scarce. There were many pieces with an antique look, not anything that you'd find in your typical mall store.

"Well hello," said Mr. Milton, stepping out from the back room.

"Hi," Karsen replied softly.

"This is Mrs. Wood's daughter. She's trying to find out if her mother purchased anything from us."

"Oh dear, I'm sorry about your mother," said Mr. Milton, offering his condolences.

"Thank you."

"Your mom did purchase several pieces over the years. Any piece in particular you were wondering about?"

"Yes, actually." Karsen's eyes rose to meet his. She pulled the chain from beneath her shirt and held the charm in her palm. "This."

Mr. Milton moved closer, adjusting his glasses on the brim of his nose. He scooped the piece into his own palm and turned it tenderly. His eyes squinted as if to admire the minute detail of his own handiwork.

"Well, doggone. I haven't seen these in years," he said almost wistfully, releasing the necklace back to Karsen's grasp.

"Then you made the three charms, right?"

"I did indeed. Well," he raised his hand to his chin and rubbed it in a moment of reflection, "that must have been over twenty years ago."

"Such an endearing idea," Mrs. Milton added. "These days people seem to find more reasons to disown their families than connect with them. So sad, today's society." She shook her head.

"Very true," Karsen agreed. "Mr. Milton, do you keep records of each piece, by any chance?" She wasn't certain exactly what to ask. When finding a needle in a haystack, it's helpful to know you're looking for a needle.

"Yes," he replied hesitantly, "but…that was an awful long time ago."

"We've never transitioned to the age of computers, you see," explained Mrs. Milton. "With our small little shop, everyone was happy with a hand-written receipt. Going back so far, well, certainly you understand."

"I do." Karsen's heart sank, realizing her efforts had produced no fruit. As a last resort, she asked, "Mr. Milton, you probably don't, and that's okay, but, do you remember if all the charms fit together? You know, linked?"

He valiantly searched his fading memory for an answer. His eyes brightened finally and he said, "I believe they did. Yes, I think so," he reiterated confidently. "Your mom had an old piece that we made a mold from."

"Okay then." Karsen smiled and thanked them for their time. She pulled a pen and scrap of paper from her purse. "If you think of anything else, here's my cell number. Call me anytime."

"All right then," said Mr. Milton, picking the paper off of the counter and staring at her number as if trying to make sure he could read her handwriting. "Have a good day, young lady."

"Thanks. You, too." Karsen left and headed home feeling defeated.

⌒⌄

Karsen spent Sunday morning resting and trying to relax before her flight. She started by making breakfast for her dad, a feeble attempt to distract him from asking her additional questions about her whereabouts the day before. She could tell he was still suspicious of her motives for coming home, but she wasn't ready or willing to divulge the truth.

Later that night, Hanna stood against the wall of the airport terminal, latte in hand. She scanned the exiting flock of passengers as they scurried through the gate. An older couple bickered at each other, dressed in bright yellows and oranges. The man wore a wide brimmed hat, and the woman sported black sunglasses the size of two cantaloupes. Typical tourists, Hanna smirked. She watched as another woman and toddler raced to welcome a man, a soldier returning from deployment. The couple embraced passionately with the child clinging to the pant leg of his military fatigues. Karsen trudged behind the pack, worn out from the whirlwind trip.

"Thanks for picking me up." She hugged Hanna lethargically.

"No worries. Caffeine helps. Could your flight have been delayed any longer?" Hanna whined jokingly.

"Sorry." Karsen glanced at her watch. It was almost midnight.

"Brad's waiting in the car. His performance last night rocked the house. I think he celebrated with one too many Coronas, though."

"Nice." Karsen managed a weak grin.

"I should forewarn you, he's pretty pissed about your little excursion. You should have at least called him."

"He's my brother, not my father," Karsen grumbled.

"Still, he's worried about you."

"You didn't tell him, did you?"

"No, not about that."

"Good. Thanks," Karsen said, relieved.

"Have you decided anything?" Hanna inquired hesitantly.

"No. Strangely enough, I barely thought about it at all."

They broke off their conversation once they reached the car. Karsen flung her bag into the open trunk and slammed it shut. She climbed into the back seat. She listened as Brad scolded her like a schoolgirl who broke curfew. All she could do was apologize. Whether she felt it was warranted or not, she knew in her heart that he was sincerely worried about her. She didn't know how she could she fault him for that.

"How's Dad holding up anyway?" Brad asked as he pulled the car away from the curb.

"He seems to be doing okay. Which reminds me, I need to call and let him know I made it."

She powered up her cell phone. A small envelope appeared in the upper corner indicating she had messages. While Brad and Hanna chatted in the front, she sank back against the seat and hit send.

First unheard message: "Hi. It's Hanna. Got your message. I'll be there to pick you up at nine-thirty. Flight 347 from Chicago. See you then."

She pressed delete.

Next unheard message: "Heellloooo? Karsen?" An old gentleman's voice quivered, uncertain how to proceed. Her mind immediately sparked. Mr. Milton?

She heard some fumbling on the other end of the line and then nothing. The caller had disconnected.

Anxiously, Karsen listened to the next message.

"Karsen?" Yes! It was the same male voice again. "This is Mr. Milton. You said to call if I thought of anything else. If I recall, you mentioned three pieces were made. I believe I actually made four. There were three closer together, then one..." Beeeep!

Karsen heard the allotted voice message time cut him off. Damn. She saved the message then listened wearily as the phone reported, "You have no new messages." She hit disconnect. Before dialing to leave the voice message for her dad, she felt an adrenaline rush surge throughout her. She sat, now wide awake, the number four bouncing around in her head. *Poor Mr. Milton*, she thought. *He must be confused.*

~ **16** ~

A chain saw revved outside Karsen's window.

"Damn landscapers," she mumbled, inwardly pleading with them to go away. She glanced at the clock. It was just before six Monday morning, giving her ample time to make her eight o'clock class. Feeling the churning in her stomach, she groaned and reached, too tired to move anything but her arm, for the sleeve of Saltines on the nightstand and lugged them across her chest. Crumbs fell and scattered indistinguishably upon the white cotton sheets. She didn't care. There would be no one entering her bed but her anytime soon.

She collected herself enough to complete her morning routine before heading off to campus. Shower, check. Deodorant, check. Make-up applied, check. She gave herself a complete once-over in the mirror. Not bad. That is, not bad if you don't mind blood-shot, droopy eyes. Cute on a bloodhound puppy maybe, but on a college girl, not exactly attractive. She shrugged, shaking the bottle of eye drops and squeezed one last dribble into the corner of each eye.

Something about Mr. Milton's phone message from the night before stuck in her head. She recounted it again. He sounded totally confident, not uncertain as he had at his shop.

She pulled up the call log. With one click, the phone began dialing.

"Hello?"

"Hi, Mrs. Milton? It's Karsen Woods. Is Mr. Milton available?"

"Yes, dear, just a minute." She placed the phone on the counter. There was no fancy phone system or hold music. Karsen could hear activity in the background.

"Well, hello again, Karsen." Mr. Milton's voice sounded as if every day were a holiday.

123

"Hi, Mr. Milton." Her voice sounded sad in comparison. "You said something in your message last night that I wanted to call and clarify."

"Yes, and what was that, dear?"

"You said that you made four charms. That's not possible. My grandfather made three, and there are only three more."

"No, dear, I'm quite certain I made four. I remember there were three closer together in years. Then, there was another. I believe your mother was expecting you when I made the last one."

"I'm sure that can't be," Karsen replied, growing a little uncomfortable.

"Well, dear, I almost forgot about the first one. It was the year our store opened, 1969. We'll be celebrating our fortieth year in business – and maybe our last – next year," he said, going off on a tangent.

"That's certainly an accomplishment, Mr. Milton." Karsen couldn't imagine doing anything for forty years. "If there was a fourth charm, though… you must have made it for someone else then?"

"No, I don't think so. I know my clients like family. Your mother, she was a beauty back then. Looked a lot like you do now; you both have a certain glow about you."

"If you did make another charm for my mother, did she say who it was for?" Karsen drew in a deep breath and held it, not sure she wanted to hear his reply.

"Well, honey, it was a long time ago. I reckon it was for a boyfriend. She did have one boy she seemed smitten with. Handsome fellow. Left around the time of Vietnam if I recall correctly."

"Did you know his name?"

"Sorry, I'm afraid not."

"Okay, Mr. Milton. Thanks again for your time. You take care of yourself," And she hung up.

Karsen sat absorbed in thought. Perhaps her mother thought she was in love and had a charm made for her high school sweetheart. But if that were the case, why would she have kept it a secret?

෴

A knock at the door interrupted Addison's train of thought. Marjorie had not announced anyone. She looked up. The door opened slightly and a hand holding two tickets appeared, followed by a familiar face. A broad smile spread across her lips.

"What are you doing here?"

Pleasantly surprised, she attempted to conceal her delight.

"Stealing you away for a night on the town?" Russell wore cargo shorts, dark brown leather sandals and a deep navy flowered shirt that intensified his crisp, ocean blue eyes. Addison admired his casual look, thinking he could look sexy in anything.

"It's Monday."

"So?"

"So what makes you think I'm available?" she teased.

"Just a hunch. You have a well-oiled machine of a company, complete with a fully capable staff that you compensate above any market-value industry threshold. I'm certain they can hold down the fort for one night. And seeing that your mother told cancer who is boss - I suppose all that practice raising you over the years helped her hone those skills – I figure she can make it through one night without you, too." He gave her a quick wink.

"So, unless you have another hot date with two premiere tickets to *Spamalot* and reservations at Restaurant One, NY, I'm guessing my offer sounds enticing?"

Addison paged Marjorie. "Didn't I tell you to keep the crazies out?"

"You sure did, Ms. Reynolds. That's what I used to tell your father before he let you move into that office," she bantered back. "Didn't work then, didn't work now."

"So, is it a date?" Russell moved in closer to her desk.

"Yes. It's a date," Marjorie's voice chanted from the hallway. "And if she doesn't accept, would you consider an old broad like me?"

"Any time, Marjorie," he yelled back.

Russell's eyes lingered on Addison awaiting her reply. She was beautiful, her light olive skin flawless. He'd heard the rumors of her non-committal history; the tabloid reporters often compared her to a female playboy. He didn't see it. There was something about her he found irresistible. She challenged him and that alone enthralled him.

"Well?"

Addison finally acquiesced. "Okay. It's a date. There, happy now?"

"Yes, actually." He smiled his crooked smile that she was starting to adore. "I'll pick you up at six." He leaned across the desk and kissed her. His mouth lingered just long enough to arouse her. He smelled uniquely good. She inhaled, trying to place the masculine scent.

She straightened up in her chair. "Now go. Unless you happen to need a full-page advertisement running twelve issues in *Urbane*, that is. In that case, sign here." She pushed a pile of papers toward him and held her pen in his direction.

"Can it be a personal ad for you?"

"I'm sorry, we're not that type of publication."

"How about I just see you tonight then."

Smiling, he turned and shut the door behind him.

಄

Four dresses sprawled across the bed, each with their merits and shortcomings. The fifth, Addison evaluated in the mirror. *Sexy but not too revealing*, she thought. Typically, she was not this indecisive. She stripped off the dress one last time and again tried on dress number one. The dress was a sleek black number dipping low in the back with the length falling just over her knees. *Elegant and sexy. This is the one.*

She scoured her drawer for the appropriate lingerie and proceeded with getting dressed. She pulled her hair into a loose, flowing up-do, making visible the sleek skin of her shoulder blades all the way down to her lower back.

Russell arrived promptly at six. She opened the door and ushered him in. "Wow!" His eyes widened. "You look great."

He leaned toward her and kissed her cheek.

"Thanks."

He followed after her into the kitchen. He noticed the vase of orchids still on the table from their first date. The robust birds of paradise and greenery remained, while the more fragile flowers she had obviously pruned out. He was pleased she had cared for them enough to preserve their longevity.

"By the way, you don't look too shabby yourself," she said. He was dressed impeccably in a dark gray suit tailored perfectly for his powerfully built physique. She imagined him in the boardroom, exuding confidence and strength. The thought excited her.

"Flattery will get you everywhere," he said playfully.

She blushed slightly and took the last sip of water from her glass and set it in the sink.

"I'm ready if you are. Just need to grab my coat."

She moved toward the hallway. He jumped ahead of her, opened the closet, took the coat off the hanger for her and held it open. She turned her back to him and slipped her arms into the sleeves. His hands squeezed her shoulders lightly then moved seductively down her back, pulling her hips toward him.

"Mmmm." He moaned slightly, nestling his face into the nape of her neck. She could feel the masculine scruff of his unshaven cheek and allowed herself to melt against him for a moment. He felt strong, safe. She squeezed her eyes tight and soaked in the moment before straightening up and turning to face him.

"We should go," she smiled demurely, thinking to herself, *before we can't.*

৩৬

They arrived back at Addison's loft just after midnight. She was rarely up this late during the week. The usual stress-induced fatigue escaped her, though, replaced by a rather giddy, energized state.

"Who would have imagined Monty Python on Broadway?" she asked, dusting off a few lingering snowflakes before placing her coat back in the closet. "I couldn't stop laughing. I think that was better than any ab workout I've ever tried."

Russell didn't comment. Instead, he grasped her arms gently, turning her to him. He lifted her into a long, passionate kiss. She welcomed his brazenness with exhilaration and suddenly couldn't remember what she'd been saying as she lost herself in his embrace. She stopped kissing and stared into his eyes, trying to read his intent. Was he falling for her? Was she falling for him? Grabbing his hand, she led him silently to her bedroom.

৩৬

Morning arrived swiftly as the sound of Addison's alarm resonated through the room. She hit the off button and snuggled back onto Russell's shoulder. He stirred.

"Good morning," he said in a raspy, just-woke-up voice.

"Morning," she replied, always unsure how to act the first morning after. He turned his head and met her lips. She pulled away and held her hand over her mouth. "Morning breath, sorry. Let me go brush my teeth."

"Uh-uh." He pulled her hand down gently and kissed her anyway. In a swift movement, he rolled, positioning his body over her. He held the weight of his body with his arms as his lips moved lower to explore. She hadn't meant for him to stay the night. She needed to maintain control, yet she felt his strength radiating a feeling of protection around her. Too easily persuaded, Addison relented.

∽ 17 ∽

A fourth piece.

How was that possible? Karsen mulled the information around again and again in her mind as she sat like a zombie in class. Surely, Mom would have told us if she had made another charm. She didn't know whether to question her mother's honesty or question her own sanity. A twinge of anger crept into the pit of her stomach. She did her best to squelch the feeling. Now that she was gone, the last person Karsen wanted to be upset with was her mother.

The professor handed back her latest chemistry quiz. A large, red 'C' appeared on the top. Karsen stared in disbelief. A C? She had never received a C before. Ever. She placed the paper in her bag before Hanna caught a glimpse of the grade. At least it was only one quiz. She knew the trend would continue if she didn't get her focus back soon.

After class, the two made their usual trek across campus to the student center for lunch. Suddenly, Hanna tugged on Karsen's arm, pulling her hurriedly in the opposite direction.

"Ouch! What are you doing?" Karsen exclaimed.

Hanna kept walking. "I forgot something." She pulled at Karsen's sleeve harder, making her stumble and drop her bag.

Irritated, Karsen shook herself free. "Well, then I'll meet you there."

Before Hanna could stop her, Karsen turned around and instantly it all made sense. There before her eyes was James. He had apparently wasted no time. His hand brushed a loose hair from a girl's cheek and placed it behind her ear. Karsen couldn't help but stare. The girl's radiant dark brown hair was cut into a trendy bob that lay just above her shoulders. She looked young, perhaps a freshman or sophomore, Karsen figured, noting the weather was a bit cold for the mini-dress she was wearing.

"Sorry." Hanna rubbed her hand in a few small circles on Karsen's back.

"It's not your fault." Karsen continued to stare at them.

"Come on. Let's go. You don't need to watch this." Hanna picked up Karsen's bag and held it out to her, but she didn't take it. Instead, Hanna watched as Karsen, filled with an unusual confidence, sauntered directly to where the two were flirting.

"James! Helloooo!" She sounded calm, sophisticated even. As if she were approaching a highly regarded friend that she hadn't seen in ages.

A look of alarm crossed his face.

"Hi," he mumbled. His body tensed and his smile faded as he waited in anticipation of whatever was coming.

"Funny running into you here." Karsen flashed a phony smile. "Shouldn't you be at work?"

Slowly, he answered in what Karsen thought to be the most rehearsed verbiage he could muster. "I decided to explore my employment options some more. The position wasn't... well...it wasn't the right fit for me." *A nice way of saying you got canned and are now unemployed,* Karsen thought smugly.

She turned to the girl, who stood with a look somewhere between confusion and annoyance, no doubt assuming Karsen's intentions were to step on her territory.

"Silly James, aren't you going to introduce us?" Karsen said pretentiously. Before he could, Karsen extended her hand out to shake. "Hi, I'm Karsen. You are?"

"Josie," said the girl tentatively. She grasped Karsen's hand, her light grip flimsy against Karsen's athletic strength.

"Nice to meet you, Josie." Karsen said. Josie smiled slightly and nodded, not knowing how to react.

Karsen turned back to James.

"So, did you think about our discussion any further?" His eyes flashed in rage.

"I thought the situation was settled," he said tightly.

Karsen's insides boiled, yet she maintained her composure. If he thought he could simply move on without any repercussions, she'd show him.

"No, James, I'm sorry. WE haven't settled anything." She clenched her fists in her pockets and dug her fingernails into her palms. She had to maintain control of her emotions. "However, it appears you're certainly clear on YOUR part."

James unease grew. He fiddled with his fake designer watch. "I should probably be going now. Josie, I'll see you later." He hoped to conclude the conversation before Karsen's ambiguous discussion turned more candid. Unfortunately for him, it was too late.

"Josie, you see, James here..."

"Karsen!" His temper flared and his tone implied for her to stop.

"Maybe I should be the one going," Josie said uneasily.

"No stay, please, Josie. I assure you. You'll want to hear this." Karsen glared at James and continued. "As I was about to say, James here wants me to have an abortion."

A deep blush rose in James's face, turning it fire engine-red instantly. Josie stood, bewildered.

"Yes, that's right. I'm pregnant with his child and he's here seducing you. If I were you, I'd run along and don't hesitate to tell all your friends about this one. He is not an honorable man."

Glaring at James with contempt mingled with satisfaction Karsen turned and hurried back to Hanna. Behind her, Karsen heard him mutter "bitch" under his breath before pleading with Josie not to listen to a word she said.

"OMG!" Hanna mouthed as Karsen approached. Karsen grabbed her bag and they giggled as they hurried away.

"I can't believe you did that!" Hanna gasped as they entered the food court.

Karsen swept her hand through her hair. A sense of empowerment radiated through her, reminding her of the inner strength that had been dormant for months.

"Me neither," she giggled, feeling just a little more fulfilled.

༜

The next morning, Karsen sat anxiously in Dr. Warren's office. An oversized, stylish clock with numbers only at the quarter marks read approximately eight-thirty. She had not spoken to Dr. Warren since the ultrasound and was no closer to knowing what to do than she was then. She was faced with a series of negatives. Her head pounded and her eyes grew tired from stress every time the topic crossed her mind.

"Hello, Karsen." Dr. Warren entered the room, quietly pulling the door closed. "How are you feeling?"

"All right, I guess." She wasn't really all right. In reality, she was really quite a mess.

Dr. Warren eased into her black leather chair, crossed her legs and folded her hands softly in her lap.

"'All right' is a bit vague. Let's start with how are you doing physically? Is the morning sickness bothering you still?"

"It's manageable. I never want to see another cracker again, but I'm getting by."

"Understandable." Dr. Warren smiled, glad to see a spark of humor in Karsen's response. "And how are you holding up otherwise? Have you thought about your options?"

"If you're referring to abortion or adoption, then yes, I've thought about them. At least a little. But, I still don't know what to do." She studied Dr. Warren's face trying to read whether she thought she was a lost cause.

"What about the father?" The doctor's voice softened. "Is he still in the picture?"

"Not any more." Karsen shook her head indignantly. She refused to cry. "He wants me to terminate the pregnancy."

"Sounds like you're hesitant to do so."

"Not necessarily, I mean…I haven't ruled it out. I just don't want to regret it. But then I think, what will I do with a baby? I'm not stable. I haven't graduated. I have little to no income. I just don't see any way… " Karsen felt her heart rate increase.

"There is adoption. Good, secure couples are searching for children every day."

Karsen closed her eyes. The picture of her child with another family tore into her. "I know. I just don't know if I could live knowing I have a child out there. I can't win. Any way I look at it, there is more negative than positive. I just don't know what to do."

Karsen put her face in her hands trying not to cry again.

Dr. Warren attempted to comfort and guide Karsen during the remainder of their session without making a decision for her. Karsen left feeling more confused than when she arrived. There was no right answer. She was scared. Scared to tell Brad and her dad, both of whom would be disappointed in her. Scared to make the wrong decision. Resentful she had to make it alone.

On the way home, Karsen dialed Brad and invited him over for dinner. She didn't know how she was going to tell him about the pregnancy, but she felt it was time. As much as she valued Hanna, she needed another source of advice and she respected her big brother's opinion as much as she would have her mother's. He'd be a secure sounding board at least once the initial shock wore off.

∽

Curious glances abounded as Addison entered her office the morning after her date. She was never late. Jacob eagerly awaited her arrival, almost pouncing on her the moment she arrived.

"Addison, Adelaide's photos are adorable! I need you to select which one you prefer so we can finish the layout." He shuffled an array of photographs on top of her desk before she even had time to remove her coat.

Her ears heard him, but her mind remained elsewhere. She flung her new Prada purse upon the credenza behind her desk, hung up her coat and reclined back in her chair. Her arms stretched behind her head and her foot bounced like a fishing bobber where it crossed at her knee. She glanced at the photos on her desk and noticed he'd also fetched her morning latte. She looked up without a word and scrutinized Jacob from head to toe. He stood motionless. For the first time, she felt it odd that he appeared nervous around her. Regretfully, she realized she'd been more domineering than empowering towards him.

She tapped her finger against her lip.

"Why don't you choose, Jacob?" Her eyes twinkled. She saw something in him. Something that reminded her of herself. His subservient character aimed to please much like she had her father, but masked his gifted abilities. He was sharp, talented. How had she not seen this before?

And the rest of her staff, had she stifled them, too, out of her need to be in charge?

"Really?" he said, shocked, before realizing the lack of confidence he was portraying.

"Really. And have Marjorie get my coffee tomorrow. Tell her you're busy."

He smiled and left the office, a feeling of fulfillment escalating inside him. Addison Reynolds had just empowered him to finalize a layout!

Marjorie's head popped through Addison's door. "Are you ill?" she demanded. Addison's face flushed.

"I take it the date went well then?" Marjorie asked.

"Get back to work, Marge."

"Since you're in a good mood today, can I have a raise?"

"How about we discuss that after I drink my coffee. The usual please, with whip."

"What's wrong with the one on your desk?"

"It's missing the whip." Addison smiled. Marjorie rolled her eyes sarcastically. "You better get going if you want that raise."

"You did have a good night," Marjorie said, arching her eyebrows knowingly and smiling.

"Later, Marjorie." Addison blushed as she waved her hand dismissively to shoo her out.

⁊

That evening, Brad arrived at Karsen's apartment with a bag of Chinese food in hand.

"Are you sure you're okay?" he asked, surveying the once immaculate space. The entry alone looked as though a tornado had hit. Her shoes, usually neatly tucked away, sprawled across the floor. Three days worth of dishes were piled in the sink. The only thing that looked in order was the bed, which appeared untouched like she had been sleeping on the couch instead.

"I'm fine," she uttered by rote. She pulled two plates out of the cupboard. "Thanks for picking up the food. Want something to drink?"

"Sure. A Coke if you have one. Or water. Whatever."

She opened the fridge and pursed her lips, feeling embarrassed for having offered drinks she didn't have. She took a glass from the cupboard and filled it with tap water.

"Sorry. It's all I've got. Guess I need to get to the store, huh?"

Brad simply shook his head. He pulled out two square boxes by their little metal handles and set them on the counter. Karsen handed him a fork and opened the second box. She'd read that greasy food exacerbates morning sickness, but she'd experienced the opposite. She scooped a pile of orange chicken onto her plate and then added a portion of pork-fried rice next to it.

"So," she smiled broadly trying to ease her way into an appropriate moment to break her news. "How are things going with Hanna?" She stabbed a piece of chicken with her fork and popped it into her mouth. The heat radiated inside her mouth, stinging her tongue. She grabbed her glass of water and swished the cold liquid around like mouthwash until the burn dissipated. "Yowsers! That's hot." She set her fork down across her plate to wait for the food to cool before attempting another bite.

"Yowsers? What are you, twelve?" Brad taunted her.

"Leave me alone and answer my question."

"Off to a good start, let's say. It hasn't been that long," Brad said to appease her. He knew he couldn't avoid the conversation entirely.

"But you two seem to spend a great deal of time together," she pressed, wanting details. Of course, she'd heard Hanna's take on the relationship but she wanted his.

"I'm sure you two talk." He assumed Hanna shared every detail. Well, hopefully she didn't share everything.

"Come on…" she prodded, still stalling while her insides wrestled in angst.

"It's good. She's …," he hesitated. He'd talked to his sister about his girlfriends before, but this time was different. Hanna was Karsen's best friend. "She's incredible, really. She is beautiful and she gets me. She even laughs at my jokes." Karsen noticed how his face beamed as he spoke.

"She is pretty cool," Karsen winked at him.

"Yes, she is."

"Speaking of your jokes, whatever happened with the reality show? I'm sorry I've been so preoccupied," She stammered, "with the break-up and all... I haven't even asked you about it. I know Hanna said your last show went gangbusters."

"The reality show? What reality show?" he teased for a moment, glad for the segue to his big news...

"So...?"

"I leave for Hollywood in two weeks!"

"Holy crap!" She jumped out of her seat and hopped onto the couch, jumping up and down like a hyperactive toddler. "That's incredible!"

He motioned for her to sit down. "You know what happened to the monkeys jumping on the bed?" Karsen laughed as she jumped to the floor.

"Yes, they fell off and bumped their heads."

She plunked down on the couch, pumping her legs up and down, unable to restrain her new found energy. "Have you told Dad?"

"Not yet. I wanted to tell you first. Except, well..."

"Hanna knows?"

"Yes."

"I guess I'm going to have to get used to playing second fiddle, huh?"

"Sorry." He shrugged.

"No worries. I like that you're happy. And now, oh my goodness! You're going to Hollywood! My brother the star!"

"Don't get ahead of yourself, sis. I'm not even on the show yet. There are forty called to Hollywood. Only ten make the actual show."

Karsen just smiled, unable to control her excitement. She knew he'd be one of the ten. She held her tongue on her situation for the remainder of his visit. She couldn't bear the thought of ruining his good news. Everything else could wait.

⌒〜⌒

Brad kissed his sister on the cheek as he left. "Call me if you need anything." He was worried about her. He knew she'd been through a great deal, but so had he. He sensed there was more going on with her but if she wouldn't open up to him, he didn't want to force it. At least not yet.

Closing the door behind her brother, a ray of happiness broke through the storm cloud hovering within Karsen. She couldn't help but share in Brad's excitement and elation. She was thrilled for him. His success gave her hope, hope she desperately needed to weather the stormy events of her own life. She could tell Hanna had kept her secret thus far. Otherwise, Brad would never have avoided the topic. He would be furious. The guilt of lying to him festered within her. She hated having secrets, but she couldn't tell him now. She knew her brother and she knew what he'd do.

She popped her daily prenatal and chased it down with a long gulp of water. The teakettle whistled, and she poured herself a cup of hot tea before settling down on the couch. She snuggled a blanket around her waist and tucked her legs underneath, finding comfort in its warmth. This had become her usual routine as a newly single woman. While most girls her age hit the nightclubs, she sat watching her shows – alone – from her favorite spot on the couch.

She logged onto her laptop, the screen scrolled to life with her family's photo set as the background display. She remembered that day vividly, everyone scurrying to get ready. Her mom couldn't get her hair quite right. Her dad sat patiently waiting without so much as a word, while Brad and she fought over the mirror in the bathroom. In the photo, their family appeared united and content, the preparation issues resolved.

"I need you, Mom," Karsen whispered to the screen, lightly brushing her mother's image with her fingertips. "I can't do this alone. Please give me a sign showing me what to do. And when I say a sign, I mean huge blaring green and red lights."

She surfed the web aimlessly for the next two hours, scanning for information on babies and pregnancy. The amount of information available overwhelmed her.

Maybe James was right. Maybe it would be easier to end the pregnancy.

She hated herself for even thinking what that meant. She'd listened as her mother had lectured her about abstinence and safe sex. She felt as though she had failed her. If she terminated the pregnancy, she could avoid telling Brad. She could avoid telling her dad. No one but Hanna would ever know. But, how could she? She didn't know if she could carry that burden. This was not how it was supposed to happen. She had always dreamed of having a family. How could she choose not to keep the baby?

～ 18 ～

"What you need is some good old-fashioned retail therapy," Hanna declared after listening to Karsen's depressed tone. "I'm coming to pick you up. Be ready in ten."

Hanna hung up before Karsen could decline. Although Karsen appreciated Hanna's concern, she'd much prefer to hide in her apartment and not come out until this whole fiasco was over.

Hanna appeared as promised and honked the horn obnoxiously. "Get your booty out here, Karsen!" she shouted out from the driver's side window. "We're hitting the mall!"

Karsen ran to the car and held her finger to her mouth like a mother to a baby, "SHHHUUSSH!" She climbed into the car. "The last thing I need is to get evicted. Could you keep it down?"

"A little noise never hurt anyone."

"So, where are we going?" Karsen was less than excited to be going anywhere, but she knew Hanna well enough to know she would have drug her out by her toenails if she had declined. She'd rather avoid the scene or else, with her luck lately, find the police at her door breaking up a domestic dispute.

"Scottsdale Fashion Square. I thought we'd grab some lunch and then I need to see if I can find a new pair of black pants. On sale, of course. And then…I have a surprise for you."

"A surprise?" Karsen wrinkled her nose.

"Yes, and you can't say no."

"Tell me what it is."

"That would take all the fun out of it, now wouldn't it? Let's just say, you need it."

At the mall, the girls wandered through several stores, mostly window-shopping as neither had a great deal of expendable income. But something about trying on new shoes and browsing through racks of clothes seemed to be working, as Karsen's fears subsided – at least temporarily – and she felt almost normal for the first time in what seemed an eternity. *Thank goodness for Hanna*, she thought.

They took the escalator up to the third floor.

"Here we are!" exclaimed Hanna, her dimples deepening as a bright smile brimmed across her face.

Karsen looked around. "Nordstom? We can't afford anything here."

"We're not here to buy anything," Hanna said, grabbing a hold of Karsen's shoulders and turning her to face the entrance of the in-store spa.

"I can't afford spa treatments either, Han, you know that."

"Surprise! You have a massage booked in twenty minutes. It's already paid for. And, as I said in the car, you can't say no."

"Yes, I can. And I will. You can't afford that either, although I must say I do appreciate the gesture."

"I said it's paid for. If you don't use it, then a hundred and fifty dollars is wasted and I'll be pissed."

"Hanna, no! I can't, really," Karsen protested.

"Look, K, don't worry about it. I bought used books this year instead of new. I've halted my expensive make-up habit, and I set aside some extra money for an emergency. Just go take your mind off your life for an hour. I meant it when I said you really do need it, and I want to do this for you."

"But what if you have an emergency?"

"This IS an emergency, Karsen. You ARE the emergency," Hanna said with terse impatience. "You need this more than I need extra money lying around. I'd probably waste it on some too-expensive gift for a boyfriend anyway." *Even though for Brad it would be worth every penny*, she thought to herself. "Now, just go. PLEASE! They said it's completely safe for pregnancy, and you can sit in the lounge and drink lemon water and eat fruit until you pop. I'll meet you back at the food court in a couple of hours."

"Okay, okay. One massage sold to the neediest girl on the street," Karsen said sarcastically. She gave Hanna a kiss on the cheek and looked her in the eyes. "Thanks. I owe you one."

"You don't owe me anything."

Karsen smiled and entered the frosted glass door leading to the spa. For one blessed hour, she was free of her anxieties and fears.

~

By Saturday the snow had cleared, but the air was still brisk outside Addison's parents' home as bubbles floated weightlessly through the air. Not simply one or two, but what seemed like hundreds of dainty circles dancing together in an assortment of sizes. Adelaide's little gloved-hands extended, fingers open wide as she attempted to catch each one without success. She giggled continuously as she pranced in circles around the lawn.

"Why didn't we have machines like this when we were kids?" Emily inquired of no one in particular.

"You tell me. I blew into that flimsy plastic wand for hours when Addison was a toddler. She could never get enough," replied Mrs. Reynolds from her rocking chair on the porch. For the most part she was back to herself, but her energy still lagged and she had to rest more than she liked.

"These machines just make lazier parents," Addison said, sticking her tongue out at Emily so she'd know she was teasing. She took the lid off the large pink jug sitting beside her and poured more bubble solution into the plastic machine. She watched Adelaide and with every movement she felt her heart drew closer to her. She looked so wonderfully content. So full of innocence. Addison couldn't help but be mesmerized, wondering why adults couldn't live in the moment like children do.

But Adie's antics were not the only thing mesmerizing Addison. Through the blur of bubbles she watched coyly as Russell rolled the handle of one of her father's new drivers between his palms. He wound it cautiously behind his head and took a slow motion practice swing. Addison lost herself in the moment, imagining his powerful arms wrapped back around her.

"Ad-di-son…" Emily exaggerated each syllable, bringing her back to reality.

She flung her head back toward her friend. "What?"

"You're drooling."

Addison's cheeks flushed.

"Whatever," she replied, embarrassed.

"He is unbelievably gorgeous. I'd drool too, but my husband's here," Emily sighed and they both laughed. "Thank you again, Addy, for inviting us over. Greg looks like he's enjoying the male bonding. He needed this."

"Oh, the joys of being a parent." Addison smiled. "No need to thank me. You are always more than welcome, Em. And anyway, it's nice to see Greg. I know how hard he's been working lately."

Emily glanced at Greg who was standing next to Russell and Mr. Reynolds. "Yes, he has. It's nice to see him relax for once. I feel guilty sometimes knowing he's sacrificing so much so that I can stay home with Adie."

"You've got yourself a wonderful husband there."

"And you could soon, too."

"Let's not get ahead of ourselves…Anyway, c'mon. Dinner should be close to being ready. Let's go in." Addison replaced the cap on the bottle of bubbles.

"Adelaide, let's go wash your hands. It's time to eat." Emily walked toward her still dancing daughter, extending her hand for her to hold and follow.

"No, Mommy! Bubbles! More bubbles!"

"Adie, sweetie. Aren't you hungry? You can do more bubbles later, okay?"

"NO!" The little voice screeched. She folded her arms and tilted her chin down in an overstated pout. "I don't want to eat. I want bubbles!"

"Adie. Now!" Emily's voice was stern. Addison watched the interaction with a mix of envy and relief. She could enjoy Adie's antics without having to struggle with the discipline. Addison ached for the bond of a child but watching Emily she questioned if she were capable of being a good mother.

"NO!" Adie continued to defy her mother. She pointed her finger to the empty chair on the porch. "Time out, Mommy!"

"What did you say?" Emily asked, astounded.

"TIME OUT, MOMMY!" Adie's gestures grew more theatrical.

Addison held her hand over her mouth to hide her laughter.

Emily squatted in the lush green grass, taking herself down to Adie's level.

"Look at me." She held Adelaide's hands still against her sides and waited for her to make eye contact. "That's good thinking, Adelaide, however Mommy doesn't do time out. Now, it's time to eat."

Adelaide's lower lip began to quiver as she painfully maintained eye contact with her mother, a crocodile-sized tear brewing in the corner of her eye.

Catching the tail end of the interaction, Greg scurried toward his wife and daughter to help.

"Adie, listen to your mother." He grabbed her hand and Adelaide finally surrendered. Emily turned off the bubble machine and grasped Adelaide's free hand. Addison watched as the family of three proceeded toward the two-story, white house. Against the landscape they appeared idyllic, like a sample photograph in a picture frame where no one has a care in the world. No disagreements, no abandonment. Nothing but pure, uninhibited happiness.

Still across the lawn with Mr. Reynolds, Russell watched Addison as she gazed at her friend's family. He wondered if she wanted a family as well. He did. He'd spent years building his career. Where there was once fulfillment, there was now a void. The money, the material rewards meant little with no one to share them with. He knew he'd distanced himself from relationships before, never allowing a woman to distract him from his career. But Addison was different. She was definitely a beautiful, intelligent and welcome distraction.

Addison turned and Russell met her gaze. She smiled, embarrassed he had caught her daydreaming. He smiled warmly and winked as he continued toward the house. He knew there was more to her. Whatever it was, he was not going to let her get away.

☙

Following dinner, Emily scoped an opportunity to approach Russell alone. She had wanted to talk to him all afternoon. Maybe it was none of her business, but she thought if he had a warning of Addison's tendencies perhaps he could ward them off. She wanted to see her friend happy and if a little intervention was necessary, than so be it.

While Addison helped her mother back to her room to retire for the evening, Emily found her opportunity. She followed Russell outside where he had taken a seat on the patio steps. "Hey, Russell," she began, uncertain how to gingerly broach the conversation. She sat beside him.

"Hello, Emily. I was watching Adelaide play earlier. You and Greg have a beautiful daughter."

"Thank you. She is something else, that's for sure." They both laughed understanding the insinuation behind the comment. "It's a good thing she's cute, or Mommy may have sent her back to the stork."

"Never. She's an absolute doll, really. You are very blessed."

"Yes, I have to admit you're right there," she concurred. She paused, contemplating whether or not she should proceed. She knew Addison would be livid if she stuck her nose in where it didn't belong. Still, she couldn't sit and watch Addison sever another relationship. Now that knew about Addison's secret, she knew it was inevitable that she would push Russell away sooner or later. Emily was bound and determined not to let that happen.

"So Russell, you and Addison seem to be doing well." She did it. She opened the door.

"Yes, I suppose so."

"Not too certain yet I take it?"

"I'm certain I think we're progressing. Or at least I am. I'm just not sure on her end. She can be hard to read, as you already know." He hesitated to offer too much information.

"Her reputation precedes her," Emily smiled dolefully. "I see her look at you. She is smitten. It's been a long time since I've seen her like this. She always…" Emily stopped herself short.

"She always what?" he asked.

She hesitated. "Oh, never mind…Perhaps we should join the others." Her conscience weighed on her and she tapped her foot nervously, attempting to end their conversation.

"She always what? I want to know. I need to know what cards are stacked against me if I'm going to make this work." His curiosity piqued, leaving him interested in extracting any information that could potentially secure a more promising future.

"Let's just say that she has a tendency to push people away before she allows herself to get too close. Call it a defense mechanism."

"So she passes her comfort level and then pulls away?"

"More like pushes the emergency button like an ejection seat on an F14. The man usually doesn't see it coming and is crashing and burning before he realizes what hit him."

"I see," Russell said.

"I didn't understand what was going on until recently," Emily continued in a rush. "She shared a part of her past that even I wasn't aware of, but it's not my place to share. I'm really sorry. I've probably said too much. I'm regretting this conversation already. If Addison knew what we were talking about, she'd kill us both."

"Yes, you're probably right."

"But I think you're good for her, and I don't want to see her sabotage herself again."

"I understand. Neither do I." He said. "Why don't we head back inside? They're probably wondering where we disappeared to." Inwardly, he wanted to press her for details. He knew Emily had Addison's best interests at heart and would be hard-pressed to blatantly disrespect her friend's trust. However, his determination to make the relationship work required knowing what pushed Addison's eject-button. That may require some reconnaissance of his own.

∽

Karsen looked for Hanna at the food court. Her massage left her feeling refreshed but also a little lethargic. She yawned as she scanned the crowd, finally spotting her fifth in line at Starbucks.

"Feel better?" Hanna asked as Karsen joined her in line.

"Yes. That was so relaxing. I can't thank you enough." Hanna ordered a mocha frappachino while Karsen salivated, knowing the caffeine was a no-no. Instead she opted to play by the rules and ordered a fruit smoothie.

The two scavenged for an empty table to no avail, so they settled for sitting along the edge of the water fountain by the concierge. Karsen watched as two children playfully threw coins into the water. She wondered what wishes they'd made.

"Hanna?" Karsen paused, dejectedly, as her eyes turned downward, focusing on the floor. She felt a drop of water splatter on the back of her neck. "I don't think I can do this."

"Do what?"

"The pregnancy." She felt defeated. Hanna put her arm around her and Karsen laid her head on her friend's shoulder. Hanna didn't speak. She wrapped her other arm around her and listened.

"I have no money. I haven't graduated. I have no support structure. How could I afford daycare? Food? Diapers? Formula? I can barely take care of myself."

Hanna couldn't stop the tears forming in her eyes, knowing there was little she could do to console her friend. Grabbing both of Karsen's hands, she looked directly into her friend's eyes.

"Karsen. I know you don't believe this, but you are the strongest person I know. I'm not saying you have to have the baby. I'm not saying you have to keep the baby. If you follow your heart, you'll make the right decision. But, you have to make your decision based on facts. And the facts are that you would be, will be, a wonderful mother whether now or ten years from now. If there is a way to make it work, you will; if it's not the right time, I'll go to the clinic and help you through. Understand? You tell me when you're sure."

Karsen nodded, trying not to melt down completely in public. She sniffled and wiped the edge of her eye with an index finger. She scanned the area and was relieved to see no one took much notice of their unusual interaction.

"The Karsen I know does not give up," Hanna said assuredly. Her head tilted down but her eyes held Karsen's gaze. "And you do have a support system. You have Brad, your dad, and you always have me. I think I'd make a pretty good aunt." She released her hands and saw Karsen give the tiniest smirk.

Karsen raised the back of her hand against her nose to blot another sniffle. "Hanna?"

"Yeah?"

Karsen exhaled heavily. "Do you think my mom could have had a secret like this? I mean, something she didn't share with anyone but her best friend?"

"I don't know." Hanna blinked twice contemplating what she knew of Karsen's mother. "Maybe. Why?"

"When I was home, I followed your advice. I found the jeweler that my mom used to make the charms. Except, he said that he made four pieces. If it's true, then my mom had another one made that she didn't tell me about."

"Did you tell Brad?"

"No. He's been preoccupied lately."

"Oops. Sorry," Hanna interrupted knowing, at the very least, she was one source of preoccupation.

"I keep telling myself it's nothing and to just drop it. Not like I don't have enough to worry about." She swiped her hair behind her ear. "But, there is this feeling in the pit of my stomach, you know? My gut just can't let it go."

"Did the jeweler give you any indication of who she made it for? He obviously knows you."

"Not really, except that it was made 18 years ago. He also mentioned she had a boyfriend, although I can't imagine her making one for just a boyfriend. Unless, it was serious… I couldn't think of where to look next. Until now."

"Why's that? What are you thinking?" Hanna asked.

"If we have this secret, maybe she confided in someone, too."

"Maybe. Do you remember anyone she mentioned? Anyone she kept in touch with from her high school? Anyone who'd know who she dated?"

Hanna slurped the last drop from her straw.

"The only person I can think of is a friend she used to e-mail. She lives in upstate New York, I think. I've seen pictures of her, but I don't remember seeing her at the funeral. Actually, I wonder if she even knows. I thought my dad had contacted everyone, but maybe he thought we called her. How could we miss one of her closest friends?"

"Did anyone check your mom's e-mail after the accident?"

Karsen fiddled with her straw, turning it in circles between her fingers. "Not that I know of. I didn't even think about it. I honestly couldn't think about much of anything those first few days."

"Well, maybe it's time we take a look-see. Can't hurt, right?"

Karsen shrugged sheepishly.

"K, I know you well enough to know you're not going to let this rest until you get some answers. Come on, let's go. We have some hacking to do."

∾ 19 ∾

The girls returned to Karsen's apartment and booted up the laptop. Karsen impatiently tapped her foot as the search engine connected to the Internet. She knew her mom kept a free e-mail account. She clicked on the "Mail" tab and entered the front half of her mom's old e-mail address into the box.

"I think that was her user name."

"Do you know her password?"

"No, but I know what she liked. She wasn't all that computer savvy, so I'm guessing it's nothing too complex."

Karsen thought for a moment and then typed in the dog's name: Belle.

Invalid Password.

"Crud," Hanna and Karsen chimed simultaneously.

Karsen typed again. This time she keyed in Lilies.

Invalid Password.

"Hmmm." Karsen thought, then typed a third time: Lilies17.

"How did you come up with that?" asked Hanna.

"Her favorite flower and favorite number."

Welcome Katherine!

"Ah!" Karsen pointed her finger at the screen. She didn't know what to think about what she'd just done. Right or wrong, she was staring at her mom's e-mail account.

"Seriously?" Hanna's eyes popped wide open in disbelief. "That's almost scary how easy it was for you to get in."

"I know. And it's not almost scary, it is scary." Karsen sat back against her chair. She was staring into her mother's private e-mail. The sudden urge to curl back into bed and shut out the world fled through her, realizing the life her mother left behind.

"You okay, K?"

"Yeah, sorry." She fought to hold back the tears ready to pour out like rain from her eyes. She focused on the screen. There were 271 messages in her mother's inbox.

"Holy crap. Over two hundred messages?" Hanna gasped.

Karsen scanned down the first page. "It looks like most of the messages are just spam. She probably didn't know how to set it up to filter."

Karsen clicked checks in the boxes to the left of any item that looked illegitimate. Coupons from several stores marketing online, numerous work-from-home offers, and a few offers for enlarging her penis.

"Got to love spam." Karsen shook her head and hit delete.

There were fifteen messages left that appeared valid. Karsen felt like she was snooping behind her mother's back. She didn't want to intentionally invade her mom's privacy. One e-mail had been from her. She grimaced realizing her mother never received it. All the little monotonies of daily life, her mom would never do again. Just like that. One moment here, the next gone. Like most young adults, Karsen had an unintentional invincibility complex. That, yes, death occurs but later in life. Not while you are still making plans. Her mother's death had made her contemplate her own mortality and that scared her. Not so much the fear of dying, but on missing out on the future.

She scanned down the subject lines. There were two messages from her father and a few from Brad. Additionally, Karsen noted three jokes and two apparent 'real' messages forwarded from the same e-mail address: margaretNY@bmail.com. The subject line of the first message read "Photos from the Bahamas." Karsen clicked and the message popped opened.

Hi Kat.

I hope things are well with you. Thought I'd forward you a few photos from the cruise. It was so much fun. We even drank a few margaritas in your honor. I wish you could have joined us. How are the kids?

Love,
Meg

"That's her," confirmed Karsen, as Hanna read over her shoulder.

Karsen opened the first photo. A slightly overweight woman in her late fifties was dressed in a conservative black one-piece swimsuit covered by a black sarong with tropical blue flowers. The view in the background was so perfect Karsen pictured the image being artificially enhanced like they are in magazines. The water glistened a pure crystal blue with the sunset a perfect orange hue.

She closed the message and opened the next. The subject line read "HHEEELLLOOO?"

Hi Kat.

I'm sure you're busy, as usual, but I haven't heard from you in over six weeks. Where are you? Is everything okay?

Write soon,
Meg

The weight hit Karsen like a brick. Her fears were confirmed. Meg didn't know. She thought about how hurt she'd felt when she'd been told the news. She knew Meg would be crushed. Her mom and Meg had been friends for decades. She turned to Hanna, feeling a sudden pang of fear. The idea had seemed novel, but it hadn't occurred to her that they'd actually be able to hack in, or that they'd actually have to contact her mom's friend and break her heart.

"What do I do?" Karsen looked helplessly at Hanna. Her stomach began to churn.

"I don't know. Do you know her phone number? Or even her last name?"

"Crawford. I feel bad calling her. It's been months. Shoot. Shoot. Shoot." She fidgeted with the mouse. "Do you think I should really call her?"

Hanna looked at her confused. "What do you mean?"

"I mean hacking into e-mail is illegal. What if I get in trouble?"

"You're not going to get in trouble. I think you're being paranoid. You have to call her, K. It's only your mom's email. Who's going to care and if anything happens, I'll take the blame," offered Hanna.

Karsen sat up and curled her leg underneath her in the chair. "Really?"

"Of course. I'm sure Meg would rather hear the news from you, and you need answers. If they're out there, then we need to try to find them."

Karsen nodded. She'd never let Hanna take any blame, but she also knew she needed to find the truth. She opened a new window in the browser. Typing in www.yellowpages.com, she did a search for Margaret Crawford in New York. One record appeared. Taking a deep breath, she nervously dialed the phone.

"We're sorry. You've reached a number that is no longer in service."

"Figures," she said annoyed, slumping into her chair. "Everyone's number is unlisted nowadays."

Hanna hugged her from behind. Karsen reached up, grabbed her arms, which were crisscrossed in front of her and held them while she decided her next move. After a few moments she straightened up, returned to Meg's last message and hit reply.

Meg,

I need to talk to you and I have a new cell number. Can you please call me at 480-555-3632.
Hope you are well.
K

Her finger floated hesitantly over the "Send" key.

"She's going to know this isn't my mom," Karsen muttered miserably.

"Maybe. But, you can't e-mail her that her best friend died. What if …" Hanna stopped herself mid-sentence. She couldn't bring herself to say the words.

"What if…?"

"What if something happened to one of us? Would you want to find out I died via e-mail?"

Karsen inhaled then blew out a long breath, puffing out her cheeks. She felt utterly disheartened. "Why do you always have to be right?" She clicked send.

"What do we do now?" Hanna asked.

Karsen folded her hands into a prayer position and pressed them against her lips.

"We wait."

❧

The pink-jeweled Blackberry vibrated against the wood of the bed-side table. Karsen looked at the clock. It was just past seven o'clock. Her textbook displayed a small wet spot where she had drooled. *Yuck,* she thought, realizing the last time she looked it was around six-thirty. She had opened her chemistry manual right after Hanna left. Trying to study seemed to be the only thing that cured her insomnia lately. She was start-ing to believe the semester was a lost cause.

She hurried to reach the phone before the call went to voice-mail. She hit the button to answer, but her half-asleep hand tingled and she clumsily dropped the phone onto the floor. She stretched her arm down, fumbling for the phone and bringing it back up to her ear. "Hello?"

"Oh, hi. I'm sorry to bother you. I must have the wrong number." The voice on the other end sounded unsure.

"Wait," Karsen said. "Who is this?" She settled her tone.

"Meg Crawford. I thought I was calling Katherine Woods. I must have misdialed. Sorry again to have bothered you."

"No, wait, wait…Don't hang up." An urgency rose in Karsen's voice.

"Who is this then?" Meg asked, flustered.

"I'm Karsen."

"Katherine's Karsen?"

"Yes. I'm sorry. It was me that sent the e-mail." Karsen didn't know quite what to say.

"Oh." Meg had thought it odd that the letter was signed K. Katherine usually signed off Kat. Confused as to why her daughter had asked her to call, she asked, "Is your mother there? Is everything okay?"

"I didn't want to… I just couldn't tell you over e-mail."

Meg's concern escalated. "Tell me what, dear? What's going on?"

Karsen trembled. All the feelings she felt when her father called her flooded back to her memory. Her voice cracked as she spoke. "I really don't know the right way to tell you this."

"Karsen, what is it? What's wrong, dear?"

"Meg, my mom died in early January." She choked out the words. "It was unexpected and somehow you got overlooked when the funeral arrangements were being made. I'm so, so sorry."

Karsen overheard a gasp in the background followed by a loud sob.

After a long silence, Karsen wondered if the line had been dropped. "Meg?"

"I'm sorry." Meg's voice cracked. "What? How? Oh, dear Lord no!" Meg's muffled voice pleaded for information.

"There was a car accident and ... I'm so sorry to be the one telling you this," Karsen spoke as tears streamed down her face like she had just heard the news herself. "She spoke of you so fondly, and I thought we'd contacted everyone until today. I thought my dad had contacted you. Maybe he thought Brad or I did. I don't know how we missed you. I'm so sorry."

Meg's voice wavered. "I understand. It's not your fault. I just can't believe it. I mean... I knew it was unlike her not to e-mail. I had tried calling her cell, too, but I just figured she was busy and I've been traveling a lot lately. Oh, I just can't believe it."

"I'm sorry." Karsen apologized again that no one had contacted her earlier as she struggled to explain about the accident and funeral in more detail.

"How horrible! Oh, Kat...no, no, no..." Meg whispered in disbelief.

"The police said the accident probably happened so fast she didn't realize..." Karsen couldn't form the words. "I try to believe that. I have to believe that. I can't stand the thought of her being in pain."

"Oh, Kat!" Meg repeated.

Karsen and Meg sat silently, both crying on their end of the phone. Several minutes passed before Karsen spoke again. She knew the timing couldn't be worse, but she also needed answers and knew she might not have another chance to ask.

"Meg, I hate to ask you this under the circumstances. But you knew my mom in high school, right? I mean before my dad, before us kids?"

"Yes. Your mom and I had been friends since we were kids."

"Do you know if she had a boyfriend back then?"

"She had several." Meg let out a slight giggle through her sadness thinking back to their early high school days. "Why?"

"Anyone serious?"

154

Meg hesitated. Had Kat told her daughter? Meg had sworn not to tell anyone Kat's secret. She certainly couldn't betray her now. "Not really. Why, sweetheart?"

"Well, you knew about her necklace, right?"

"Of course. She hardly ever took it off."

"Well, this might sound crazy, but I have reason to believe there might be another piece out there. A piece that she never told the family about. She wouldn't have told you anything about it, would she have?"

"No, I'm sorry, but it's not ringing a bell," Meg stammered slowly.

"It was just that the jeweler who made them thought it might have been for a boyfriend."

"Oh," Meg paused. "Huh. I'm sorry, honey, nobody specific is coming to mind. I'll let you know, though, if I think of anything, okay?" She sniffled.

"Thanks," Karsen said, the frustration of another dead end rising up through her again. She knew it wasn't Meg's fault. Who could expect her to remember her mother's boyfriend from forty years ago?

"Meg?"

"Yes?"

"I'm sorry again about the funeral. My mom would have wanted you there."

❦

Russell and Addison made their goodbyes as they left her parents' house. Her mother whispered, "He's a keeper," in her ear as she hugged her.

When they arrived at Addy's loft, Russell barely allowed her through the door before whisking her passionately into his arms. He pressed her body between his and the wall. Watching her with her family had escalated his attraction. He now knew he wanted the whole package, for better, for worse. He knew she was what he had been waiting for. She exhibited a down-to-earth sincerity that most women who grew up in affluent households lacked. He couldn't put his finger on what it was exactly or why, but it spoke to him of humility.

He lifted her up. She wrapped her legs around his waist and kissed his neck as he carried her to bed. He laid her on the bed, kissing her first on her lips and then her neck, moaning softly as he inhaled her scent. She ran her fingers through his hair. He drew back and gazed at her face.

"I've fallen in love with you," he whispered.

Addison stared back, the words resonating within her head. Her heart and her head were torn in separate directions. She wanted to respond. She wanted to say, "I love you, too." Instead, she placed her hands on the sides of his face and kissed him firmly, avoiding a response. Those words, so powerful, frightened her. Her own biological mother gave her away. The only man she allowed to get close to her broke her heart. How easy it would be for Russell to leave her, too. She was not worthy of accepting his love no matter how much she yearned for it. She wouldn't say those words back to him, even though her heart wanted to.

⁊

"Wake up, sleepy head."

Russell kissed Addison's forehead and placed a breakfast tray over her lap. The arrangement looked as though it were delivered from a personal chef. She inhaled the warm, sweet scent of syrup.

"Hope you like French toast," he said, easing back into bed beside her.

"It looks delicious. Thank you." She felt rejuvenated from a full night's sleep. She could not remember the last time she'd woken up without an alarm.

He scooped a dollop of whipped cream onto his finger and placed it in her mouth. She seductively obliged, sucking the sweetness between her lips. The feeling excited him.

She wished she could erase the words from being said. Those three little words changed things. She couldn't allow herself to be vulnerable. To do so opened her up for more hurt than she was willing to endure.

"Addison." Russell lifted her chin toward him. "I meant what I said last night. I love you."

"Russell, don't. Please." She felt her emotional walls going up.

"Don't what? Tell you how I feel?"

"Yes, don't," she pleaded.

"Why not? I know it may seem fast, but we're adults, not teenagers. I know what I want."

"You may think you do, but…"

"But what, Addison? All you have to do is let me in. I can't read your mind."

"I can't do this," she said, setting the tray aside and climbing out of bed. She grabbed her robe.

"Addison." He crossed the room, catching her hand and turning her toward him. "I won't let you push me away."

"Russell, you don't want me." She tugged at her arm, but he wouldn't let go. "I can't do this."

"Why not?" He stepped closer, peering down into her eyes.

Her answer was silence.

"Why not?" he demanded again. "You can't tell me last night wasn't… incredible. Why are you doing this?"

"I…," she looked him in the eyes. "I don't love you."

She spoke purely out of desperation. Of course it wasn't true. She hated hurting him. She hated hurting herself, but reasoned it was better for it to happen now, on her terms.

"I don't believe that. I see it in your eyes. I feel it when we're together." He released her and she stepped back.

"Don't do this, Russell."

"Don't do what? Tell you that I love you? Fight for us?"

"I think you should go." She dropped her gaze to the floor. She wouldn't let him see her cry. She tucked her hands under her arms so he couldn't see them tremble.

"Whatever hurt you in the past, whatever makes you feel that you are unworthy, you have to let it go."

"WHAT?" Her head snapped to attention. "What did you just say?"

"You can't allow your past to dictate decisions in your future. Eventually, you are going to have to stop shutting people out. Or, you will end up alone."

"What the hell do you know about MY past?" she steamed.

"Nothing. Forget it."

"What do you know, Russell?" she pressed angrily.

For better or worse, he had her attention. He hesitated reluctantly, not wanting to throw Emily under the bus. "Emily just said that there was something in your past…"

"What else did Emily say?" Addison interrupted, feeling betrayed.

"Nothing. She didn't tell me anything specific."

"What did she say, Russell?"

"Nothing. I came to my own conclusions. Can we just let it go, Addison?" He grabbed her hand again. "Please, just let me in."

"I think you need to go." He resisted and attempted to pull her into him. She closed her eyes and pushed away. "Just go now. Please, Russell." She lowered her voice for fear of it cracking.

"Fine," he said sternly. He took one last look at her perhaps waiting for her to change her mind. Addison stood motionless, eyes closed. She listened to him gathering his things until he left the room. Her body jerked as she heard the front door slam behind him.

⚬ **20** ⚬

Sunday evening, Karsen returned to her apartment after going on a long run to clear her head. She'd made her decision. She needed closure. She needed to start over and thus justified to herself that there was only one solution. Tomorrow she would call the clinic and schedule an appointment to terminate the pregnancy. She would let her mother's memory rest in peace and end her search for the missing charm. That was how it had to be. She would put it behind her and move forward. She placed her hands on her abdomen and sighed heavily.

"I'm sorry," she whispered.

She wiped the sweat from her brow with a paper towel and threw it in the trash. She needed to call Hanna and tell her she'd made her decision. She picked up her phone and noticed the red blinking light indicating a new message. It was a text from Meg.

CALL ME

She sat down on the couch and stared at the phone. Perhaps it was nothing. Her apprehension grew. Holding her breath, she highlighted Meg's number and hit send.

"Hello?"

"Hi, Meg. It's Karsen."

"Hi, Karsen." Meg's voice sounded solemn.

"I got your text. Did you think of something else?" Karsen asked eagerly.

"Is this a good time to talk?" Meg asked, not wanting to subject Karsen to life changing news at an inopportune time.

"Yes. I just got home."

"Well, all right then." Meg contemplated where to start and questioned one last time if she should disclose the secret at all. She'd struggled with this since they'd spoken the night before. *Forgive me, Kat.*

Silence.

"So, was there something you wanted to talk about?"

"Yes, I'm sorry, Karsen. It's just hard, you know. Your mother and I knew each other since we were five. We were more like sisters than friends."

Karsen could tell Meg had been crying. "I'm so sorry again, Meg. I hated having to be the one to tell you about my mom. I know how close you were."

Her heart burdened with the thought that she was about to betray her best friend's confidence, Meg continued. "We shared everything from clothes to secrets. I want you to know that she loved you kids more than anything and would never intentionally hurt you."

Karsen contemplated where this was going but didn't interrupt.

"You asked me about another charm. I promised Katherine, your mom, that I'd never tell. I don't know if it was the right choice or not, but it was her choice so I abided by her wishes."

"What are you trying to say, Meg?"

"I'm saying that you *are* right. That there *is* another charm."

"But, why wouldn't she have told us that? Why keep it a secret? I don't understand."

"She didn't want to hurt you. She didn't want to relive the past. She didn't want to upset the family. I don't know all her reasons, Karsen, but just know everything she did was out of love. She loved you so much, Karsen. You and Brad and your dad. You meant everything to her."

"So, she gave a charm to a boyfriend. Why is that such a big deal? Why did she think we would care? I mean, yes, the tradition was meant for our family, but it's just a silly tradition."

"Well…you are right. I mean…the jeweler was right." Meg stuttered trying to figure out how best to explain. "You see, there was a boyfriend. His name was Alex. I don't remember his last name, but your mother was head over heels in love with him. I remember he worked on his dad's farm. He was quite handsome. Your mom was taken with him from the moment she saw him and they must have dated for close to a year."

"Really? My mom never said anything about him."

"Karsen, it was 1969. Well before she met your dad, of course. The Vietnam War was in full swing. She was devastated the day he told her that he had been drafted. No one we knew came back from Vietnam, so she made a decision. In ways she regretted it and in ways she didn't, but she lived with it nonetheless. So she slept with him. He left the next day. Just up and skipped out on her, the country, everything. The jerk deserted her. She never did find out what happened to him, but she figured he ran to Canada."

"Wow. I had no idea. She never said anything...not one word."

Karsen thought of James. Perhaps that was why her mother never approved of him. Her mom's first love had broken her heart. Still, Karsen didn't understand why her mother wouldn't have shared this with her. She remembered her preaching to her about premarital sex, but maybe she didn't want to admit she'd done it herself.

"Your mom was crushed. She hardly left her bed for a week."

"Oh? Then why would she make a charm for him?"

"Karsen, the charm wasn't for him."

"Huh?"

"Katherine...I mean your mom...got pregnant."

"What? No! You're making this up!"

Karsen's eyes filled with tears. Pressure welled around her forehead making her head throb. She couldn't think.

"I'm so sorry, dear. I'm sure this is a shock, but I assure you, I would never make something like this up. Back then the stigma of unwed pregnancy was much different than it is today. Abortions were riskier. Her parents were destroyed. They insisted she put her up for adoption."

Karsen was speechless. Her mother? A baby? Meg referred to the baby as "her." A sister? Everything in her reality jumbled.

"The charm?" she choked.

"The charm was for the baby. She had it made to match hers and left it with her when they took her away."

"Where is she? Did my mother know where she is?"

"That, unfortunately, I don't know and neither did your mom. She never looked for her. I know she named her Lily, but I would imagine the adoptive family changed her name. After she and your father had you and Brad, she was so afraid, Karsen. Afraid of hurting your family. Afraid of hurting the adoptive family if she tried to find the baby and get her back. She regretted giving her up, but her love for you and for Brad held her back. If you believe anything, believe that she loved you too much to hurt you."

Karsen couldn't help but wonder if her mother were still alive if she ever would have told her. Lily, lilies - her mom's favorite flower. Her mom would buy a vase full of lilies every April seventeenth. It all finally made sense.

"Karsen, I know you may not understand, but she thought she was doing the right thing."

Karsen was too distracted to respond.

"Karsen, I mean it. Call me if you need anything. Okay?"

"Okay." Karsen echoed in shock.

They hung up. Could what Meg claimed be true? Did she really have a sister? Her mother had made a choice. And now she faced the same choice. Knowing now what her mother had gone through she wondered more than ever if she was making the right decision.

Karsen sat emotionless, in utter disbelief for the next five minutes. She stared at the phone deciding what to do next. She dialed home. Her dad did not answer. She tied her key back onto her shoestring and left her apartment. Phone in hand, she started running toward Hanna's. The two-mile distance between her apartment and Hanna's house felt as if it took the time to run a marathon. When she arrived, Hanna's sorority sister opened the door.

"Is Hanna here?" Karsen panted, her face red from exertion.

"I think she's upstairs in her room. Brad's up there, too. I'd knock first." She smiled. "Do you need some water?"

Karsen didn't respond. She plunged past her and skirted up the steps two at a time.

Knock. Knock. Knock. She pounded on the door.

"Who is it?" Hanna's voice sounded muffled through the door.

"Hanna, it's Karsen. Let me in."

"I'm kind of...busy. Can we talk later?"

"No! I know Brad is there. Open up. Come on."

"Okay, okay. Hold on." Hanna wriggled back into her shirt and Brad straightened his own before she opened the door.

"Sorry." Karsen barged through the doorway.

"K, you're red as a beet! Sit down," Hanna demanded, handing her an already opened bottle of water. Karsen took a long drink. She sat heavily on the pink chair in the corner trying to slow her heartbeat. She was unsure whether it was racing from running or from stress.

"You okay?" Brad asked anxiously.

Karsen nodded, still catching her breath. She held her Blackberry in front of her. "Red and green lights," she spoke, sounding like a crazy person.

"Huh?" Hanna and Brad looked puzzled.

"I asked for Mom to give me a sign. You know, for what I should do."

"Okay …??" Brad looked even more clueless.

"Brad, I've been tracing the missing piece, you know, from our charms. I was about to let it go, but then I saw this. The green light flashed on the Blackberry."

"Are you for real, Karsen? I have no idea what in the hell you're talking about," Brad said.

"Karsen, maybe we should talk in private?" Hanna offered.

"No. It's okay. He needs to hear this." Karsen paused. "I know it sounds crazy. But, I asked Mom to give me a sign, jokingly adding the red and green flashing lights like a traffic light. Maybe I'm losing my mind, but when I came home the Blackberry was flashing red. There was a message from Meg. So I called and talked to her and now it's green."

"You can't be serious, Karsen. Are you?" Brad asked.

"Yes, I am. I'm not stupid. I know the light changes for all messages. But, I asked Mom for a sign and I believe this is it. Mom wanted me to talk to Meg. She wanted us to know."

"Meg, Mom's friend Meg?"

"Yes. Meg knew about the charm." She looked her brother in the eyes, tears welling in hers. "Brad, Mom had a baby that Mom and Dad never told us about. We have a sister."

Brad's back muscles tensed.

"No! Stop this nonsense, Karsen. There's no way! Mom would have never kept a secret like that. And at any rate, she wouldn't have kept it from Dad and he would have told us."

"Well, he didn't and Meg said he knew. Now I get why he wanted to bury the charm." Hanna sat on the bed speechless as Karsen explained about tracking down the missing piece.

"I don't believe you!"

"Brad, I wouldn't make this up. Call him!" Karsen shoved her phone at him. "I'm telling you. He knows." Brad hesitated. "CALL HIM!" Karsen yelled, pushing the phone into his chest.

Brad grabbed it and scrolled to their home number. Visibly shaking, he hit send.

Their father answered.

"Hi, honey! I saw that I missed your call…"

"No, Dad, it's Brad."

"Oh, hi, son. Is everything okay?"

"Yeah, I mean, Karsen's right here."

"Oh, okay. I was at the grocery store or I would have answered when she called earlier. Just wanted to get home and put things away before I called…your mom always took care of these things."

"Dad," Brad stopped him, "Karsen has some ridiculous idea that Mom had…that Mom had another child." The words sounded false. He couldn't believe he was even speaking them aloud.

Silence.

"Dad, can you reason with her?" Brad demanded.

Silence.

"Dad? Dad?"

Finally, he heard his father say, "I told her secrets only postpone the inevitable."

On the other end of the phone, Carl rubbed his face with his hand and sighed in anguish.

"It's true?" Stunned, Brad sat down heavily on the bed. He did not respond to his father, but instead held the phone back to Karsen.

"Daddy?" she asked quietly.

"She thought it was best," he mumbled feebly, trying to explain while defending his wife.

Karsen instantly felt resentment toward both her parents. Even though her father had finally validated her suspicion about the missing charm, the validation provided no solace. Instead, her pent-up emotions spewed out uncontrollably.

"You knew? All these years and you didn't say anything? We have a sister we never knew about and you thought that it was okay to keep it from us? What else did you lie about? What else did Mom lie about?"

She unloaded relentlessly. There was no response on the other end. Her clamorous tone drew the attention of Hanna's sorority sisters, three of which were now peering inquisitively through the door.

"I'm sorry," her father said, his voice full of regret.

Karsen looked at Hanna for support. "What am I supposed to do?" she pleaded with her friend, her question still audible through the phone.

"I don't know, sweetheart," her father replied on the other end.

Hanna raised her shoulders expressing her own uncertainty, her eyes wide with doubt.

Focused on Hanna, Karsen spoke again without thinking.

"Mom put her baby up for adoption and now look what happened. What do I do? I can't have this baby!"

Brad gasped, comprehending her statement. Realizing what she'd said, Karsen dropped the phone, turned, and ran out of the room and out the front door.

Brad sat paralyzed. His father's panicked voice emanated from the Blackberry on the floor. "What? What do you mean? Karsen? Karsen, are you okay?"

Hanna picked up the phone and articulated the only words that came to mind, "Mr. Woods, I'll have Karsen call you later."

~ 21 ~

Monday morning, Addison arrived at the office before dawn. She couldn't eat. She couldn't sleep. A mere twenty-four hours ago she was enjoying breakfast in bed with Russell. The scene repeated again and again in her mind with the outcome always the same. She and Russell were over and no matter how much she hated to admit it, she hurt. She had ignored the two messages Russell had left on her cell phone since she asked him to leave. She listened with a heavy heart to the last of the three messages she now found from him in her office voice mail.

"I've called five times, Addison. I won't call again."

Addison pressed delete.

She scrolled through the proposals for the new issue, tracking her revisions in red. An hour – maybe more – passed, and she started hearing her staff roll in and the office outside her door start to bustle with activity.

"Good morning, Addy," Marjorie poked her head through the door. Immediately noting her employer's unusually lackluster appearance, she shook her head and said, "Oh no, Addison. You broke it off with him, didn't you?"

Addison looked up from her desk with an expression clearly warning Marjorie not to go there.

"You're going to end up alone like me," Marjorie muttered under her breath just loud enough for Addison to hear. She nodded her head and backed out of Addison's office, closing the door behind her.

Addison kept cover in her office the majority of the morning, speaking only to Jacob via online messenger. It was getting close to lunch time when Marjorie's voice came through the intercom.

"Line 1, Addison."

"Who is it?"

Marjorie hesitated, knowing she'd decline.

"Emily."

"Tell her I'm busy."

"I'm not going through this again, Addison. She's already called twice. You tell her." She transferred the call.

"Hello?" Addison answered disgruntled.

"Addy, what are you doing?"

"Working."

"No, you know what I mean. Russell called. Are you really this stupid?"

"Stay out of my business, Emily. I'm a big girl."

"Then perhaps you should start acting like one. He loves you."

"What makes you think I love him?"

"Because I know you," Emily said.

"You think you know me. Perhaps you should stop meddling in my business," Addison vented. "What did you tell him anyway? I trusted you."

"You didn't trust me. You blurted it out by mistake. Besides, I didn't tell him anything except that you have a history of pushing people away."

Addison didn't respond.

"Addy," Emily softened her voice. "You can hate me. You can shut me out, but I'm your friend, your best friend – maybe your only friend – and I won't sit around silent while you destroy your chance at happiness. I love you and I can't live with that."

"I've got to get back to work," said Addison dismissively. "Can we talk about this later?" she asked, meaning as in never.

"You tell me when you're ready. And, Ad, please call Russell before it's too late." Emily hung up the phone.

Addison stewed. She knew Emily was right. She would lose him. But that was for the best, no matter how much her heart ached.

❧

Monday passed slowly for Brad, Hanna, and Karsen. Hanna attempted to call Brad, but he avoided her calls. At the same time, Karsen avoided all of his.

Brad's anger swelled. His foundation – his family – was crumbling around him. He felt betrayed, first by his mother's secret and now knowing Karsen's. Pregnant? How could she allow that to happen? And now? The timing couldn't be worse. He was supposed to leave for the audition any day. How could he depart for Hollywood and leave her alone? Even if he did, his focus would be compromised. His natural instinct to protect and help her as he always did now conflicted with a growing resentment. "Damn it, Karsen!" he shouted, picking up a framed family photo and flinging it across the room.

The glass shattered against the wall.

❧

Karsen opened her purse and pulled out the photo of the baby she'd brought from home after her recent visit, realizing now that it was that of her sister. She held the photo to her lips feeling as though it could speak to her. Karsen knew "Lily" had been adopted as an infant. She wondered, though, if her sister knew about her, if she knew she had another family other than her adopted one. Or if she knew she was adopted, would she even want to find her birth mother? Did she resent her mother's decision? Would she welcome at her age – Karsen figured the now-grown woman to be in her late thirties – the fact she had a brother and sister? Maybe their mother felt she couldn't or shouldn't seek out her first born, but Karsen had to know the answer to these and so many other questions. She had to know how Lily felt about her life. Was she happy? Did she love her adoptive family? In her heart, Karsen needed to know whether giving her baby a chance at life was worth it even if she couldn't be in it.

With a sense of urgency, Karsen pulled her laptop off the counter and booted up the system. She wasn't sure where to start searching for a person, but in her blog readings on the ancestry.com site Karsen recalled remnants of advice. The first was to trace the person through the state they were adopted in. Each state had different laws regarding access to adoption records. She also remembered something about intermediary services. She logged on to the web and searched for "adoption in Indiana." What if the adoption had taken place elsewhere? She reasoned she had to start somewhere. Her stomach churned thinking she very well may be on an impossible quest. She wondered also if Brad would approve of her search. Not that she really cared at this point. She was the one in her mother's shoes, and she needed to know.

The screen brought up the Indiana Adoption History Registry. She clicked on the link and skimmed the text. As a birth sibling she had rights, but consent had to be granted from her sister. She wondered if she had already consented. If she had not, the way Karsen interpreted the information was that an independent party could contact her for consent. The registry offered this service and it was known as a confidential intermediary. She searched for a contact e-mail, but could only find a brick and mortar address for contact. Great, snail mail, she thought sarcastically as she opened up Word to type the letter.

March 20, 2008

Indiana Adoption History Registry
Attn: Registrar, Vital Records Division
Section B-4
2 N. Meridian Street
Indianapolis, IN 46204

TO WHOM IT MAY CONCERN:

My name is Karsen Woods. I have recently learned that my mother Katherine Marie Woods placed a baby for adoption around the time of April 17, 1969. My mother has passed away and I am seeking to find my half sister. My mother's birth date was May 4, 1953. I believe at the time of birth she may have resided in Wayne County. Please contact me at the number provided.

Sincerely,
Karsen Woods

She printed the letter bolding her contact information in the header and then addressed the envelope. Before placing it in the mailbox, she prayed for a rapid reply.

⌒

Brad stood outside the science building in the warm afternoon sun. He wore baggy, cargo shorts and brown flip-flops. Heat radiated through his striped polo shirt and he could feel sweat trickle down the middle of his back. He didn't care. It had already been three days, and he refused to let his sister avoid him any longer. He felt guilty about distancing himself from and ignoring Hanna, too. He knew they would be in class together and headed toward them hastily as soon as he saw them walk out of the door.

"We need to talk," he said to his sister. Looking at Hanna, he smiled and gave her a quick kiss on the cheek. "I'll call you." She nodded and walked away.

He put his arm around Karsen and grabbed her bag.

"Let's go somewhere more private."

They walked through campus and arrived at a shaded bench. A few students lounged under trees studying nearby.

"Sit," he directed her, and she complied. He wanted to tell her how disappointed he was, how he was tired of sacrificing his life to pick up hers. But he didn't. She was his baby sister, and she'd been through enough.

"I'm sorry," she said, nervously fiddling with her necklace.

"I know."

"Brad, I wanted to tell you."

"You should have."

"Hanna wanted to tell you, but I begged her to keep my secret until I could figure things out. Please don't be mad at her. "

"I'm not. I know you two are close."

They sat quietly for a moment.

"What about James?"

"Exactly. What about James?" she said bitterly. "He wants me to have an abortion. And, from the last time I saw him, it appears he's taking no time moving on."

"Figures."

"I was going to schedule one, this week actually. But then I got the call from Meg. I need to find her, Brad." Two girls walked by and she waited for them to pass beyond earshot. "I feel like Mom wants me to find her. Our sister, not Meg. I don't know what the right decision is, but I need to do this and fast. I don't know if talking to her will help me make a choice or not, but I have to see."

"How far along are you?" He asked.

"Right around ten weeks." Brad understood the urgency. There was a point of no return when three options turned into two. He knew she was scared and he was scared for her.

"How can I help?"

"You can't. You're leaving for the show."

"No, no...Karsen, I'll just tell them I can't participate. This takes precedence." He could hear his own words coming out of his mouth and felt his dreams disintegrating.

"Oh, Brad, you can't! I can't...I won't let you do that!"

"K, you can't do this alone. I promised Mom when you decided to come to school here that I'd take care of you. Now that she's gone, I won't go back on that promise."

Karsen knew what this sacrifice meant. This opportunity may not come again no matter how talented he was. This was his shot. She leaned forward, placing her forehead on his chest. His lean, track-built body was small compared to many men, but the size of his heart overcame his stature. She felt safe against him.

"Have you talked to Dad?" he asked.

"Not since the phone call. Seeing that it's been over a week, he's probably pretty pissed at me."

"Maybe. But you owe him a phone call."

She straightened up and tried to compose herself the best she could under the circumstances. "I know. And you owe Hanna a phone call."

◌

Karsen dialed tentatively, hoping her father would not answer so she could sheepishly leave him a voice mail.

"Hello?" answered the soft, familiar voice.

"Hi, Daddy." She held her breath, waiting for him to speak, not knowing exactly what reaction to expect.

"Are you okay?" he asked. No scolding, no anger penetrated his voice.

"Yeah. I mean, I guess, considering." She weighed her words. "Daddy, I'm sorry."

"I know, sweetheart. I'm sorry, too." There were few intimate moments between them. They both hesitated uncomfortably considering what to say next.

"Mom would be so disappointed in me."

"Maybe a little. She didn't want you to face the same decision she had to make. It tore her apart. But don't believe for a moment that disappointment undermines love. We both just wanted the best for you, Karsen."

"I'm angry at her, Daddy. I keep thinking I shouldn't be, but I can't seem to let it go. She should have told me."

"I know you can't understand, honey. But, right or wrong, she did what she thought was best."

"I guess."

"Karsen, your mom had a small amount of life insurance. I had planned to put it away for you and Brad. I wanted to help when you got married or bought a home. But if you need it...I mean if money is weighing on your decision, you can have it now. I'm not your mother and I don't have all the answers, but I'll do what I can to help."

"I know, Daddy...thanks. I'll think about it."

∽

The women stared at Brad as he entered the sorority house. The scene in Hanna's room had tickled its way through the entire clan like a bad game of childhood telephone where the story is hardly recognizable by the end. Brad wondered how distorted the account of his family had become through the layers of gossip. He scaled the steps and tapped on Hanna's door.

"Come in."

"Hey."

"Hey." She sat at her desk with her laptop open. "I was just downloading a movie. Thought it might take my mind off things for awhile."

He walked over as she stood from her chair. His arms embraced her tightly. "I'm sorry," he said, not letting go. "I didn't mean to push you away. It's all just too much. My Mom, this whole mess with Karsen."

"I know. You don't need to explain. I don't blame you." Hanna pressed her cheek into his chest until she could hear his heartbeat. She closed her eyes and lost herself momentarily with his arms curled around her. She couldn't stand the thought of losing him.

"I withdrew from the show," he said in a faint voice, which Hanna hardly heard.

"You what?" She pulled back and looked into his eyes with disbelief.

"I withdrew from the show," he repeated.

"Brad, you …you can't!"

"I had to."

"But…"

"But nothing. Karsen shouldn't be my responsibility, but I can't let her go through this alone."

Hanna rested her head back against his chest. "I know."

"I could kill James."

"You're telling me."

She pulled back again. "Brad, maybe it's not too late. I can help Karsen. This could be your big break. Call them and tell them you made a mistake."

"I can't. Even if I went, I'd be too preoccupied to concentrate. At any rate, it's already done. I called the producers before I came here. They've probably already filled my spot."

Hanna could see the disappointment in his eyes. She reached up and pulled his face to hers. Her fingers felt prickly stubble over his typically smooth shaven skin. She kissed him softly. He responded immediately, kissing her passionately in return.

"I can't lose you," he whispered with a sense of urgency. She pulled away. He stood for a moment alone, wondering if his words frightened her off and watched as she quietly walked to the door. He sighed and smiled with relief as she closed it and turned the lock.

She walked back and stood in front of him.

"You won't," she whispered back into his ear.

He kissed her again. Together, they moved toward her bed.

∾ 22 ∾

"Slide, Mommy! Slide!" Adelaide chanted.

Emily held her daughter's hand as she slid down the playground sliding board, giggling with delight. Reaching the bottom, she slipped free of her mother's grasp and raced back around and up the steps, then slid down again, over and over.

Addison smiled as she watched at Emily's side. She had agreed to meet Emily because she missed her goddaughter, but Emily dared not tread on uneasy waters. Russell had not been a topic of conversation since their phone call at the office and Addison wanted it to stay that way.

Addison's phone began to ring in her purse.

"It's probably the office," she said, and began to rummage through the Louis Vuitton for her cell.

"Let me take it," Emily said in an attempt to stop Addison from being pulled into a lengthy business conversation. She knew her friend needed a break as much as she did, but Addison never seemed to turn off.

"Me talk! Me talk!" Adie bounced off the bottom of the slide and ran toward Addison.

"Hello?" Addison raised the phone to her ear, turning away from the toddler. Adie began to scream.

"MEEEE TAAALLLKKK! MEEEE TAAALLLKKK! WHAAAAAAAHH!!"

Emily grimaced and grabbed her by the hand.

"Adie, no! Aunt Addy is talking on the phone. Let's go slide again."

"Hello?" Addison repeated, as Emily dragged Adie away kicking and screaming.

"Ms. Addison Reynolds?" a man's voice questioned.

"Yes, this is Addison Reynolds." *Great*, she thought, *what now?*

"I'm Nicholas Ross with the Indiana Adoption History Registry."

"Who?" Addison froze.

"Nicholas Ross, ma'am."

"What's this about?" Addison's anxiety rose, her smile replaced by a less attractive scowl. Emily could tell by Addison's expression that the call was not what she expected.

"I'm a confidential intermediary. You are aware that you were adopted, correct?"

"Yes?"

"Well then, ma'am, we've been contacted by a member of your biological family. By law, they cannot contact you without your consent. Are you aware of the procedure?"

"What? NO!" Addison shouted. Emily's head turned hearing the harsh tone in her voice.

"No, you are not aware, or no you do not consent?"

"No, I do NOT consent. I'm sorry," stammered Addison, trying to regain her composure.

"Certainly, Ms. Reynolds, I understand. If you were to change your mind, you can call me back at this number, or our contact information is listed online."

"Thank you." She ended the call and hurriedly stuffed the phone back in her bag. Rising from the bench, she walked over to Emily.

"Who was that? Is everything okay?"

"Someone tried to contact me," she said, visibly flustered.

Emily looked confused.

"Who tried to contact you?"

"My mother maybe? The man said he was an intermediary from an adoption registry service. He said someone wanted to contact me, but they can't without my consent," Addison continued.

"What did you say?"

"No. I said no."

❦

Karsen didn't recognize the number on her phone, but answered quickly.

"Hello. May I speak to Ms. Karsen Woods, please?"

"This is Karsen."

"This is Nicholas Ross from the Indiana Adoption History Registry."

"Yes?" Karsen's heart skipped a hopeful beat. It had been a painfully long week since she'd written to the registry and she was beginning to wonder if she'd ever hear anything.

"We received your letter and we were able to trace your sister. Unfortunately, she declined to give us permission for you to contact her. I'm sorry."

Karsen's heart sank. The notion that her sister wouldn't want to meet her had crossed her mind, but she'd dismissed it. Maybe she wouldn't want to be best friends or call her a sister, but how could she not be curious at all?

"Are you sure? Maybe if you asked her again. Did you tell her it was her sister trying to contact her?"

"I'm sorry, Miss. At this time, there is nothing further I can do. She has my information if she changes her mind."

"And in your experience, do people change their minds?"

"Sometimes yes, sometimes no. If she reaches out, we'll notify you."

"I understand. Thank you for your time."

Time. A component Karsen was running out of.

∽

Karsen cocooned herself away for the next two days. The shades in her room were left unopened, creating a somber dark hiding place for her to seclude herself. She rarely arose from her bed except to drown her depression in a tub of rocky road ice cream, the last of which she had finished this morning. There were several unanswered voice mails waiting on her phone, including a reminder for her appointment at the clinic at nine o'clock Friday morning.

It wasn't fair. Her friends invited her out, but she didn't want to be the source of their gossip, nor did she want their sympathy. What she wanted was to turn back the clock. To bring her mom back. She wanted to ask her mom why. She wanted to scream at her for deceiving her. She wanted her to tell her what to do.

She had dozed off again when the front door opened.

"Karsen?" Brad's voice boomed throughout her small apartment.

"Go away!" she yelled out, wishing she'd never given him a key.

He entered her bedroom, followed by Hanna. "You didn't return my calls."

"I just want to be left alone."

Hanna opened the shades, brightening the room instantly. Karsen groaned and pulled her pillow over her head.

"We're worried about you." Brad sat on the edge of the bed, placing his hand on hers.

"I'm fine."

Brad looked at Hanna. She shook her head.

"You're not fine. Look at you. Look at this place," he said. Two days and her apartment looked like a fraternity house after a rush party. Empty ice cream cartons littered the floor with the spilled remnants dried in sticky blobs beside them. Furniture was barely visible under piles of unwashed laundry.

"Karsen, consider this an intervention. Come on, get up," Brad said sternly.

"NO."

He pulled the pillow off her head.

"Stop it!" she yelled, trying to hold onto it harder.

He tugged harder and the pillow flew across the room, almost hitting Hanna and knocking over a half-empty glass of milk. Hanna flinched.

"F- you!" Karsen shouted at her brother.

Agitated, Brad pulled her up by her arms. "C'mon, Karsen. I'm not kidding. Get up!"

"Wow, K, you look dreadful," Hanna said, noticing – in addition to her lack of housekeeping – Karsen obviously hadn't showered in two days either.

"Thanks," Karsen said sarcastically and glared at Hanna.

"Hey, what are friends for?" Hanna grabbed her keys from the counter and tossed them to Brad. "Why don't you run out and get some decent food. She needs to eat and there's nothing here."

"Sure. Be back in a few."

"Come on, K. Let's get you into the shower."

Reluctantly, Karsen dragged herself into the bathroom. Hanna started the water.

"It's going to be okay," Hanna said softly, and gave Karsen a hug. She closed the door so Karsen could clean up in private.

Karsen stepped out of the shower and wrapped herself in a towel. The mirror had steamed over from the heat. She toweled off a circle and peered into the mirror, analyzing her appearance. Ten weeks of pregnancy and several gallons of Ben & Jerry's were beginning to show in her face. She opened her towel and examined her body. Her typically flat abdomen appeared rounded. Not enough to be noticeable in clothing, but definitely filling in. It wouldn't matter now. She had made her decision and after Friday the weight gain would subside. The feeling of emptiness seemed ironic with her growing physical appearance. She re-wrapped the towel around her and secured one around her hair.

Hanna sat on the edge of the bed thumbing through the new issue of *Urbane*. She looked up and set the magazine aside as Karsen came back into the room. Karsen noticed that Hanna had tidied up while she showered.

"Thanks, Han," she said.

"No problem."

"I mean it. Thanks."

Karsen slumped beside her, hands folded in her lap. "Will you still go with me?"

"Of course."

"Without Brad, right?"

"That's up to you. Whatever you want. He'll understand."

"I know."

"Did you tell your dad?"

"No. I figure he'll realize when… well, when no baby arrives. I can't face the disappointment."

Hanna hugged her tightly. She could see the worry on her face and wished she could take it away. They sat in silence, lost in thought, trying to digest what Karsen's appointment meant.

⚬⚬

The next morning, Karsen sat in the clinic waiting room and filled out the routine medical paperwork. She signed her name on the last form and turned everything in to the receptionist. That was it. In one hour her mistake would be erased. Her emotions were another story.

She sat back down next to Hanna. Neither knew what to say. Karsen's nerves boiled within her. The medicinal smell irritated her already queasy stomach. She stared blankly over Hanna's shoulder as she flipped through the issue of *Urbane* she had brought from Karsen's apartment.

"Karsen Woods?" the nurse called from the doorway. Hanna looked up toward the nurse then at Karsen, expecting her to get out of her seat. Instead, Karsen's eyes burst open.

"Wah…wait!" she exclaimed. "Go back!"

Startled, Hanna looked at her concerned. "What?"

"Karsen Woods," the nurse repeated.

"No, go back!" Karsen reached across Hanna's arm to flip back the page. She could hardly believe her eyes.

"Karsen, she's calling you…," Hanna started.

Karsen impatiently pointed at the page. "Look!"

Hanna looked down again and her jaw dropped when she saw what Karsen was pointing at. There on the editorial page was a photo of *Urbane*'s CEO Addison Reynolds. Visible in the open neckline of her blouse was a silver puzzle piece charm.

∽ 23 ∽

Addison held the phone away from her ear. She knew her mother would be upset once she learned about Russell and she was right. Garbled in the background she could hear her rattle on about how she was going to ruin her life and how she needed to beg him to come back. She brought the phone in only to utter a few "Uh huhs" and "Yes, Mom. I understand," anything to appease her until she felt they could move on. Addison almost felt as if the lack of a date for her mother's charity event was the greater issue. The appearance of her only daughter still single at thirty-nine must cause undue whispering in her mother's social circle.

"Yes, Mom, I said I know. Now, I really need to get back to work." Addison pushed. "I'll see you soon." She felt a pang of relief as she hung up the phone. At least the conversation about Russell was over and she hoped that would be the last.

As frustrated as she felt, still, she loved her for the mother she was. Perhaps her parents didn't fit the picture-perfect model of family, but they did the best they knew how. They'd taken her in and provided her with a lifetime of financial security. She respected them for that. Her loyalty remained to them and a birth mother had no right to find her. Not now. Not almost forty years later.

Jacob entered the office and sat a warm, frothy latte along with a hard copy of the next issue's proof on her desk.

"Morning, Addison." His voice was casual. He was becoming more comfortable with his position and with her.

"Good morning," she replied as she looked up. Perhaps for the first time, she realized how good looking he was. Not in a sexual way – he was fourteen years her junior and she was not about to venture down that road. But, he'd evolved in the short time she'd known him. As his confidence grew, his appearance transformed from boyish to manly. She smiled and nodded as he left.

Her e-mail inbox contained the usual cluttered morning mess. She sipped the latte and relaxed into her chair as she clicked through message after message, methodically and efficiently delegating or deleting each one. Suddenly she froze. She looked twice at the "From" line in the next message. KWOODS. Unexpectedly, she was on the verge of tears. Her memory files from years ago resurfaced. Katherine Woods. She had written it down when she was looking for her mother as a teen. A name she found herself never able to forget. *No, no, no.* How could she have found her? How dare she contact her? Addison's memory flashed back to when she had seen her, a loving mother with two kids toddling around the front yard. She had been written out of their family. Hadn't she just talked to the intermediary and indicated she definitely would not permit it? She did not want to be contacted! *No, no, no!* She pounded her fist on the desk causing her coffee to splatter. "Shit," she said, rubbing the sting away. She wanted to scream, but instead she gritted her teeth in frustration. Despite her initial anger and anxiety she felt compelled to open the message. Apprehensively, she scrolled the mouse over the message and clicked.

Dear Ms. Reynolds,

I know you must receive hundreds of unsolicited e-mails. This might sound crazy, but I have reason to believe we may be related. I wouldn't attempt to contact you, but this is an emergency. Please don't delete without responding.

Thank you,

Karsen Woods

Addison reread the name. Karsen. Not Katherine. Maybe it was a mistake. Maybe Karsen was just some crazy stalker who was looking for money. Maybe her last name was a weird coincidence. Karsen. Katherine. The names were too alike. In her heart, Addison knew. She knew from the day she'd gone to their home that she had a sister. What kind of emergency warranted contacting a sister you never met? Addison groaned and covered her eyes with her hands. "Urgh!" She grimaced, conflicted about what to do. They couldn't just expect her to welcome them with open arms…could they?

"I'm sorry," she said aloud, as she slid her pinkie across the button. DELETE.

❦

Hanna walked into chemistry lab and was relieved to see Karsen at their station.

"Hey, K. Anything new?" Hanna asked. She looked at Karsen hopefully. She had crossed her fingers and said her prayers hoping to hear something finally was going her friend's way.

"No," Karsen responded. With Hanna's notes and a bit of leniency from her professors, she managed to at least maintain passing grades but the prospect of producing her usual stellar GPA was looking grim. "I tried to e-mail Addison, but I didn't get a response."

Karsen opened her notebook, the tear sheet from the magazine was taped to the inside cover. "I know it's her. She even looks like us."

"What if it was a shock to her? Maybe she didn't know she was adopted," Hanna reasoned noticing the similarities in the photo.

"Maybe? I don't know."

"Did you try calling? The e-mail could've been blocked by the spam filter, or maybe she has an assistant filter her account and they just think you're some whacko."

"I don't have a number."

"Oh, gimme a break. When has that stopped you before? You found the e-mail."

"I don't know, Han. I'm just too tired. She obviously doesn't want to be contacted. I'll just reschedule my appointment. This is all just prolonging the inevitable anyway."

"Call the magazine. She owns that damn thing. I bet someone there knows who she is. You CAN'T give up now, Karsen," Hanna urged her.

❦

Following class, Karsen and Hanna found a bench on campus. Karsen dialed the number listed on the editorial contact page. Her heart raced as she waited with Hanna standing supportively by her side.

"*Urbane* magazine. How may I direct your call?"

"Yes, ma'am. I'm trying to reach Addison Reynolds," Karsen said, trying to sound as sophisticated as possible.

"One moment, please."

Her heart continued to pound as she listened momentarily to music on hold as her call was put through.

"Hello, thank you for calling *Urbane*. This is Marjorie." Her routine answer sounded rushed as if twenty calls arrived at once and she had only a moment to attend to each, which wasn't much of an exaggeration.

"Yes, um…may I speak to Addison Reynolds, please?"

"Who's calling, please?"

"Karsen Woods."

"Is she expecting your call?"

"Yes," Karsen lied with confidence.

"One moment, please." Marjorie punched the hold button and clicked Addison's line to announce the call. Another call beeped in simultaneously on line two, so she hit transfer, putting Karsen through before Addison knew who it was.

"This is Addison."

Karsen froze.

"Hi. Yes, this is Karsen Woods," she said hesitantly. "I don't know if you received my e-mail…"

Furious at being caught off guard, Addison cut her off.

"Ms. Woods, I'm not sure who you think I am, but I'm certain I'm not that person. I wish you the best, but I have to go now."

"But, wait. Please give me a moment to explain…"

"I'm sorry. Now, I…"

"Please!" Karsen pleaded.

"I'm sorry, but I can't help you."

"But… you don't know that. You have a choice and you're choosing not to listen. Choices are made every day. Some bear no consequence. Others have life-altering results. I should know. My mother made a choice. She kept a secret. Her intentions were pure. With every beat of my heart, I believe she thought keeping her secret was in everyone's best interest. She thought the secret would be buried with her, never to be revealed. She thought wrong."

"Unless I'm mistaken, you're breaking the law by contacting me."

Karsen gasped with relief.

"It is you!"

Addison said hurriedly, "Please don't call again," and abruptly hung up. Tears flooded her eyes. Her intention certainly was not to hurt anyone. She simply wanted to be left alone.

◦◦

Karsen's heart and mind raced. She couldn't understand why her sister would push her away. Wasn't she at all curious about her? About their mother? Didn't she care at all? Was Addison really that cold? Karsen was simply a bystander. It was her mother that chose adoption. Not her.

"What did she say?" pressed Hanna.

"She said I was breaking the law. She said I was breaking the law by contacting her. She knew. Hanna, it's her. Addison Reynolds is my sister."

"OMG, Karsen!" Hanna said excitedly. "What are you going to do?"

Karsen's voice did not waiver. "I'm going to meet her."

◦◦

Emily arrived at Addison's office and smiled at Marjorie who waved her on without hesitation. Emily knocked gently before opening Addison's closed office door. She peered in through the crack before entering. "Who was that?" Emily asked, witnessing the end of the one-sided conversation which clearly had upset Addy.

"No one. Just business."

"She called you, didn't she?" Emily knew Addison would never handle a business call in that manner. She'd only seen Addison cry a handful of times and never over business.

"Who?"

"Your biological mother."

"No, not my mother."

"Then who, Addy?"

"Karsen, my sister," Addison said. She didn't care what Emily knew anymore. She was tired. Tired of feeling abandoned. Tired of hiding the truth.

"You have a sister?"

"Apparently, yes."

"Any other Jerry Springer news I should know about?"

"I have a brother, too."

"And you've known this?"

"Yes."

"For how long?"

"Since I was eighteen or so. I basically ran away from boarding school to try to find my biological mother, except when I got there she looked like her family was complete. So I turned around and went home."

"You aren't even curious about them?"

"Why should I be? I was the one discarded, remember?"

"Aren't you even interested in finding out why?"

Addison shook her head. She grabbed a tissue to dry her eyes.

Emily thought about what she would do if she were in her friend's position. A part of her understood Addison's hesitation, but she'd rather know the truth. And to get to the truth meant speaking to the source.

"Addy, maybe you're being too harsh," Emily said tentatively.

"Harsh? She gave me away, Em. I made peace with it a long time ago. I know I may look like an ice queen, but what do they think? That we'll meet and hug and live happily ever after? It's been thirty-nine years."

"Wow, you're almost forty," Emily poked.

"Shut up."

"What if you got pregnant as a teenager, Addy? What would you have done?"

Addison raised her hands to cover her face. "I don't know."

"Put yourself in someone else's shoes for a change. Maybe, just maybe, it was the best choice your mother had at the time. Lots of women put babies up for adoption. Not everyone is perfect, but at least you're here."

"Understood, Em. What would you have me do?" Addison demanded.

"Talk to them."

"I can't."

"Why not?" Emily said, exasperated.

"It would tear apart my parents. I mean Mom and Dad. The only parents I know. Not to mention what would happen if the media got a hold of this. I can only imagine the headlines. And…and what would people think about me running this magazine?"

"That you're capable?"

"No, that my adoptive father gave it to me out of pity."

"Addison, you are completely crazy. I swear. I've never seen you act this irrationally."

Then Emily saw a side of her friend even she'd never seen.

"How can a mother give up a child, Em? How could she give me away?" Tears flowed down Addison's cheeks as she broke down completely. Emily wrapped her arms around and rocked her.

After several minutes, Addison pulled away.

"I didn't ask for this," she said, wiping her eyes, struggling to regain her composure.

"I know you didn't." Emily paused. "Addy, you probably don't want to hear this and I'm certainly not a shrink, but I think the only way you're going to get past this is to face it head on. You've let the past affect all of your attempts at relationships. But it doesn't have too. Not anymore."

Addison thought of Russell and every other man in her past. "I can't."

"Yes, you can. You run a billion dollar business. You have a strength within you that I could never have. You can."

Emily stood and kissed the top of her head. "I'm here for you. Whatever you need. You know that."

Addison wiped her eyes trying to erase the smudges of eyeliner. She hated letting anyone see her cry. But for once, she didn't care. The embarrassment, the weakness, whatever it was that she conjured in her mind no longer mattered. She knew what she needed to do.

∾ 24 ∾

Karsen threw a mismatch of clothing into her suitcase. Her flight left in two hours. The last minute fair maxed out her credit card, but she couldn't worry about that now. She tried calling Brad. No answer. She left a voice mail letting him know her intentions. Hanna, she knew, would fill him in on her conversation with Addison.

She hustled through security with little time to spare. Her flight was boarding the last section of seating. Breathlessly, she handed her boarding pass to the attendant and stepped onto the breezeway.

Her Blackberry vibrated inside her bag. She fumbled for it while she walked. Brad. "Hello?" she answered, against her better judgment and in no mood for an argument.

"Karsen, what the hell are you doing now?" he yelled through the phone.

"I have to see her, Brad. I have to talk to her."

"She doesn't want to talk to us. You need to accept that. You can't fly to New York on a whim. Seriously, Karsen, she already made it clear. She's not interested."

"If I see her in person, she might change her mind."

"Karsen. Get a grip. She could have you arrested."

"I don't care." Tears welled in her eyes. "I have to go."

"Karsen!"

"I'll call you when I get there."

∾

Addison apologized to Emily for cutting their afternoon plans short, and headed for her parents' house. When she arrived, her mother looked surprised to see her. She waved her in with her free hand; the other was holding a notepad with the phone tucked awkwardly under her chin. The color in her face once again looked normal and she was scurrying around finalizing details for the charity ball.

Addison brewed a pot of tea in the kitchen while her mother finished her call. Her nerves swelled. She hadn't remembered being this anxious since leading the first board meeting following her dad's retirement.

"Honey, hello. This is an unexpected visit." Mrs. Reynolds kissed her daughter's cheek.

"Hey, Mom. Sorry about just dropping in. You look like your old self again."

"Thanks, but is the word 'old' necessary?" her mother smiled.

"You know what I mean." Addison handed her a mug. "Here, I made you some tea." They each took a seat around the kitchen table.

"Thanks. Are you okay? The stars have to align in order for members of this family to tear themselves away from that magazine. Lord knows your father never left early."

"Where is Dad?"

"Golfing. Where else?"

"Figures." Addison thought about whether to wait for them both to be present, but rationalized that would probably never happen.

"Mom, someone, I mean…they contacted me."

"Who contacted you, dear?"

"My biological family."

"Oh." Her mother's hand shook as she set down her tea. She sat silently her eyes gazing downward.

"I told them I didn't have any interest in meeting them."

"I see. And do you?" Her face shifted. Addison had never witnessed an expression like this on her mother's face. She appeared sad, but there was something else. Fear?

"Not so much an interest, but a need. I need to know why."

Her mother didn't respond. She got up and walked out of the room leaving Addison sitting alone at the table not knowing what to do next. A few moments later, her mother returned. She held out a simple white, sealed envelope.

"I was waiting for you to ask."

"What is this?" Addison looked quizzically as she took the envelope from her mother.

"She wrote it. Katherine wrote it and asked if I'd give it to you some day."

"I never wanted to hurt you, Mom."

"You're not hurting me, dear. I knew this day would come."

Slowly, Addison tore the edge of the envelope and pulled out a handwritten letter.

April 17, 1969

My dearest Lily,

Today was the happiest day of my life. It was also the saddest. My heart is broken knowing that I may never see you again. For months we've bonded, you kicking me, me talking to you (under the ribs hurts, by the way). Now where there was life, there is emptiness.

I've asked your parents to give you two things. I pray that they will and that someday you'll read this and find it in your heart to forgive me. It was never my intention to give you away. I'm all but a child myself. Your father up and took off and my parents are so angry. I just want the best for you and I know I have nothing but my love to offer and, if not anything else, I know that it won't be enough. I pray that the family receiving you loves you as much as I do. If they do, then I know you'll be okay.

They may change your name, but you will always be my precious Lily, the flower that grew within me.

I love you more than you'll ever know.

Katherine

Addison's eyes blurred once more as she noticed the 'i' in Katherine was dotted with a heart, the trademark of a teenager. Her mother cupped her hand over hers. "She was only sixteen, Addy. From what I understand, your father left and her parents forced the adoption."

"Why did you wait until now to tell me?"

"I'm sorry. I guess I was afraid. I was afraid that you'd go searching for her and perhaps... she'd be a better mother to you than I ever was. The longer I waited, the harder it became."

"Mom," Addison looked up at her mother's face. "You were, you are, a wonderful mother."

"No, I wasn't. I drowned myself in activities because I didn't want to fail you. It was easier to hide behind nannies than to be a real mother."

"You didn't fail me. You did the best you could."

"Maybe." Her mom was crying, too. Addison couldn't remember the last time she saw her cry. She hadn't cried even when she was diagnosed with cancer. "Addison, I'm truly sorry."

"Sorry for what?"

"Sorry that we, that Dad and I, handled this so poorly."

"It's okay."

"It's not okay. I let my selfishness hurt you." "You didn't hurt me."

"Yes. Yes, I did. She loved you, Addy. I saw the terror in her eyes as they took you from her arms. It's an image that I'll never forget. And I...I let you think that she didn't."

"I'm fine."

"No, you're not, and it's my fault. Every time I see you on the brink of happiness, I think, maybe this time she'll let herself be loved."

Addison spoke defensively. "My relationship choices have nothing to do with me being adopted."

"Whether you believe that or not, I disagree."

She didn't want to argue the point further. "The letter mentioned two things. The letter and the charm, right?"

"Yes."

"Then why keep the letter from me? You told me the necklace was from her."

"I told you the necklace was left with you. I guess I felt the letter would push you to pursue finding her. I know it was wrong. You deserve to know the truth. You deserve to meet her."

"Mom, you know I love you, right?" Addison asked.

Her mother brought Addison's hands to her lips and kissed them. "Yes. I know. I love you more than you know." With that, her mother gently set her hands back onto the table and straightened up. She blotted the tears with her napkin and slowly reverted her face to normal, like nothing had happened.

The remaining conversation returned to a superficial subject. As Addison opened the front door to leave, her mother grasped her hand.

"Addy, he's coming to the ball, you know."

Addison understood 'he' meant Russell.

"Mom, it's over," she said softly, giving her mother's hand a squeeze. As she headed down the walkway, though, a smile played upon her lips and she silently thanked her mother for telling her, a glimmer of hope growing in her heart.

⁓

The sky was dark as Karsen exited JFK. She struggled with her bag, which seemed to grow heavier by the minute, and felt a growing uneasiness from being alone in an unknown city.

"Hi," Karsen said to the driver nervously as she climbed into a cab. A strong stench of vanilla air freshener poorly masked the smell of cigarette smoke. She handed him a paper showing the address for *Urbane*. The driver nodded and waited for her to shut her door before pulling away.

She looked at her watch. Eight thirty-five. *Please let her be working late*, Karsen thought, knowing it was a long shot. She did own the company, so at least it might be a possibility.

"This your first time in New York?" the driver asked. His accent sounded nasal. She noticed his arms were covered in tattoos.

"Yes." Karsen tried to sound confident, as if to let him know she knew what she was doing. A picture of him driving the cab down a dark alley popped into her mind.

"Here on business?

"Visiting family," she replied, hoping to give him the impression people were expecting her. She didn't know how far the airport was from her destination, but couldn't help wishing they were there already.

"Ah...very good," he nodded. They drove silently as Karsen watched the meter continue to click higher and higher. Much more and she would not have enough cash to pay him.

He pulled to the curb. "Here you go."

Karsen stared up at the building towering fifty floors above her. It looked dark, almost deserted. The fear inside her escalated and she sat paralyzed in her seat.

"You getting out or not?" the cabbie asked, impatiently looking at his watch.

"Yes. Thank you," she said handing him a wad of cash. She pulled her bag out behind her and watched him pull away, leaving her alone on the street. She'd envisioned the sidewalks filled with people, with traffic bustling, the streets a yellow sea of cabs as she had seen on so many commercials. At night, it seemed there were few around. The street was eerily quiet. She shivered. She turned and entered the revolving door of the building. On the other side, security lights dimly lit the foyer. She froze again. How impulsive she'd been. She filled with panic. Alone at night in a city where she had no contacts and hardly any money. What was she thinking?

"Hey!" A man's voice echoed through the entrance. She jumped. The beam from his flashlight blinded her eyes. "You can't be here," he continued.

"I'm sorry." She sounded like a little girl. How she wished she had listened to Brad. Her eyes scanned the empty foyer. She could run back through the door, but where would she go?

"That door should have been locked," he said approaching her. He was an older man, tall with broad shoulders. His dark blue security uniform made her feel slightly more secure. Realizing she was probably harmless, he lowered his flashlight. "You looking for someone?"

"Addison Reynolds." She clenched the strap of her bag thinking if she needed to, she could swing it into his head and buy herself some time to escape.

"Sometimes she's here late, but not tonight. She expecting you, Miss?" He could sense her anxiety.

"Not exactly. I thought...I would surprise her."

"You got a place to stay?" he asked, noticing her bag. She didn't want to tell him no. She bit her bottom lip and stared back without replying. His demeanor softened.

"Well, there's a Starbucks in the hotel two blocks down. Open 24 hours. It's usually filled with people even late at night. Ms. Reynolds usually gets in early."

Karsen thanked him and mustered a weary smile. Clutching her bag, she walked back through the door and out onto the street. Glancing back, she saw the security guard wave and nod at her as he locked the door.

She walked briskly, trying not to slip on the unfamiliar sidewalk hardly visible in the dark. A homeless man rested against the wall for the night. She walked closer along the curb to avoid him. The cold was excruciating to her thinned Arizona blood. Her light sweatshirt provided little warmth, but she hesitated to stop and pull a thicker one from her bag until she reached the coffee shop.

As she entered the hotel lobby, the familiar green Starbucks sign gave her comfort. The recognizable décor made her feel out of harm's way. The security guard had been right. There were at least ten people sipping lattes at tables in the café. A small group socialized, laughing together around a small oval coffee table. A younger guy sat alone, his eyes fixated on the screen of his laptop.

She stepped up to the barista behind the counter.

"I'll take a non-fat, one pump peppermint mocha misto, please. Grande. No better make that a venti." For a moment she hesitated about the caffeine, but figured one time wouldn't hurt. To pull an all-nighter, she'd need all the help she could get. She rummaged through her pocket to find three dollar bills.

The computer guy raised his head and laughed. She glanced toward him curiously.

"You sound like my boss," he said.

"Oh?" she said uncomfortably.

"You staying at the hotel?" he asked, noticing her bag.

"Not exactly." She noticed his tie was loose and his shirt was unbuttoned around his neck. "You?"

"No. I work close by. I like to come here if I need to work late. The office gets, well, creepy when no one else is around."

She smiled at the fact a guy would fess up to feeling uneasy in a dark, deserted office building. She certainly knew the feeling.

"Three thirty-five," the barista said.

She handed the barista her last three dollars and dug the change from her pocket.

"You want to sit down?" the guy asked.

Was he flirting with her, she questioned inwardly as she contemplated his offer? He had an honest look about him, but then again so did some serial killers.

"Okay," she said. At least she'd have company for a while. "I'm not going to keep you from your work, am I?"

"Ah, don't worry about it. Some people say if you're working over forty hours a week, you're doing something wrong. You know, wasting time – too many meetings, water cooler breaks and what not. Those people have never worked in publishing." He busted out a broad smile. Karsen giggled.

As she grabbed her drink off the pick-up counter, he rose and pulled out the chair across from him.

"Thanks," she said, as they both settled into their seats. "So, where do you work?" she asked, noticing he had the most amazing green eyes.

"*Urbane* magazine."

Karsen gasped. She swore she felt her heart stop.

"All the girls think I'm cool because I can get them the latest scoop before it hits the shelves," he continued, misinterpreting Karsen's reaction. "Don't get too impressed, I'm the bottom feeder of the company. You know, errand boy."

"And by boss, you mean...? Karsen paused for him to fill in the blank.

"Addison Reynolds."

Her face went blank and she spilt her coffee over her hand.

"You okay?" He handed her a napkin.

"Ouch!" she exclaimed, shaking her hand.

"Let me help you." He dabbed liquid off her hand before wiping the spots off the back of his laptop.

"Sorry," she said.

"Don't worry about it."

"Really, I'm sorry. Spilling coffee seems to be my trademark way of meeting men," she joked.

"Oh really? So, you do this often?" The dimple in his cheek deepened as he smiled.

"Actually, no, just once. Twice now, I suppose."

"Boyfriend?" he asked. She thought she saw a twinge of disappointment cross his face.

"Ex. But, I'm not exactly in the market right now. Sorry." *Who would be interested in a girl who's already knocked up?*

"Yeah…the pretty ones never are," he shrugged. "So, what are you doing here?"

Karsen mulled over whether to disclose her purpose. She chose not to, even though the urge to find out more about Addison built within her. She couldn't risk Addison finding out she was here. Thankfully, her phone rang, relieving her of coming up with a less than believable explanation.

"Excuse me, uh, …?" Standing to excuse herself, she realized she didn't even know his name.

"Jacob," he replied in a soft voice. She smiled and walked out of the coffee shop and into the hotel lobby, leaving her bag under his watch.

"Karsen, where the hell are you? You said you'd call when you landed. That was two hours ago!" Brad screamed. She held the phone away from her ear.

"I'm sorry. I lost track of time."

"You're alone in New York City and you lost track of time? How the hell does that happen? We're worried sick."

Karsen hoped "we're" meant only Hanna and him.

"You didn't tell Dad, did you?"

"What? That his daughter has flown over the cuckoo's nest? Are you crazy? No. He'd be driving there now."

Karsen sighed in relief.

"K, where are you? Do you have a place to stay?" Brad's tone mimicked a father's, expressing both irritation and concern.

"Kind of."

"Kind of yes or kind of no? It's past ten o'clock. Did you even book a hotel room?"

"Not exactly."

"Have you totally lost your mind?"

"It's okay, Brad. Calm down, I'm fine. I've been talking to a really nice guy."

"A guy? You've been there for two hours and you've already taken up with a guy? You are completely crazy!"

"Brad, it's not like that." He continued yelling at her through the phone. "Listen!" She raised her voice to interrupt. She cringed seeing the front desk attendant staring at her. Fearing he'd ask her to leave, she lowered her voice. "Listen...I found a twenty-four hour Starbucks in a hotel two blocks from her office. It's just one night. I'll be fine."

"Karsen, I'm just worried about you. This is craziness."

"I'm sorry you think so."

"Promise me you'll be careful."

"I promise." Reluctantly, she agreed to call him in the morning.

As he hung up, he pulled Hanna close to him and held her, resting his chin on the top of her head. They stood quietly, both understanding the other's concern. Karsen had a knack for needing help. Brad had a knack for needing to save her. Hanna felt caught somewhere between 'the moon and New York City.'

"Pack some clothes," he said kissing the top of her head. "We're going to New York."

～ 25 ～

Jacob stayed and chatted with Karsen until midnight. She didn't share details of her past relationship, or the fact that she was pregnant. Rather, they talked about her classes and his career aspirations. She shared her uncertainty about her own career. With a degree in communications, she anticipated a less than glamorous future. In reality, she had never pictured herself pursuing much of one. Most of her dreams about the future included living in the suburbs and driving kids to soccer practice.

Without Jacob's company, Karsen wrestled with exhaustion. Her eyes grew heavy and she yawned at least once every two minutes. Afraid to fall asleep, she charged another coffee to her credit card. The night barista attempted to make small talk, but she wasn't interested. Her nerves tortured her. Sitting alone left her nothing to do but think about tomorrow. No matter how hard she tried to envision a positive outcome, negative thoughts festered in her head.

"Wake up, sleepy head." A hand gently shook her shoulder. "You're still here?" He questioned, noticing an intriguing familiarity about her that he couldn't quite put his finger on.

Groggily, Karsen processed the familiar voice. Her eyes struggled to focus through her dried out contacts.

"Hi," she said.

"I'm beginning to think you're homeless," Jacob replied.

She groaned as she sat up. "No, just fell asleep I guess. What are you doing back here anyway?" She reached over her shoulder to rub out the kink. Her whole body ached.

"Boss lady needs her coffee." He lifted a travel tray with two venti-sized cups. "One for me today, too. Some girl kept me out past my bed time." He tried to fathom why she would still be there. She seemed intelligent, not like some weirdo camping out in a public facility.

"Sorry." She looked at her watch. "Shoot!" It was already well past seven o'clock. How many people had watched her drool on herself? She slunk down in embarrassment.

"You sure you're okay?" Jacob asked.

"Yeah. Go. I have a feeling we might run into each other again sometime." She attempted to smile, certain she must look a mess.

"Looking forward to it." Jacob turned to leave, thinking the chances of that happening were up there with winning the lottery.

Karsen stared at herself in the ladies' room mirror. Her mascara had smudged, leaving dash marks around her eyes, and her ponytail holder had slid down and now dangled two-inches from the end of her hair. This was not how she wanted to present herself, certain the 'Hi, I'm your homeless sister' look wouldn't make Addison long for a reunion. She changed into fresh clothes and pulled out her make-up bag, trying every trick she knew to cover the dark circles under her eyes. Two ladies entered. They grimaced at her in disgust as if she truly were living in the hotel lobby.

When she felt remotely respectable, she stuffed her belongings back into her bag. She closed her eyes and visualized a positive outcome one last time. "See it. Believe it. Receive it." Wasn't that the latest self-help catch phrase?

She backtracked the two blocks from yesterday. People scurried around her, glaring in annoyance at her snail's pace. Last night, she couldn't get there fast enough. Now, her feet felt like they were burdened by cinder blocks. Maybe Brad was right. She second-guessed her actions and for the first time she questioned her sanity. Addison had clearly pushed her away. What if she did so now? What if she had her arrested? Then what?

She entered the building, looking around her in amazement. She even double-checked the address to make sure she was in the same place. The lobby, so desolate hours ago, bustled with activity. Daylight allowed the lavish ambiance to emanate through. Marble floors meticulously shined. The black granite reception counter glistened as Karsen approached.

"Hello. I'm here to see Addison Reynolds." She felt awkward lugging her travel bag with her.

"Certainly, Miss. Take the elevator to the thirty-seventh floor. You'll see the *Urbane* reception desk. The receptionist will help you from there."

"Thank you."

Karsen boarded the elevator and squeezed in among a flock of business executives. Her casual dress appeared amiss alongside their stark black suits. As she reached for the console to push the button for the thirty-seventh floor, her bag swung uneasily into the shin of a woman, the zipper snagging her panty hose.

"Oh, I'm really sorry!" Karsen sputtered, mortified at her klutziness. The woman grimaced, giving Karsen a withering look as the door mercifully opened onto the next floor and she exited.

Karsen continued to ride up floor by floor, thankfully with no further incidents. The door chimed as it opened into the lobby of *Urbane*. In front of her, a semi-circular black, granite desk stood. Behind it there was a large glass wall etched with the *Urbane* logo.

"Hi. I'm here to see Addison Reynolds." She told the girl behind desk, who looked younger than she did.

"Down the hall, third desk on the left is her assistant."

Karsen stepped around the entryway and into a vast field of cubicles, quite desolate looking considering the creativeness of the publication. An incessant surge of phone calls penetrated the area, making it sound like the clatter of a casino floor.

She reeled her way around the floor as the receptionist had directed her and waited for the woman behind the desk to end her call.

"May I help you?" Marjorie asked, the phone still tucked under her chin.

"I'm here to see Addison Reynolds, please."

Marjorie punched a few strokes on her keyboard. She squinched her nose surveying Addison's schedule before looking up. "Is she expecting you?"

"Not exactly." Karsen wobbled unsteadily on her feet, trying to adjust her bag strap back onto her shoulder.

"I'm sorry. She's not in at the moment. I can let her know you were here." Marjorie said, making a mental note to explain to the new receptionist up front that *she* is supposed to be the gatekeeper.

"Oh. Okay."

"And you are?"

Karsen couldn't help it. The tears welled up over the brims of her eyelids. "Never mind." Her voice cracked as she turned and ran, retracing her path to the elevator. The door opened and Karsen kept her gaze toward the floor to avoid all of the stares. As one foot stepped across the threshold, a hand grasped her arm, whisking her around slightly. The face staring back at her was graced with the familiar features of her own. Both stood, unmoving.

"You look like me," Addison gasped, then stared. She wasn't expecting Karsen, but an unusual feeling swept through her and she intrinsically knew who she was as soon as she saw her.

"Addison?"

"What are you doing here?" Addison asked, knowing for certain to whom she was speaking.

"I'm sorry. I had to come. Please don't call the police."

"Come on." Addison stepped into the elevator, pulling Karsen the remainder of the way in. "Not here."

They rode silently to the lobby. As they passed the reception desk, Addison took Karsen's bag from her and handed it to the attendant behind the desk. "Can you watch this for us?" She turned back to Karsen, "Don't worry, they'll make sure nothing happens to it."

The two walked out onto the sidewalk and Addison hailed a cab. Karsen followed trustingly, zipping her coat the remainder of the way up. Climbing into the cab, she shivered more from anxiety than the cold. She knew Brad would not approve of her climbing into any vehicle with what basically was still a stranger, but she had come too far not to. The cab navigated the congested streets until they arrived at Central Park. Neither spoke along the way. Addison paid the cabbie and led Karsen down a tree-lined pathway. As they walked, Karsen marveled at the size of Central Park. She'd seen only the glimpses of it in movies. The park was more extensive then she could have imagined. Addison stopped at a secluded bench where people were still visible but not close enough to eavesdrop. They sat down facing one another. Karsen's body tingled with nerves.

"Wow." Addison spoke first. She scanned Karsen meticulously. The once-over would have been considered rude in any other situation, but Addison couldn't help herself. She felt as if she were looking into a mirror that took her back eighteen years.

Karsen hesitated to speak. She stared back at her sister in disbelief. She didn't know what to expect. At least Addison hadn't thrown her out. Maybe there was a chance for them to connect or to at least hear her out.

"I was going to e-mail you back," Addison finally said. "I'm sorry if I came off harshly before. It wasn't my intention."

"It's okay. I guess I understand."

"I can't believe how much you look like me. I'm gobsmacked."

Karsen couldn't help but smile. "You could imagine my thoughts at realizing you were my sister."

"How did you find me anyway?"

Karsen reached into her purse and pulled out the magazine photo of Addison.

"I saw this."

Then she reached in and pulled the chain out from under her shirt. She held her charm for Addison to see.

"Oh, I see." Addison paused. Her posture relaxed as the reality set in. She looked less like a businesswoman and more like a friend. She slid the glove off of her right hand and pulled her own charm out from around her neck. "Why now? Why you?" She felt a sudden surge of confused emotions envelop her. Here she was sitting in front of her sister. A sibling she always wished she'd had. But also the sister her mother chose to keep when she had been given away.

"She never told us," Karsen said. "My mom. She never told us about you."

"Oh." Addison's face reflected her disappointment. Her mother hadn't been interested in finding her after all.

Karsen sensed her distress. "If I had known." Her voice shook. "If I had known I had a sister, I would have found you. I'm sure she would have wanted to find you, too. I believe she thought she was protecting everyone, Addison. My mom, our mom," she corrected, "was the most compassionate person..."

"Was?" Addison interrupted.

Karsen felt her eyes well up. "She passed away in January."

"I see... I'm sorry" Addison didn't know what to say. She felt deflated. She laid her hand on Karsen's. Her heart ached with longing for the mother she'd never have an opportunity to meet. The mother Karsen had obviously deeply loved.

"Me, too," Karsen said. She explained the details of the accident, how she discovered the missing charm, and the subsequent journey that had brought her to New York.

Addison no longer felt guarded. She justified her prior actions to Karsen. She shared her fear of hurting her adoptive parents. "I went back to find her once. I saw her...Katherine. I saw her with the two of you. You were just a baby. You were all playing in the yard and looked like the picture-perfect family. I suppose I felt rejected. She could love you, but not me. I couldn't bring myself to approach her." Addison felt more tears emerge. "And now, I've lost my chance."

Karsen listened intently. She could hear the pain in Addison's voice. One she couldn't imagine until the day of her mother's accident.

"Karsen, I love my life. I love my family, but the money, the work. It all took away from the closeness," Addison continued. "My dad worked fourteen-hour days. I was in bed before he came home. He was gone before I got up. My mom loved me. But she was involved in so many activities. Charity events. Luncheons. I dreamed of trading it all for a chance to have what I saw that day."

Both sniffled as their tears faded. Karsen felt the connection between Addison and herself building as they talked. She had found her sister and within her lay the answers she needed to help make her choice. She vacillated about whether to disclose her pregnancy. She worried Addison would misinterpret her actions as an attempt for a handout. She didn't want her money. All she wanted was to know that Addison felt her life was worth living. If that were true, she could give her child a chance at life even if that meant she wasn't in it.

ᏯᎧ

Hanna stared out the window as their flight made its descent into JFK. She had never visited New York and was a bit disappointed this trip would not allow for some sightseeing. They were on a strict mission: Find Karsen and take her home.

Hanna squeezed Brad's hand as the loud swoosh of the brakes subsided and the plane lulled to a halt. She didn't know what to say to ease his anxiety or brighten his mood.

Grabbing their single carry-on, they exited the plane. Brad led Hanna by the hand through the maze of the terminal and outside where they hopped into the first available taxi. Uncertain where to begin, Brad handed the driver the address for *Urbane*.

"You okay?" Hanna asked. He had been withdrawn since they landed. Brad attempted a smile and raised her hand to his lips. The kiss warmed her but his expression reflected otherwise.

His concern grew. He had tried Karsen's cell four times since they landed, and she had not answered. He had not spoken to her since the night before. Rationally, he knew she was an adult who, for all practical purposes, should be able to take care of herself. Emotionally, she was his baby sister once again in need of protection.

Arriving at *Urbane*, Brad and Hanna entered the lobby and were directed as Karsen had been just a few hours earlier. Hanna felt more than a little self-conscious as she found herself at the center of the world's leading fashion magazine, knowing she must look a sight after flying all night.

"We're here to see Addison Reynolds, please," Brad said.

Perplexed by the odd recurrence of strangers looking for Addison, Marjorie wasn't sure what to think. "I'm sorry, she's not available at the moment."

"When will she be?" Brad asked.

"I'm sorry, but I'm not at liberty to give out her schedule. Perhaps you'd like to schedule an appointment?"

"Urghhhh." Brad's frustration rose.

"I'm sorry, it's been a long day," Hanna interjected. Which in reality, it had been. So long, that Hanna's stomach growled, sustained by only a black cup of coffee and a small bag of pretzels she'd eaten on the plane.

Three lines rang simultaneously. "Excuse me," Marjorie said quickly, picking up the receiver.

"She's not here," Hanna whispered to Brad, pulling at his arm to go. "We can try again later."

"Do you realize how large this city is? I don't even know where to start looking for her," Brad practically hissed, his voice filled with urgency.

"Try her cell again," Hanna said. He pulled out his phone and dialed. The line clicked straight to voice mail.

"Maybe her battery died?"

"Great. So we won't have any way to find her." He tapped his fist on Marjorie's desk.

"Yes, sir. Certainly. I will have her call you. Goodbye." Marjorie's voice pleasantly ended the phone conversation. Fueled with frustration, her tone immediately reversed.

"Look, I'm sorry Ms. Reynolds is not available. You really are going to need to come back another time. I can let her know that you were here and she'll contact you if she so chooses." She grabbed her pen to note his pertinent information. "You are?"

"Apparently, I'm her brother. I'm looking for my sister. Actually, I'm looking for both of them. The sister I've never met and the sister who ran off to find her."

Marjorie stared blankly at him, processing his claim. Her long-standing history as Bryce's assistant had left her privy to information most were unaware of. She knew Addison had been adopted. She recalled the seemingly unending chain of futile fertility appointments interrupting his work schedule. Marjorie had promised her lips were sealed.

Hanna cringed at Brad's bluntness. His behavior was uncharacteristic of his usual well-mannered nature. Before anyone had a chance to speak, a tiny voice billowed behind Hanna.

"Mar-zie! Mar-zie!" Adelaide's smile was graced with a large gap between her two tiny front teeth. She rested her chin between her hands on the desk, peering over.

"Marjorie is busy, honey." Emily said as she pulled her back and attempted to lift her onto her hip. Adie struggled for freedom. "No, Mommy!"

"Fine, Adie. Stay right here." Emily set her squirming daughter back on the floor.

"Hi, Emily. Addison isn't here. Was she supposed to meet you today?" Marjorie knew they had a rather consistent play date set up every Friday, but today was Thursday.

"Yes, we rescheduled because Adie has a doctor's appointment tomorrow. She hadn't said otherwise, so I assumed we were still on." She tried to recall any conversation where Addison rearranged when to meet again, but to her dismay she could hardly remember what she had for breakfast. Adelaide had been frequently waking up in the middle of the night, leaving her in a brain fog.

Marjorie redirected her attention back to Brad. "I can have her call you when she returns."

"Fine. Brad. My name is Brad Woods." He recited his number as Marjorie scribbled it down.

"Let's go. We can try to call Karsen again." Hanna squeezed Brad's hand.

"Did you say Karsen?" Marjorie asked.

"Karsen?" Emily repeated. She knew immediately that Addison's brother was standing before her. Addison had not known his name, but he was looking for Karsen and Emily knew that Karsen was her sister's name. Not a common name to be showing up at Addison's office.

"Yes. Why?" Hanna asked.

The day was finally starting to make sense to Marjorie. She remembered the name from Addison's calls. "That must have been her here earlier. Addison wasn't here though. Actually, I don't know where Addison is. She left earlier this morning and never returned."

"Addy? Wer ar u Addy?" Lost among the fracas, Adelaide wandered. She first peered into Addison's office. Not seeing her, she shuffled her shoes adorned with big pink and black polka dot bows along as she headed into the maze of cubicles. The adults were oblivious.

"She, Karsen, ran off before I had gotten her name. She seemed extremely upset," Marjorie added.

"Where did she go?" Brad asked exasperated.

"I have no idea," Marjorie shrugged. "I didn't know who she was."

Just then a siren blared throughout the building. Hanna shielded her ears with her hands. "What the hell?" she asked. A flood of people rose from behind their desks and scattered toward the doors.

"Fire alarm," Marjorie yelled. "Probably a drill."

"You got to be kidding me?" Brad yelled over the pandemonium.

Emily scanned the area. "Where's Adie?" she screamed. Her throat clenched with fright as she didn't see her anywhere. "Adie! Where are you?"

"Emily, I'm sure she's close. No worries. I'm sure it's just a drill," Marjorie tried to calm her.

Emily didn't stop. Her motherly instinct wouldn't allow it. "Adelaide! She's hiding. She's probably scared. I know she's hiding. Adelaide!"

The room went black except for the flashing lights of the alarm.

"ADELAIDE! ADELAIDE!" Emily screamed again.

❧ 26 ❧

Addison ignored her phone the first time it rang. By the third, she knew it must be something urgent. Marjorie knew not to bother her more than once.

"Excuse me, Karsen. It's the office."

"Of course, go ahead." Karsen said. She was content to wait all day.

"Hello?"

"Addison! Thank goodness! Where are you?" The distress in Marjorie's voice caught Addison off guard. Her breath labored to get the words out. "The office…it's on fire! Where are you?"

"What?" Addison stood in shock. The call dropped. "Damn it!" Frantically, she dialed the number back.

All circuits are busy now.

"Shit!" Addison hit redial again.

While Addison tried to reach Marjorie, Karsen powered up her own cell phone and scrolled through the call log. There were five missed calls, all from Brad. She called voice mail and started to listen to his messages. She only partially heard the first message, too preoccupied by Addy's sudden mood change. By the second, she disconnected the line.

"Addison, is everything okay?"

"Come on! We have to go NOW!" Addison grabbed Karsen's arm and started running toward Fifth Avenue. "There's a fire at my office!" Karsen stumbled as she ran to keep up.

"What?" Karsen's face went white instantly a she gasped. "Brad is there!"

"What?"

Her words sped together in panic. "Brad left me a message. He's at the office with Hanna. They came looking for me. Oh my! Oh no, Addison! How bad is it?"

"I don't know yet. Marjorie sounded frantic. The call dropped before she could give any details." She flagged down a cab and they hurried in. "I'm sure it will turn out to be nothing." Addison lied unconvincingly. She had never heard Marjorie sound so distraught. She tried to hide her distress for Karsen's sake. She could tell she was worried and maybe this all would turn out to be nothing. She could only hope.

Don't panic. Everything will be okay, Karsen told herself as the cab crawled through the midday traffic. It had to be. She couldn't take any more.

扰

"I won't leave until I find her!" Emily screamed as Brad and Marjorie pleaded with her to go, the smell of smoke seeping into the air, getting thicker. "Adie!" Panic-stricken, Emily raced through cubical after cubical, searching under every desk. By now the work areas were deserted as people piled into the hallway and stairwells.

"Someone probably found her. She's probably already out of the building," Marjorie tried to assure her.

"That's not good enough! You don't know that. I can't leave without her! Adie!"

Brad turned to Hanna.

"Go! Take Marjorie and go now!" Hanna shook her head. "There isn't time to argue, Hanna! You have to get out of here. Go!"

"No, I won't leave you!"

He kissed her. His voice softened, trying to calm her. "You have to. I'll be fine. Go now, please."

"He's right," Marjorie said, coughing from the smoke as she pulled a golf towel embroidered with *Urbane* on it from a recent tournament from her desk. "Put this over your mouth!" she instructed.

Hanna held the towel up, covering her nose and mouth. Her eyes peered over the top and she looked one last time at Brad. They could still hear Emily screaming for Adie as they entered the stairwell.

∽

Police guarded the area as the crowd of bystanders gathered. Curious on-lookers prodded for information. Associates searched for friends and family. Answers were few. Only time would tell how the blaze began or how it spread so quickly.

Flames sputtered from windows and black smoke billowed into the sky as Karsen and Addison jumped from the cab and pushed through the crowd. "Let me through!" demanded Addison, as Karsen weaved closely behind. As soon as Addison saw the chaos, she knew her worst fears were realized. The fire was anything but insignificant.

"I'm sorry, Miss, you can't go past here." An officer held his arm out, stopping Addison from crossing his path.

"This is my building! Let me through!" Just then a thunderous boom resonated and glass shattered down, hitting the sidewalk.

"Oh my God!" She stumbled backwards, shielding herself from the falling glass with her arms. Karsen dropped her phone as she caught Addy from behind.

"You need to move back." The officer reiterated, his arms spread-eagle forcing them farther from the scene. Karsen swept down to grab her phone before it was trampled on. As she rose up again, her unstable body lurched forward and she grabbed Addy to steady herself. Both women stood shell-shocked in the moment. Not knowing what to do next, they turned back helplessly to their phones.

Addison called every office line she could think of to no avail. Karsen frantically dialed Brad's number. Please answer. He's out. He's fine. She consoled herself. If she wouldn't have ran off, he wouldn't have come. This was her fault. The phone rang but Brad did not answer.

Unable to connect with Marjorie or Brad, both Karsen and Addison watched as people poured out of the building. *Thirty-seven floors to come down.* Addison, thought, knowing her floor would be one of the last to evacuate. She shivered although she didn't feel the cold. She felt numb, deadened, anesthetized. She watched, a helpless bystander, as her associates, her building, her world teetered on the verge of destruction. There was nothing she could do but watch and wait.

Firemen entered and exited the building working diligently with utter disregard for their own safety. Flames danced in a wondrous flurry of devastation seemingly engulfing each and every floor from the thirtieth floor upward. Karsen watched as Addison stood in shock. She dug down in the pit of her being and drew an unusual strength from within.

"Everyone is going to be okay," she looked Addison in the face to reassure her, while trying to do the same for herself. They stood hand in hand, eyes fixated on the doorway. Addison felt some relief as she recognized several of her employees exit. Not Marjorie. Not Jacob. Where were they?

∽

Inside, Marjorie and Hanna inched slowly down the steps. Some pushed past rudely fearing for their own lives. Others coughed and panted as their bodies overexerted themselves to exhaustion. Hanna checked her watch. Thirty minutes and by her estimation they had only descended ten stories. The unknown horrified her. Where was the fire? How long could they inhale smoke? Had they found Adie? Had they even started down?

Too worn-out to continue, an elderly woman sat on a step against the wall burying her face in her hands. Her hair was a shimmery-silver and the wrinkles in her face told stories of their own. "You've got to keep moving." Marjorie placed her hand on her shoulder.

"I can't."

"You must. Come on. We'll help you. You can do this."

Hanna and Marjorie each reached under one of the woman's arms and pulled her up. They continued down, one step at a time, burdened by the extra weight. Neither of them cared. Even if they made it out, they wouldn't be able to look in the mirror if they left her behind.

Finally, overcome by smoke and exhaustion, the three stumbled out from the building's entrance and onto the sidewalk. Hanna and Marjorie transferred the elderly woman to paramedics waiting past the door as they hurriedly fled further from harm's way themselves. Karsen spotted Hanna and scanned the door for Brad. He wasn't there.

"Hanna!" Karsen screamed. Addison's body shuddered with relief as she recognized Marjorie. Both Addison and Karsen darted through a gap in the crowd and made their way toward them. Addison embraced Marjorie and Karsen did the same to Hanna. She squeezed her into a bear hug and wouldn't let go.

"Where's Brad?" Karsen asked.

"He stayed behind," Hanna said clearly worried.

"Adie," Marjorie choked. "They can't find Adelaide."

"She wandered off before the fire. They couldn't find her and Emily wouldn't leave. Brad stayed to help. He wouldn't let her stay alone," Hanna added.

"What?" Addison asked in agonized disbelief. A lump swelled in her throat as she swallowed. She had forgotten Emily's play date. She felt the ground shift beneath her. Only it wasn't the ground, but her knees collapsing underneath. She sank to the sidewalk. She did not know what started the fire but she couldn't help but feel responsible. She should have been there. She should have responded to Karsen's first request to meet. Maybe then, just maybe, none of this would be happening. Adelaide, that beautiful innocent child would be safe. Emily would be safe. Brad would be safe. *Oh God, this is my fault.*

"It'll be okay," Karsen bent down to hug Addison and help her to her feet. "Brad won't let anything happen. I promise you."

꙾

"We have to go," Brad pleaded with Emily. "She's not here. We've looked everywhere." There was no way to estimate how much time they had left, but he knew they had to get out immediately. The air was thick with spongy, gray smoke. Sweat seeped down his brow and he covered his nose and mouth with his shirt. Emily fought desperately.

"Adie!" her voice cracked, strained from overuse and hoarse from breathing in polluted air. Brad pulled her toward him as a loud crack sapped from above them. A devising wall fell, crushing Marjorie's desk. Ceiling tiles crumbled down around them from the impact. Brad embraced Emily to shield her.

Distraught and exhausted, she fell to the floor. She curled into a fetal position and sobbed.

He reached his arm around Emily's back and curled the other under her knees. He picked her up like a father would a sleeping child. Brad carried her into the hallway and to the stairs against her will. She wailed, flailing her arms and kicking her feet, but he wouldn't stop. She didn't have the strength to break free or she'd never leave. She'd sacrifice her life before ever giving up on her daughter.

The stairwell no longer held the mass of people as it had before. The well was dead silent with only the occasional cracks from the building as it shifted under the flames. Brad hacked as he struggled for air. Even with his seasoned runner lungs, his body craved oxygen due to the extra exertion. He moved swiftly, but with every snap he feared they'd left too late. He hoped he hadn't made a mistake by not forcing Emily to leave earlier. *I'm sorry, Hanna,* he thought, tormented by the idea that he may not see her again.

Brad continued down several flights of stairs. He carried Emily until his arms were weak. "You have to walk." He moaned setting her down onto her own unstable feet. She started running up the steps. "No!" He grabbed her ankle. Her body slammed down against the cement steps.

"Adie!" she whimpered. He pulled her down. She turned toward him. His brave face looked beaten, frightened even. They stared at each other.

"I know you don't want to give up, but you're no use to her dead. We looked everywhere, Emily. She has to be down already."

He squeezed her hand tight. White streaks striped her face from eye to chin where tears dripped down through the soot. She nodded blankly and he helped her to her feet. Together they began their descent again.

A fireman trudged past, stopping them. "Here." He handed his oxygen mask to Emily. She inhaled deeply, filling her lungs. "We thought everyone was out."

"We were looking for a little girl. She's only two," Brad explained, wheezing. Emily held the oxygen mask to Brad. He took a drag from the mask then handed it back to the fireman.

"Keep it." The fireman unstrapped the tank from his back. "I'll take one last look around for the girl. What's her name?"

"Adelaide," Brad answered.

"Get down as fast as possible. I'm not sure how contained the fire is. It could still spread." He pushed past before Brad could respond.

They trudged on for what seemed like hours, the repetitive motion and downward impact piercing Brad's knees with pain. He winced with each step. They couldn't afford to stop. Brad took an intermittent breath from the oxygen tank, allowing Emily to breathe with it freely. He held tight to her hand to make sure she couldn't turn back.

Brad had lost count of floors somewhere around floor nineteen. He knew they were drawing close to the bottom, but wasn't sure exactly how many more flights were ahead of them. With each floor the air grew thicker with ash. Brad's lungs wheezed. He felt lightheaded.

"Look!" Through watery eyes he saw the first glimpse of daylight creep through the open doorway. His voice came out a mere whisper. "We made it!" He still held Emily's hand. He could feel her hesitation knowing that leaving the building may also mean facing life without her child. Bewildered and exhausted, Brad's oxygen-depleted body collapsed as they crossed the threshold.

༒

Emily barely inhaled her first breath of fresh air before she saw Addison sprinting toward her. She sobbed as Addison threw her arms around her neck and pulled her in. At the same time, Karsen dropped to her knees beside Brad. She placed both hands on his face and lifted his head.

"Brad!" Hanna kneeled at his other side, as Emily and Addison huddled overhead.

"Brad! Don't you dare leave me!" Karsen cried.

"Please, Brad! Wake up!" Hanna begged. "Please!" She held his hand to her heart desperate to feel him grip her hand, which felt like dead weight within hers.

Two paramedics launched through the crowd. A male medic dressed in a dark blue uniform grabbed Hanna's arm and pulled her up, taking her place beside Brad.

"Move aside, please," he directed Karsen without looking up. He began working diligently. Karsen staggered slowly back and walked around Brad's body to Hanna. They wrapped their arms around one another as they watched, filled with despair.

☙

Several yards away, another medic placed his hand on Addison's back. "We need to check her vitals," he advised, referring to Emily.

"NO. I'm okay," Emily waved the medic off, weeping uncontrollably. At least she felt she was, physically. Her voice sounded spongy like she'd smoked two packs of cigarettes.

"You breathed in quite a bit of smoke, ma'am. We just need to check you out. It won't take long."

"Give her a minute," Addison said sternly. She could not console her friend. There were no words; there was nothing she could do to soothe her. She felt Emily's chest shudder against her. With every rise and fall, Addison felt increasingly nauseous. Adie was missing and flames still raged through the windows on her floor. The thought of Adie trapped inside was unbearable.

Addison felt a hand clutch her shoulder pulling her aside. "Emily!" He cried. Addison turned her head. Realizing it was Greg, she steadied Emily and stepped aside allowing him to take her place.

"Greg!" Emily cried throwing herself into his chest. "How did you find me?"

He wrapped his arms around her. "The fire is all over the news. I knew you were meeting Addy for lunch. I tried to call you again and again. When you didn't answer, I just knew I had to get here."

Emily sobbed against his shoulder.

"I couldn't bear the thought of losing you. It's going to be okay." He looked relieved. "Where's Adie?"

Emily's sobs grew stronger. "Em, where's Adie?" His face fell as his eyes gazed the surrounding area.

"Adie's missing!" Emily choked. "Oh Greg, it's my fault! I let her out of my sight. It's all my fault. I'm so ... so sorry."

"What do you mean she's missing?"

"She'd gone to find Addison when the fire alarm went off. I looked everywhere but I couldn't find her. I looked everywhere! I'm so sorry."

"No, no, no! Em, it's not your fault!" Her husband pulled her in tighter and held on for what felt like an eternity. Their bodies rocked together. "We'll find her. She'll be fine. It's not your fault. It is not your fault." He opened his mouth to speak again, but he couldn't find the words. There was nothing he could say to ease her fears, nothing he could do to protect his daughter. There was nothing he could do but wait.

໑ຉ

Paramedics strapped Brad onto a backboard and whisked him directly into the ambulance. Karsen and Hanna watched in horror as they strapped on an oxygen mask on him and connected an IV. Addison turned toward Karsen. Just hours before, they were no more than two strangers - two individuals that would have passed each other on the street with hardly a greeting. Now they instantly had been bonded into family. They grasped each other's hands, holding on for dear life. Brad's life. The brother Karsen had always known and had always loved. The brother Addison had barely met, but that risked his own life to save a child he didn't even know.

"It's not your fault, Karsen. You know your brother. He'd save anyone. It's just who he is," Hanna whispered, her voice muddled with tears. Karsen listened to the words, but they didn't pacify her. She couldn't lose him.

໑ຉ

"Addy! I find u, Addy!" The familiar voice twinkled in Addison's ears. For a moment, she thought she was dreaming.

"Adelaide!" She turned around. "Oh, thank God! Adie!" She swooped Adie into her arms, hugging her so tight she could hardly breathe. "Oh, child!"

"Where's Mommy?" Adie coughed, struggling for air.

"She's here, honey. She's right over here." Addison couldn't stop the fat tears stinging her eyes. She carried Adelaide as fast as she could across the sidewalk to where her parents prayed and waited.

"Mommy! Mommy!" Adie chimed with the innocence of a child unaware of the immensity of the event that had just occurred. Addison

217

set her down and Adelaide ran to her mother smiling like it was any ordinary day.

"Adie?" Emily questioned softly like she'd heard the voice of an angel.

"Adelaide!" Greg shouted.

"Oh, Adie!" Emily picked her up and embraced her. "Adie! My baby! Adie! Where have you been?" Adelaide wrapped her arms and legs around her tightly.

"I sorry, Mommy," Adie said sounding as if she'd just come out of time out.

"Oh, sweetie. Mommy missed you so much!"

"Mommy hurt?" Adie inquired, seeing the tears drip from her mother's eyes.

"No, not hurt, sweetie. Not now." She held her against her body. She couldn't bear the thought of letting her out of her arms. Emily looked at Addison for answers to her question.

"Jacob," she said. "He said she came to his desk before the alarm looking for me. He tried to find you, but in the chaos thought it better to get her out of the building."

"Oh, thank goodness!" Emily said. "Where is he?"

"The paramedics are checking him out, just routine he said. He's fine. He said they were out quickly."

"I need to find him. How will I ever be able to thank him enough?"

"There will be plenty of time for that. Let's just get you home." The sight of Emily and Greg reunited with their daughter overwhelmed Addison. She was relieved to see Adelaide safe and sound, but a wave of regret flooded over her. She longed for Russell's strong embrace as she scanned the crowd longing for a glimpse of him. Maybe he had heard the news. Maybe he still cared about her enough to come. She glanced back at the building as black smoke swirled above as she wondered what her future held.

⌒♡

Now only Brad remained a concern. Karsen knew his lungs were strong from years of training, but even so he'd been inside for forty-five minutes, taking little to no precautions for minimizing the amount of smoke he inhaled.

She stepped away from the others and fell to her knees. "God, if you're listening, please don't take him now. I know I've depended on him too much, but I need him now more than ever. Hanna needs him, too. I can't have a baby without an uncle to watch over it. Please don't do this."

She closed her eyes, covered her face with her hands and sat blocking out the commotion revolving around her. She envisioned her mother. *He's needed here, Mom. Please don't take him yet.*

◦◦

A hand lay gently upon Karsen's shoulder. She didn't look up. She didn't want to be bothered. "Let's go home, K." The voice sounded weary, but she'd recognize it anywhere. Could it be? She reached her hand and placed it over top of his. She felt a squeeze against her thumb. She stalled, momentarily worried that when she got up it would be someone else.

"You're okay?" She questioned, looking up at him in disbelief.

He nodded. "The paramedic said I'll be fine. I didn't let them take me to the hospital."

"Are you sure?"

"I'm sure. I want to be here. Now, come on." He pulled at her hand. *Thank you, Mom.*

When Karsen rose, she saw a new image through her eyes. For the first time in months, her family didn't appear in pieces. She saw Brad, Hanna, Addison, even Adie. Some related by blood, some not. It did not matter. There was a bond of love between them, a love that conquered and persevered. At that moment, a sense of strength emerged within her and she realized her problems might not be as insurmountable as they seemed.

"Nice to meet you," Addison held out her hand to Brad. He pulled her in and hugged her.

"And I thought I could draw a crowd," he joked.

∾ 27 ∾

The next morning, Addison sat on the enclosed porch at her parents' home. Knowing Karsen, Brad and Hanna had nowhere to go, she'd invited them back to stay for the night. It seemed strange to have her biological siblings under the roof of her adoptive home. But, to her amazement, her parents welcomed them openly.

As the others still slept off the trauma from the day before, Addison was lost in thought. Creating an inventory of the business personal property was going to be a nightmare. She had already contacted the insurance company, but she knew that was only the beginning of what was inevitably going to be a long and arduous process to rebuild her business. She'd watched as the family business turned to ash before her eyes, all because of an electrical fault on a light fitting on the floor below. She was told the magazines in her storage room had provided fuel for the fire to burn fast and hot. This month's issue was lost. There was no way to have another to press in time for distribution. All the workstations had been demolished. She could already make a list of to-do items a mile long, but that, she decided, could wait another day or two.

Brad woke and gently climbed over Hanna, taking care not to wake her. He pulled a gray t-shirt with navy trim over his bare chest and stepped into a faded pair of jeans. He slipped quietly through the bedroom door and crept down the stairs, trying not to wake anyone.

"Hey," he said to Addison, stepping onto the porch. He wasn't the first one up after all. He crossed his arms and began rubbing them up and down for warmth.

"Good morning," she replied softly. "There's coffee in the kitchen."

"Thanks."

"There's another blanket on the couch if you want to come out." She wasn't quite sure what to say, but inviting him to chat seemed reasonable.

"Great. Be right back." Brad went back in and followed the smell of fresh-brewed coffee into the kitchen. He returned coffee in one hand, blanket in the other and took a seat in the chair across from Addison. She looked younger, more vulnerable cuddled beneath the blanket. Her hair was pulled loosely back into a messy ponytail, her face flawless without an ounce of make-up.

"Thanks for letting us crash," Brad said. He saw a glimpse of his mother as she smiled.

"No problem. It was the least I could do after what you did for Emily."

"It was nothing, really. Anyway…thanks." He sipped his coffee. The morning was peacefully quiet. They both stared across the lawn still shy in each other's company.

Addison could see from the corner of her eye that he'd gaze curiously at her then shift his attention back to the yard trying not to let her catch him. She spoke without looking at him.

"I'm sorry I caused this."

"What do you mean? You didn't cause the fire." Brad said. He turned toward her and looked at her intently. There was no sense in placing blame. Not on Karsen, not on himself and certainly not on Addison.

"No, but I caused Karsen to fly out here on a whim. If I had just talked to her when she called…"

"You had no way to know she'd come. She's usually, well, usually she's got a good head on her shoulders. She's been through a lot lately and I think she's just grasping for answers."

"Who could blame her?" Addison shrugged. She raised her mug to her lips and inhaled the warm aroma. Brad smiled.

"What?"

"It's just that…"

"Just that…?"

"Karsen does the same thing. She holds the mug up to her face to smell the coffee."

They both laughed. Brad finished his coffee and got up for a refill.

"Would you like me to top yours off?"

"Actually, this is my third cup. I better not."

"Okay. Say, is there a computer I can log on to check flight times?"

"Oh. Sure, in the study. It's down the hall, third door on the right." A sense of disappointment flooded over her. She realized she wanted more time to connect, to learn about their lives. What they liked. What they didn't. What they had in common with her.

"You okay?" Brad asked, noticing the change in her demeanor.

"Yes, I'm fine." She forced a smile. Brad turned back and took a step toward the door.

"Brad?" She stopped him and he turned back to look at her.

"Yeah?"

She hesitated. "Why don't you stay a few days?"

He looked at her quizzically.

"I mean, it's Friday. I know Karsen and Hanna have class tonight, but with the time change, even with an afternoon flight you won't get in until late. They'll both probably be too beat to absorb anything anyway. And hell, I've got a corporate jet sitting at the airport with nowhere to go."

"Seriously?"

"Absolutely. Might as well fly back in style. At least you can get a drink without being charged an arm and a leg for it. And if you're nice, I won't even charge a baggage fee." She felt relief trickle through her as he laughed.

"Thanks. I really appreciate it, Addison, but there's no need. We'll be fine."

"Oh Brad, why not? There's no sense spending money on airfare. Let me do this for you. For all of you. I want to." She had not anticipated him declining her offer. "It will give us more time to get to know each other a bit more, and tomorrow night's my mother's charity ball. You guys could come and be my 'dates' since my mother is pissed I don't have one."

"I don't know that I have anything to wear," He said realizing too late that he sounded like a girl. She burst out laughing. He rolled his eyes at her. "Thanks. I'll talk to the girls when they get up."

"I can't imagine they'll pass up the opportunity to get gussied up in formal dresses...that we'll have to go shopping for today," she added, confident she'd reeled them in.

"Probably not."

"It's really the least I can do. Now, go refill your cup and come sit back down. You've got, what, twenty-two, twenty-three years to fill me in on?"

As Addy expected, Hanna and Karsen were more than thrilled about the prospect of staying. Karsen welcomed the extra time getting to know her sister and Hanna could never pass up the opportunity to shop.

"What do you think?" Hanna asked, exiting the dressing room and entering the spacious waiting area where Karsen waited on a plush, plum-colored couch. Hanna twirled, the skirt of her dress floating around her. The white halter-top accented her sculpted shoulders and the bodice cinched in perfectly around her size two waist. Her lightly tanned skin gave her enough color to pull off the light color, even at this time of year.

"I bet if you sang 'Happy Birthday' you could make the president swoon," Karsen said. "How about Brad?"

"Hell, he'd swoon if you were wearing a paper sack. Really, you look absolutely amazing, Han. That dress is perfect."

"Too bad I can't afford it. Can you believe we're actually shopping at Barneys? In New York?" She tiptoed toward Karsen, pretending she was wearing heels. Reaching inside the armhole of the gown, she pulled out the price tag.

"Shit!" Karsen exclaimed as she leaned in to see the price. The sales associate shot her a disapproving glare.

"Sorry." She lowered her voice and whispered to Hanna, "Addison said to pick whatever we want."

"But K, come on. I could never accept this. I could pay six months of rent with the cost of this dress."

"But it does look fantastic on you."

Hanna twirled again and moved closer to the three-way mirror mounted on the wall. She twisted her neck like an owl to view the back of the dress.

"Stunning!" Addison exclaimed, rounding the corner. "So, Hanna, is that the dress, or did you want to try on some others? Karsen, did you try on any yet? I'm so excited. You're both going to need shoes, too. We can hit the shoe department next. Add some strappy, five-inch heels, Hanna, and we'll have to scrape Brad's tongue off the floor."

Hanna smiled and examined herself one last time in the mirror.

"I love this dress, but as much as I appreciate your offer, Addison, I really can't accept it."

"Nonsense."

"It's too much."

"Hanna, I invited you to an event. You need a dress for it. Now, is this the one you want, or should we keep looking?"

Hanna glanced at Karsen. Karsen rose from the couch and mouthed, "Just say thank you," while touching her right hand to her chin and bringing it down in front of her.

"I do know some sign language, Karsen. You know, baby signs are hip these days. Adie loves them."

Hanna laughed. Both Karsen and she had learned a few signs from babysitting. Sounds like they all had the same educational source.

"Okay then!" Hanna squealed, clasping her hands together and feeling like she'd landed in the middle of a fairy tale. "Thank you, Addison!"

Addison signaled to the sales lady to gather a few selections for Karsen.

"Your turn, Karsen. What do you think?"

An instant energy surged through Karsen. For the first moment she could remember since her mother's accident, she felt pure and utter bliss. She wrapped the first dress around her arm and hugged it to her. Her eyes sparkled with excitement. "I'll be right out."

Inside the dressing room, Karsen pulled the dress on and attempted to fasten the zipper. She heard a stitch pop. "Shit!" she murmured. She squeezed out of dress and called out to Hanna.

"What's wrong?" Hanna asked, entering the dressing room and peaking in Karen's door.

"It's too small," Karsen whispered.

"But you always wear a four."

"Apparently not any more." Karsen's expression went flat.

"Oh. Right. Don't worry, I'll be right back." Hanna took the dress from Karsen and returned with the next size.

Karsen re-emerged, shimmering from head to toe. The pale blue evening gown transformed her appearance from a pretty, young college girl to a sophisticated, elegant woman. She wasn't going to let a few excess pounds ruin this experience. If anything, the curves added sex appeal to her muscular build.

"Wow!" Hanna beamed at her friend.

Addison turned to look. "Karsen! You look absolutely amazing!"

Karsen bit her lip as she admired herself in the mirror. She ran her hand over the slight bulge in her tummy. Addison didn't notice.

"Do you like that one then? Or do you want to try another?" Addison asked. "It's completely up to you."

Karsen felt guilty accepting the dress. Hanna thought hers was expensive. This dress was almost double the cost.

"Stop thinking about the price. Do you like it or not?" Addison walked up behind Karsen and placed her hands upon her shoulders. She looked in the mirror from behind her.

"I love it. I feel like Cinderella." She turned to face Addison. "Thank you."

"You're welcome. Now, get changed. We have more shopping to do."

Karsen scurried back into the changing room. "Poor Brad. All he gets is a rented tux," Karsen yelled to Hanna over the door while wiggling out of her gown. She carefully placed the dress back on its hanger then squeezed back into her jeans.

"Are you kidding, K? Right now he's golfing at the most exclusive, private country club in New York. He'll be fine."

"But he gave up so much. It's my fault he's not on the show."

"What show?" Addison asked. Neither Karsen nor Hanna answered immediately. Karsen opened the door and walked out carrying the dress over her arm.

"What show?" Addison asked again. She lifted the dress from Karsen's arm and handed it to the sales associate to ring up with the other.

"Brad auditioned for a reality show. He does stand-up comedy," Karsen explained.

"He's super talented," Hanna enthused. "Not that I'm biased; he's really funny."

"He was supposed to be in Hollywood right now, but with everything that's happened recently, he withdrew."

"You mean, you coming here because I didn't want to see you?" Addison again felt as if she were at fault.

"No, he withdrew before that. Trust me if it's anyone's fault, it's mine."

"Why do I get the feeling there's something else you're not telling me?" Addison asked.

⚭

Three hours later, the ladies arrived back at the house having brought new meaning to the term 'shop till you drop.' Karsen held dress bags in both hands and Addison carried several additional bags filled with accessories and shoes.

"My feet are killing me!" whined Hanna, plopping down on the couch, sprawling her arms to both sides. She laid her head back against the cushion and closed her eyes.

"Can I see?" Brad asked sitting down beside her.

"No. You can't." Hanna replied, opening her eyes. She straightened up and crossed her legs Indian style. He looked adorable in a blue and green striped golf shirt, khaki pants and cap. Hanna had always loved the way men looked in ball caps. Perhaps that was why she had dated half of the university's baseball team.

"It's not like this is a wedding," he said.

"No, but it's more fun as a surprise. Trust me, you'll like them." Hanna leaned over and pecked him on the cheek.

ↄ◡౦

"I'll go hang these upstairs. I've got to pee like a racehorse anyway." Karsen headed toward the staircase. Addison carried the packages she held into the kitchen.

Finding a moment alone, Brad reached his hand behind Hanna's neck and pulled her face toward his.

"I missed you," he said quietly, his voice heavy, craving her touch. The fingers of his free hand tucked her hair behind her ear and lingered, cradling her face. His warm lips brushed the corner of her mouth then slowly covered hers.

Lost in each other, they didn't hear Addison return. She stared, momentarily frozen, her face flushed with embarrassment as the two kissed. She quickly fled back around the corner. She pressed her head against the wall and closed her eyes trying to make heads or tails of her emotions. Was it jealousy? Sadness? There was a pure, uncompli-cated nature to their relationship that she had never known. She'd never allowed herself to. She'd never given over to trust, and without trust she'd never truly allowed herself to love. The hurt she'd tried avidly to protect herself from for so many years had finally found her. The pain was relentless. Her heart hurt with an overwhelming feeling of emptiness. The reality of the fire had not fully set in yet. *What would she do if the business couldn't recover? She had nothing.* She pushed the thought out of her head.

"AAAHHH!" A scream came from upstairs.

"AAAHHH! Hanna! AAAHHHH!" Karsen shrieked again, this time even louder.

Addison sprinted up the stairs, while Brad and Hanna jumped off the couch and immediately followed close on her heels. They stood, breathless, outside the bathroom door.

"Karsen, are you okay?" Hanna banged on the door.

Karsen unlocked the door and opened it a crack.

"Hanna, come in here," she sobbed, concealing herself behind the door.

Hanna turned and gently pushed Brad back. Her hand lingered over his chest. "Give us a minute," she whispered. Her eyes met his and he understood. Addison took Brad's arm as Hanna squeezed through the opening and closed the door behind her.

Karsen was squatting against the wall, hugging her knees to her chest. Hanna knelt beside her. She could see terror in Karsen's eyes.

"There's blood," Karsen sniveled. "I'm bleeding. The baby..."

Dumbstruck, Hanna thought for a moment.

"How bad is it?"

"I don't know. It's not heavy, but I don't think it's normal. You're not supposed to bleed when you're pregnant, right? Oh no, Hanna. What do I do?"

"Does it hurt?"

"No, a little crampy maybe, I don't know. What's any of this supposed to feel like?" She looked at Hanna. She was tired of hurting, tired of crying. Her eyes pleaded for answers. "I'm scared."

"I know." Hanna wrapped her arms around her shoulders and held her. "I know. Let's get you to a doctor."

~ 28 ~

Twenty minutes ticked by as Karsen, Hanna, Brad and Addison sat in the plush waiting room that resembled more of an upscale spa than a medical office. A faint vanilla scent filled the air. The office differed greatly from the bleak free-clinic waiting area filled with brochures on STDs and pregnancy options on the campus back in Tempe. The only brochure here was on three-dimensional ultrasounds that allowed parents to view and gather photos of their unborn children. The atmosphere made family life seem uncomplicated, as Karsen had once thought it was.

She curled her legs underneath her on the chair, leaned her arms onto the arm of the chair and buried her head into them. She felt for the charm around her neck and pressed it against her heart. *Please let my baby be okay,* she prayed, trying to stay calm.

Brad thumbed through a magazine on motherhood, baffled by the arsenal of products advertised for babies.

"What's this?" he asked Hanna in a quiet voice, pointing to a picture of two clear, plastic cones with handles attached to bottles.

"It's a breast pump," Hanna whispered. Brad burst out laughing.

"SHHH!" Hanna raised her finger to her lips like a mother would to hush a child.

"Does it make them bigger?" He raised his eyebrows curiously.

"No!"

"Too bad."

"It's for pumping milk."

"Like milking a cow? Moooo."

"Hush!" She elbowed him in his rib.

"Ouch!" He pulled away. "That hurt. Can you kiss it?"

"No. You don't get kisses for injuries you deserve."

"Oh, come on. You never know when I might need to know about these things."

Hanna's eyes gleamed. Was he insinuating that he might need to know these things if they had children together someday? She had never been one to daydream about romantic futures, but everything about him captivated her. She reached over and wove her fingers into his.

A petite, blond girl in blue scrubs appeared in the doorway. "Karsen Woods?" she called in a light, wispy voice. Addison reached over and helped her to her feet. "I'll go with you, if that's okay?" she asked.

Karsen nodded.

When they entered the exam room, the nurse instructed Karsen to undress and handed her a paper sheet to drape over her legs. As she did, Addison glanced through a pamphlet to give her some privacy. When she was settled, Addison came and stood beside the table. She rested the palm of her hand on Karsen's forehead, like a mother feeling for a temperature.

"You should have told me." she said, her expression concerned.

"I didn't want you to think I came to find you for a handout," Karsen said apologetically.

"What makes you think I would have thought that?"

Karsen shrugged. She felt as though every decision she'd made recently, even with the best of intentions, had turned out horribly wrong. "Besides, before I came to New York, I'd decided I wasn't going to have the baby. But…"

Karsen felt ashamed. The last thing she wanted to admit to Addison was that she intended to terminate the pregnancy.

"Oh," Addison said a bit confused.

"…but now, I don't know. I see you and the life you have and imagine if my mom hadn't had you. That's why I had to come here. I had to meet you, talk to you. And now that I have, I don't think I could not have this baby. Even if I put it up for adoption, isn't their life worth living? The thought of losing this baby…"

Addison squeezed her newfound sister's hand. She finally under-stood Karsen's urgency for wanting to meet her. She had a choice to make. Now, no matter what she decided, Addison felt she had to live with it, too.

"Why don't we see what the doctor has to say? There's no need to worry until then."

The minutes crept past as they waited. Karsen fidgeted, flipping restlessly through an issue of *Home & Gardens*. Addison sat, legs crossed staring blankly at a "Stages of Pregnancy" chart on the wall. In forty-eight hours her life had turned upside down. She wanted to help Karsen, but how? Only yesterday she felt as though she had all the answers, the omnipotent author of her own destiny. She had never imagined the powerlessness she felt now.

There was a light knock on the door.

"Hi, Karsen. I'm Dr. Gallegos," she introduced herself as she entered the room and approached Karsen. "How are you doing?" she asked, flipping through Karsen's file.

"I don't know."

Dr. Gallegos smiled reassuringly, then turned to greet Addison.

"Hello, Addy. It's good to see you." Clearly, the two women knew each other, although Dr. Gallegos didn't pry as to what Addison's connection to Karsen was.

"You, too, Olivia," Addison said. "Thank you for squeezing us in."

The doctor set the file on the counter and focused her attention back to Karsen.

"Karsen, I'm assuming since Addison is in the room you want her here, correct?"

"Yes."

"All right then, lay back, please. So you're experiencing some cramping and bleeding, correct?"

"Yes," replied Karsen, as she reclined per doctor's orders.

"Is the bleeding heavy or light?"

"Light, I guess? Sorry, I'm a bit nervous. I don't really know what is considered light or not."

Dr. Gallegos squeezed her hand.

"It's okay. Try to relax. Anxiety will only stress the fetus more, okay?" Karsen appreciated that she seemed truly concerned, not as if she was sending her through the system like another no-name patient.

"Your chart said you should be coming up on twelve weeks, correct?" Dr. Gallegos pressed gently on Karsen's abdomen, feeling for the size of her uterus.

"I believe so."

"Has anything unusual happened recently? Have you had inter-course? Any strenuous activity, or under any undue stress?"

"Stress..." Karsen glanced at Addison. "Definitely stress."

"Sometimes stress can cause spotting to occur. From what I can feel, everything appears on track. However, I would recommend we do an ultrasound just to take a look. We have one here so you won't have to go anywhere else."

"All right," Karsen agreed apprehensively.

Dr. Gallegos pulled a cart holding the sonogram machine closer to the bed. Another monitor was mounted on the wall so Karsen could watch. Karsen lifted her shirt exposing her bare belly.

"Oh, that's warm!" she giggled nervously.

The glob of clear jelly smeared across her skin as Dr. Gallegos guided the wand around searching for the fetus. The doctor smiled, "Yes, we warm the bottle. It's much more pleasant than ice cold jelly."

"Breathe, Karsen," Addison reminded her.

Karsen tried to relax, but she couldn't. If she miscarried, the decision no longer would be hers. Maybe it would even be for the best, but why then was she desperately and suddenly hoping to see a heartbeat among the fuzzy black and white image on the screen? She turned to Addison.

"I want my baby, Addison! I want to have this baby!" Karsen pleaded.

"I know," Addison grasped her hand and prayed silently to herself, *Please let there be a heartbeat.*

ᕤᕤ

Brad paced in the waiting area. He had already read through every available publication and his patience had worn thin.

"Sit down, honey," coaxed Hanna.

"I can't. They've been back there over an hour. What if Karsen's not okay?"

"She's going to be fine."

"You don't know that."

"And you don't know that she's not. But, I do know wearing a path in the carpet isn't going to help, and quite honestly, you're driving me crazy. Whatever is meant to be always happens anyway."

Logically he knew she was right, but he couldn't help it.

"Brad, sit. Please," she said sternly.

"Fine." He slumped down in the chair beside her.

"She's strong, you know. You don't give her enough credit."

"Probably not. I just… I just can't let anything else happen to this family."

"At some point, you have to take care of yourself. What happens when you have a family? I mean, what happens if we have a family… someday? Are you still going to be saving Karsen?"

The words came out before she realized what she was starting. She saw anger cross his face. The scowl lines deepened in his forehead and his lips pursed. She hadn't intended to initiate a serious conversation. She just needed to know he'd put her first someday.

"I'm sorry." She tried to retract her statement before he could speak.

"That's not fair."

"I said I'm sorry." She regretted broaching the topic at all. He turned to face her, but she looked only at the floor. Her last intention was to start their first fight, and in public, no less.

He knelt down in front of her and leaned in.

"It's not fair that you compare Karsen to you. Karsen is my sister. We've always been close. But you…"

He paused. "Look at me."

She raised her eyes to meet his.

"I love YOU."

She stared at him in shock. She hadn't expected to hear the word love. They'd been close, intimate even, but neither had actually verbalized the "L" word.

"I want to be with you. I want to have a family with you someday. But right now, she needs me, and I know as her friend you understand that."

"I do know. I'm sorry." She tried to withhold the tears forming in her eyes.

"I love you," he repeated, wiping the tear from her cheek.

"I love you, too."

"You two are going to have to stop being so lovey-dovey all the time."

Addison stood looking down at them. Brad got up and they both smiled sheepishly.

"What's the word?" Brad asked, trying to sound calm and collected.

"Karsen's doing fine," Addison assured him. She knew 'fine' wasn't what he wanted to hear, but the details were not hers to tell. "She'll be out in a minute. I'll let her fill you in."

༄

Karsen finished dressing. She was filled with a newfound hope as she walked down the hallway, smiling at the photos aligning the walls. All infants delivered by Dr. Gallegos. *How lucky they were to have had such a compassionate doctor*, she thought.

Brad and Hanna stood anxiously as Karsen re-entered the waiting room. She embraced Hanna in a warm hug, holding her tight.

"Thanks," she said into her friend's ear as she held her.

"Are you okay?" Hanna asked.

"Yeah, I am now."

"So?" Brad asked, not sure what really he was asking.

Karsen took a step back from Hanna. Her lips pressed together into a peaceful smile as she thought about what to say.

"I'm fine. Dr. Gallegos said I need to start taking it easy."

"Does that mean ...?" Hanna asked expectantly.

"The baby is fine." Karsen's eyes lit up as she took Brad's hands. "I guess it means you're going to be an uncle."

"Seriously?" Brad was taken aback. His focus had always been on Karsen's well-being. Hearing the word "uncle," he realized he'd be more than a big brother now. He had a new role to play. "Are you sure about this?"

She smiled confidently. "Absolutely. I know it won't be easy, but I want to keep the baby."

"Hear that Hanna? You're going to be an auntie," Brad winked at her.

"What about me?" Addison interrupted. "What am I, chopped liver?"

"If it's a girl, you'll be her new best friend, Auntie Addison. After all, she heard you took Adelaide shopping at Barneys. Better have them increase your credit limit."

They all laughed.

"I haven't seen you smile like this in a long time, K." Brad sounded relieved.

"I know." She tilted her head slightly, looking up at him. He pulled her in and squeezed her shoulder in an awkward brother-sister, one-armed hug.

"I hope it's back for good," he said.

"Me, too."

❧ 29 ❧

The ballroom glittered from the crystal balls sparkling against the dimmed lighting. There were immaculately set, circular tables with place cards indicating who would sit where. Lilies rose from slender glass vases surrounded by candles making the air sweet with their scent. Soon the room would spin with two hundred attendees. For now, Addison admired her mother's efforts alone.

"I changed the arrangements at the last minute." Her mom approached her from behind. Addison jumped. "Sorry dear, I didn't mean to startle you."

"They're beautiful, Mom. The whole place looks gorgeous." Addison smiled slightly. Her eyes lacked the twinkle of optimism they usually contained.

"Thank you." Mrs. Reynolds looked at her daughter. "Are you okay?"

"I'm fine," Addison replied, her voice sweet but sad.

"That didn't sound too convincing. What's wrong, dear?"

Addison pulled out a chair and sat. Her mom followed suit, sitting in the adjacent chair facing her.

"For once, Mom, I don't know. Insurance will help rebuild *Urbane*. My newfound brother and sister are fantastic. My friends and family are safe, and Karsen's baby is going to be okay. Everything seems to have worked out, so why do I feel so empty?"

Her mom took a deep breath and exhaled slowly. "Addy," she said softly, "I think it's because you're lonely."

"I'm not lonely," she said defensively. "Especially now. If anything, my family just got bigger."

"But they'll be returning home tomorrow. Brad and Hanna have each other. Karsen will have the baby and what about you? What is fulfilling Addison?"

"I don't know. I'll reestablish *Urbane*."

"Addy," her mom stood looking down at her. Her hand reached and gently tipped her chin up slightly so their eyes met. "I think you know what you want." She paused. "And it's not just *Urbane*." She stroked Addison's cheek; Addison closed her eyes and soaked in her mother's touch.

"You'll figure it out, Addy. You always do. Now, I've got to finish up a few preparations before our guests start arriving. Why don't you go get dressed?"

She kissed Addison's forehead, turned and began walking toward the door.

"Mom?" She waited for her to look back. "Thank you for the lilies."

Her mother smiled pleasantly. She raised her hand to her mouth and blew Addison a kiss.

෭ඁ

"Hanna, look at all the silverware. I'm going to embarrass myself, I know it." Karsen stared at the properly set place settings.

"You'll be fine."

"Have you ever seen anything like this? Makes my prom look like it was held in a barn."

"It was in a barn," Hanna laughed.

Karsen whacked her shoulder with her purse. "Smart ass. You've been hanging around with Brad too much. Think you're a comedian now, do you?"

"Who's been hanging on me? Oh, I mean around..." Brad popped out of nowhere and slid his arms around Hanna's waist from behind. He lowered his face to her neck. "Mmm you smell good."

"Addison bought us a new perfume while we were out shopping. It's called Sexy. You like it?"

"What's not to like?"

"Ick. I can't wait until you two get out of the PDA phase," Karsen teased.

"I second that." Addison approached, her appearance significantly changed from the casual jeans and sweater she'd worn earlier. Her hair was pulled into a loose up-do that flawlessly framed her face. She wore a deep garnet satin gown that plunged deep enough to be tastefully seductive. The girls' mouths dropped noticing the six-carat diamond choker gracing her neck.

"Unbelievable!" Hanna said, feeling as though she was standing next to a movie star on Oscar night.

"Hi, Addy. You do look hot," Brad interjected. "If you weren't my sister..." He was stopped by the sharp jab in his side. "Ouch, Hanna." They all burst out laughing.

Addison touched her necklace. "This may be expensive but..." She reached into her dress and pulled her puzzle necklace out from where it was tucked inside, "...this is priceless."

Karsen pulled Addison into a strong embrace. Addison closed her eyes. It felt open, honest. She couldn't remember when she allowed herself to feel a pure connection such as this. Maybe her emotional walls could be torn down after all.

She opened her eyes and blinked, noticing the man standing just past the ballroom's entrance. His back was facing her, but the familiar silhouette caught her attention. Karsen felt her shudder.

"You okay?" Karsen asked.

Addison pulled back and tucked the charm back in her dress.

"Not sure."

She continued to stare across the room. Karsen turned to see what she was looking at. The man looked toward them. He was dressed in a black tuxedo with a dark gray bow tie and matching vest. A row of black buttons polished off the shirt. Karsen thought for an older man he was devastatingly handsome.

"You know him?" Karsen asked.

"You could say that." Addison recalled the conversation with her mother regarding sending him an invitation. She knew there was a possibility he'd attend. She figured it would be the same old routine as when she ran into any other ex. She had not anticipated her reaction. Her adrenaline soared, constricting her chest and clouding her thoughts. She couldn't decide whether she wanted to stay or flee.

He caught her gaze from across the room. Her face remained blank. He strode toward her. With each step her heart skipped. *Could she let him in? Would he still want her to?*

"Addison," he greeted her, leaning in to kiss her cheek.

"Hello, Russell." She tried to sound indifferent in an effort to evaluate his feelings before she breached any unforeseen boundaries. An uncomfortable tension filled the air as the others looked on.

"You look radiant."

"Thank you."

They both stood silently for a moment.

"Russell, this is my sister, Karsen." Karsen shook his hand. "And this is my brother, Brad, and his girlfriend, Hanna."

"Hi. It's a pleasure to meet you." Brad extended his hand to shake. Russell grabbed it firmly, looking at Addison perplexed.

"Hi." Hanna held her hand up in acknowledgment.

"Perhaps you'd like to get yourself a drink and then maybe we could talk outside?" Addison suggested. He looked at her with a guarded expression that she couldn't read.

"All right. Would you like anything? Glass of merlot perhaps?"

"That would be lovely, Russell. Thank you."

He nodded, then swiveled around and headed to the bar.

"Nice," said Hanna, once Russell was far enough removed from earshot.

"He's hot. Way to go, Addison," Karsen added.

"I'd do him," Brad said. They all looked at him simultaneously. "Just joking of course." He grinned.

"Sorry, Brad, but I think he's already spoken for." Karsen winked at Addison.

Addison's cheeks turned a cherry red.

"I'm not so sure about that," Addison said, trailing off under her breath. "...and I can only blame myself."

Karsen responded at an equally quiet decibel. "Then only you can fix it."

She peered at Karsen.

"He could have any woman he wants. At any rate, he's probably already moved on."

"I think you're wrong," Karsen said.

"Me, too," Hanna declared.

"Really." Addison paused, intrigued at their confidence. "What makes you think that?" For a moment, she couldn't believe she was asking advice from two women almost half her age.

"First of all, he's here alone," Hanna said assuredly. "Second, he beelined his way directly to you and didn't hesitate when you suggested you two talk."

"And lastly," Karsen added, taking the words straight out of Hanna's mouth, "you can see it in his eyes. He's in love with you, Addison."

"Honestly, you really think he's still interested?" Addison asked, genuinely thrown. She couldn't believe she might get a second chance. Not after how she'd behaved.

"Yes!" They retorted in unison. "Now go!"

❧

"I heard about *Urbane.* I'm sorry," Russell said meeting her outside and handing her a large round glass filled with wine. He watched as she swirled the wine like a professional sommelier. She raised it to her lips. The nose of the wine smelled of a sweet harmonious fusion of black cherry and plums. She pursed her lips against the brim and allowed the burgundy liquid to saturate her palate.

"The important thing is that no one was hurt. It could have been a tragedy."

"I'm glad to hear you're keeping it in perspective. I know how much *Urbane* means to you." He sipped his drink, a smooth shot of scotch. He held back telling her how he had come to *Urbane* the day of the fire. How he had wanted to sweep her up into his arms. How he watched from the side lines, not letting her see him.

"I don't know how you drink that straight." She shuddered at the thought of the potent liquid burning her throat.

"Drinking it any other way would ruin it."

They stood beside each other, an awkward silence hanging overhead like a thick storm cloud. Addison watched several couples interspersed across the balcony. She admitted to herself the atmosphere was quite romantic. The sky was striated with wispy clouds. Underneath the muffled voices, the gentle trickle of the waterfall provided a calming hum.

"Addison." He placed his drink on the railing then slid hers from her hand and set it beside his. He took her hand and lifted it slightly more out of an act of compassion than of romance. He met her eyes with his. "Is this what Emily was referring to? I mean, your past...I thought you were an only child." His voice strained as he searched for clarity.

She stood motionless, holding his hand. A sudden familiar urge to conceal the truth, to walk away, swept over her, but she knew running away now would defeat the purpose of initiating this interaction. If there was a chance to rectify their relationship, no matter how small, she had to divulge the truth. She'd been hiding for far too long. Without turning to face him, she nodded. He patiently awaited her explanation.

Addison recounted every detail from the moment she found out she was adopted to the present. He listened intently, allowing her to speak without interruption.

"I'm sorry, Russell, very truly sorry. I know my actions for all these years may have been based on an immature false reality, but to me my feelings were real."

"I had no idea, Addy. I wish you could have trusted me with this."

"I'm sorry," she repeated.

He paused. "Me, too." He squeezed her hand before letting go. "Should we go back inside? They're probably about to serve dinner."

She wanted him to take her into his arms. She wanted him to tell her everything was okay, but her courage failed her. Instead of asking him if there was still a chance, she simply nodded in agreement. Russell turned to leave.

"Russell?" She stopped him. "Before we go in, can I ask you a favor? If it's not possible, I'll understand. But, there is something I thought you might be able to help me with." She explained her proposal.

"Absolutely," he said, managing a cordial smile. "I'll see what I can do."

 ∽

"Soooo?" Karsen asked as Addison took the seat next to her at the table. Addison forced the corners of her mouth into a slight grin and shook her head, not wanting to cry in front of everyone. Both surprised and disappointed, Karsen scanned the room for Russell. He had taken his seat and she could see that he'd entered into a conversation with the elderly couple sitting at his table. She couldn't help but continue to watch him. *Give me a sign. Any sign.* Just then he looked their way and, noticing her attention, tipped his glass toward Karsen. *He is still interested!* she thought with a satisfied smile.

After dinner, Karsen fashioned her own agenda. Excusing herself from the table, she walked across the room.

"Would you like to dance?" Karsen placed her hand on Russell's shoulder. Her boldness surprised even her.

"Certainly." He placed the napkin from his lap onto his plate and walked beside her to the dance floor. "It's Karsen, right?" He remembered from their brief introduction.

"Yes."

"Karsen is a unique name. Very pretty, I like it."

"Thank you." She faced him, suddenly struck with the thought that her dancing skills consisted of holding her boyfriend's neck while swaying back and forth, hardly the waltz. He grasped her hand lightly keeping a comfortably platonic distance as if she were his daughter. She placed the opposite hand upon his shoulder and felt a trace of relief as he began to lead.

"So, I'm guessing there is something on your mind other than dancing," he said as he slowly whirled her around the floor.

"That obvious, huh?"

"Well, you're half my age and from what I've been told, you're expecting, so I'm guessing you're not after a one night stand."

She smiled. "No. I've had enough of men for awhile."

"I see."

"Addison, on the other hand…"

"Ah ha. That's what this is about. I figured as much. Are we in fifth grade again?"

Karsen looked at him intently. "She didn't send me. Just to be clear."

"I know. She never would. Too stubborn."

The fine lines around his eyes wrinkled as he smiled. His look was rugged but distinguished, like a model in an outdoor clothing catalogue. Karsen could see why Addison was attracted to him.

"She's in love with you."

"Did she tell you that?"

"Well, not exactly. But she is." Karsen contemplated what to say next. "You're in love with her, too."

A faint smile crossed his lips and Karsen noticed how it appeared slightly crooked, a slight imperfection which oddly made him more attractive. The same trait Addison loved. "And what makes you think that? You've known me for all of an hour."

"You've made one hell of an impression." She giggled. "But seriously. I just want her to be happy."

"As do I. And for the record, she pushed me away."

The song drew to an end. The beginning of "Let's Twist Again" transitioned the dance floor to a faster tempo. They stopped dancing and stood for an awkward moment staring at each other.

"She only pushed you away because she was afraid. Russell, you can't let her go. Please, you have to talk to her."

"Thank you for the dance, Karsen."

His voice when he spoke had a hard edge. Karsen cringed as she felt an unyielding stab of defeat. She scrutinized his face one last time. The smile he forced was unconvincing and his weathered skin tightened around his brow. The spark in his eyes contradicted his voice. Instead, he seemed sad. He kissed her hand without another word and walked off the floor.

Across the room, Addison turned and caught a glimpse of Russell just as he exited. She wanted to run after him, but her feet wouldn't move. She couldn't find the courage. Her heart ached as she let her second chance walk away.

∞

Karsen left the ballroom in search of Addison. She found her secluded, nestled in the furthest corner of the patio by the fire pit. The structure was impressive, surrounded by hand stacked stone. Two oversized wrought iron patio chairs and one loveseat faced the fire. Addison sipped her wine and allowed the soft crackles of the fire soothe her.

"Care for company?" Karsen interrupted the silence.

Addison glanced over her shoulder and shrugged. "Sure."

Karsen squeezed in next to her on the small couch. "I talked to Russell. I don't know if he's going to come around."

"You shouldn't have done that."

"I know, but that's what sisters do, right?" Karsen paused. "I'm sorry if it seems childish. I just wanted to help."

Addison laid her head on Karsen's shoulder. They sat together quietly, soaking in the fire's warmth.

"Thank you for tonight, Addison." Karsen said. "I feel like Cinderella at the ball. Although, I hope I don't lose one of my new Prada shoes." She giggled. "Think I'll still be able to wear them when I'm fat and swollen being prego in a hundred and ten degree heat?"

Addison finally smiled. "You might want to put them away until after the baby arrives."

"Will you come visit? I mean, when the baby comes?"

"I'd love to. I love Arizona. The Aji spa is my absolute favorite. Maybe I can treat you to a postpartum retreat."

"Sounds wonderful, but I'm not sure I'll be living in Arizona once the baby arrives. I'll probably have to move back in with my dad and I don't know what spas are like in Middlebury, Indiana. There's a great Amish restaurant that has pies that are to die for, though."

"Mmmm. I love pie. Do I get the whole pie or just a piece?"

"I'll take one piece, you can have the rest. How's that for sharing?"

Addison straightened up. She pulled the clip securing her hair and allowed it to flow down gracefully over her shoulders. The night was ending. Russell had departed without saying goodbye. There was little reason to remain all gussied up.

"Karsen?"

"Yeah?"

Addison's face lit up. "Why not come to New York?"

"New York?" Karsen repeated, a bit surprised. "I couldn't afford to live here. I figure I can live with Dad and get a job locally. Maybe take some classes if I can fit them in. I want to finish school, someday at least."

"Taking money out of the equation, what would you do?" Addison asked.

"I don't know. Finish school for sure. Then find a job that would support the baby and me."

"You're degree is in communications, right?"

"It will be."

Addison paused. Karsen had answered her questions unaware of where precisely she was going.

"What if you came and lived with me?"

"What?"

"You can finish school at NYU, or Berkeley for that matter, and work for *Urbane*. I have more than enough room for you and the baby, and with my help you'll be more flexible with time, or I can pay for a nanny if needed."

Karsen stared in disbelief at Addison. Had she heard right?

"Addison, I appreciate the gesture…you don't know how much I do, but I could never impose on you like that."

"Nonsense. You wouldn't be. I'm going to need all the help I can find to get *Urbane* back up and running. And, I want to be a part of my niece or nephew's life. It's win-win."

"Really?"

"Really, Karsen, I know rationally moving across the country to live with someone you've just met may seem foolish, and me, of all people. Typically I never act in such an illogical manner. If anyone asked me last week if I'd be considering this, I would tell them that they were insane. But, it feels right. Let me help you. What do you say?"

Karsen sat contemplating, her face momentarily void of emotion. She looked steadily at Addison, waiting for her to waiver, to change her mind. She released a breath, half sigh, half laugh as a smile perked across her lips.

"I can't believe I'm saying this, but let's do it. I'm going to move to New York!"

∽ **30** ∽

The next morning Karsen bounded out of bed. The dark cloud she'd had hovering above her the last few months had lifted. Within her brewed a sensation that she hadn't felt for a long time. Hope. She looked in the mirror and smiled. *Thank you, Mom. I know you'd be here if you could. Maybe there is a reason for all of this after all.*

"Hey, sunshine," Brad called from the porch.

"Good morning!" Karsen grabbed a glass from the cupboard and poured herself some orange juice before joining him. "Coffee smells wonderful. Drink some for me, would ya?"

"I'll buy you a stash of decaf when we get back to Arizona."

"Can you make it a small stash?"

"Why's that?"

"Don't freak out, okay?"

"Uh-oh. Here we go again. What's up now, Karsen?" *What could she possibly be thinking?* He thought, though he noted a happy note to her voice that had been absent for far too long.

"Addison asked me to move to New York."

"What?"

"Before you get your feathers all ruffled, hear me out. The semester is over in four weeks. I can finish my classes then transfer here for the fall. Addison offered me a position at *Urbane*. That would have been a dream job for me before. Do you know how hard it is to get hired by a major publication? The experience alone is priceless."

Brad understood the appeal. "But what about the baby? I'm not going to be close enough to help if you need it."

"Brad. I love you and I appreciate everything you do for me. I do. But I need to stand on my own two feet. I can do this. I can help Addison rebuild *Urbane*. I can finish my degree and raise this child. I'm not expecting it to be an easy road. But sometimes you have to choose the path less taken, right?"

He set his coffee down on the table. His fingers intertwined and he lifted his hands in thought to his lips. He struggled to find the right words to say. He knew she was strong enough to succeed. Protecting her had become part of his own identity, but deep down he knew she was right. He needed to let it go.

"Karsen?"

"Yes?" she said tentatively, awaiting his response. Her mind was made up no matter what he thought, still she longed for his approval.

"I'm proud of you."

∾

The late risers eventually staggered down one after another, muttering groggy but cordial greetings until their first cup of coffee kicked in. Addison's parents arranged an elaborate spread of food, putting the buffets at most five-star resorts to shame. Everyone gathered around the kitchen table.

"Thank you so much for having us," Karsen said to Mrs. Reynolds.

"I hear you'll be returning," she said smiling.

Karsen couldn't help the grin that stretched across her face. "Yes. In a month."

"I'm glad. Come by anytime."

Addison finished a bite of eggs benedict and reminded the group that they needed to be packed and ready to go in one hour. She'd arranged for her corporate jet to fly them back to Arizona. They joked about how it wouldn't take long to get ready since all of them had traveled so light. Through the chatter, they heard the doorbell ring.

"I'll get it," Addison's mother said, rising from her seat. She entered the foyer and opened the front door.

"Is Addison available?" a male voice asked. The voice sounded oddly familiar to Karsen.

"Certainly. Please come in."

He wiped his feet on the doormat before he entered then followed Mrs. Reynolds down the hall into the kitchen.

"Hello, Jacob. What are you doing here?" Addison asked with a bewildered expression.

Jacob lifted his laptop bag off of his shoulder and placed it on the table, all eyes following his movements in amused anticipation.

"Work, what else?" He grinned with pride. "I've got this month's issue of *Urbane* proofed, formatted and ready to go. Luckily, I had saved a copy on my laptop and grabbed it before I left. At any rate, Brandson Publishing has offered to lend their services. We can have the issue printed and on shelves in only a week past its usual publication date."

"Are you serious?" Addison asked in amazement.

"Absolutely. I just need your approval."

"Wow!" she screamed. "You are unbelievable! I can't thank you enough!" She scrambled to her feet and threw her arms around Jacob, knocking him off balance.

"He probably deserves a raise," Brad chimed in.

"I'll see what I can do about that." Addison bounced up and down more like a schoolgirl than an executive. She could hardly contain her excitement.

Pride radiated from Jacob's face, his eyes twinkled as he laughed.

"Just doing my job," he winked.

"Well then, you've certainly impressed the boss." Addison smiled then turned back toward the table. "While you're here, let me introduce you to everyone. This is my mother, Annabelle, and my father, Bryce."

Bryce stood and shook Jacob's hand. Jacob's face glazed over in a starstruck kind of way.

"It's a pleasure to meet you, Mr. Reynolds."

"The pleasure is all mine. You've certainly worked a miracle for my...," he paused, "my daughter's magazine," he corrected himself with a nod to Addison.

"And this is my brother, Brad, and his girlfriend, Hanna," Addison continued the introductions.

"Hi. Nice to meet you," Jacob said.

"And hiding behind the centerpiece is my sister, Karsen. She's going to start working with us next month."

Jacob leaned sideways to look at Karsen.

"You?" he said incredulously. He suddenly realized why she had looked familiar.

"Guilty as charged," she said, blushing.

"You two know each other?" Addison asked inquisitively, noticing the gleam in Jacob's eyes.

"We spent the night together," Jacob said.

"In Starbucks!" Karsen interjected. Jacob laughed, impressed with himself.

"In Starbucks," he reiterated. He glanced down at his watch. "Oh, I should get going. I'm supposed to be at my niece's birthday party by ten."

He turned to Addison, his voice returning to a down-to-business tone. "Can you get the revisions back to me by this afternoon? Also, there is space for lease in the building next door. Here's the number if you're interested. Might buy some time until you can find a new permanent location." He handed Addison a piece of paper with the realtor's contact information.

"I'll get with you about that raise," she said, hugging him goodbye.

"It was nice to meet all of you." Jacob waved and headed toward the front door.

"Wait!" Karsen called. "I'll walk you out." She rounded the table and caught up with him.

"I didn't realize you knew Addison," he said, a thousand questions swirling through his head.

"At the time, I didn't. It's kind of a long story."

"Interesting…I can't wait to hear it. Sooo, would you want to meet back at Starbucks sometime?"

She hesitated. "I would, but…"

"There is always a 'but,'" he joked. Inside he felt insecure, as though she were out of his league.

"But for one, I'm headed back to Arizona this afternoon…and two, there is something I need to tell you. And…and it may change your mind."

"Really, what's that?" He couldn't think of anything that would change his mind about a date with an attractive girl.

"I'm pregnant."

"Oh." He looked startled.

"Guess you weren't expecting that." She crisscrossed her arms across her chest, hands on her shoulders, chin on her arm as if to console herself in an embrace.

"Not exactly."

"Yeah, I kind of figured. It looks like I'm going to be a single parent, but as soon as this semester ends I'm moving here to live with Addison. She's going to help me finish school."

They both stood shuffling their feet and stared at the ground, wondering what to say next.

"How about you tell me the story over coffee when you get back in town. If nothing else, you could use a friend, right?" Jacob said hopefully.

"That would be lovely." She looked up into his eyes and smiled, still hugging herself. He smiled back.

"Well then. I'll see you in a few weeks." He bounded over the patio step and down the walk then opened the car door. She turned to go into the house. "Karsen?"

"Yes?" She turned back.

"Have I told you that I love kids?" He didn't wait for her to reply. Instead he quickly ducked into the car and shut the door. She watched him drive away and felt her heart suddenly pound against her chest. She didn't know whether it was right or wrong to feel this way in her condition, but at the very least she knew her future held promise.

ᖚ

"I can't believe we're flying on a private jet!" Hanna all but skipped toward the tarmac. A large white jet, shiny from a recent wash, stood in front of them with steps pushed up to the door for them to board. The sky was clear, dotted only with a few scattered clouds, and the sun sparkled down giving the blacktop a sleek shine.

"The flight should be around four hours. There are drinks and snacks on board. Help yourself to anything. Just try not to drink the alcohol dry," Addison chuckled.

ᖚ

At the bottom of the jet's stairs, Addison turned to face her three new friends, her new family.

"Well, I guess this is where we say goodbye." She'd never understood why people struggled with farewells, until now. Addison hugged Hanna tightly. "Please come and visit anytime. It's been a pleasure meeting you."

"You, too," Hanna said. "Thank you for everything."

"Brad." She turned and hugged him as well. "This is your home now, too. Don't be a stranger."

"I won't be," he replied, returning the hug. "I'm turning her over to you now. It's a tough job," he joked.

"I think I can handle it." Addison winked at Karsen.

Hanna and Brad climbed the steps and disappeared into the plane. Karsen stood below with Addison taking a moment for her own goodbye.

"Wait!" A voice bellowed from behind. Both Addison and Karsen spun around to look.

"Stop!" The two women stood dazed as Russell ran toward the plane, waving his hand in the air. He caught up to them and looked at Addison.

"Hi," he said, catching his breath.

"What are you doing here?" she asked, bewildered yet excited by his unexpected arrival.

"Your favor," he grinned.

"How'd you know where I was?"

"I stopped by your parents' house first. Your mom told me. Where's Brad?"

"Brad, come back here, please," she yelled up the steps.

Brad peered curiously through the doorway of the jet.

Russell looked up at him and spoke. "Brad, before you go, I can't promise you anything, but I spoke to Sam Cadence."

Brad's mind raced as he jogged back down the steps. *Sam Cadence? The producer for The Funniest Comic?*

"I explained to him why you withdrew and he's willing to allow you to audition again. It doesn't guarantee you a spot on the show, but from what I hear you can hold your own."

"How did you know about that?" Brad asked, his face showing his shock.

Russell held out a piece of paper. Brad grasped it and glanced down. Handwritten in black ink was Sam Cadence's name and cell phone number.

"Addison told me. I hope you don't mind."

Brad looked up from the paper. "Mind? This is incredible! Thank you," he whooped, calling for Hanna, who appeared at the top of the stairs. "We're going to Hollywood, baby!"

"OMG!" Hanna screamed, racing down the steps. She grabbed his hand and started jumping up and down. "Brad! You're back in?"

"Can you believe it?" He picked her up and swung her around. "WHOOO HOOOO!" he screamed as she snuggled her face into his shoulder.

Addison caught Russell's attention.

"Thank you," she said softly.

He winked at her. Her heart skipped with a faint flicker of hope.

Brad set Hanna down and shook Russell's hand.

"Good luck. I had to pull some strings for this," said Russell warmly. "Don't let me down."

"I won't," Brad promised. Grabbing Hanna's hand, they gave Addison another quick hug goodbye and headed back up into the plane. Before Karsen could follow, Russell turned his attention to her.

"Karsen. You're more like your sister than you know. Strong, beautiful and hard-headed."

"I know," she smiled.

"I hope I get to know you even better. Thank you," he said with a wink. *Why was he thanking her*, she wondered. It immediately became clear.

Turning to Addison, Russell slowly took her hands in his and asked, "Can we go home now?"

A tear trickled out of the corner of her eye. He held her face between his broad, strong hands and kissed her.

"Yes!" Karsen yelped out loud. "Oops! Sorry." She giggled, covering her mouth with her hand.

Russell and Addison didn't seem to notice. Reluctantly, he pulled his lips from hers, their noses almost touching. "Well?"

She looked deep into his eyes and for the first time, without hesitation, she said what she had felt for so long now. "Yes, Russell. Yes. Yes. Yes. I love you. Let's go home." He told her he loved her and then kissed her again.

Addison walked back to Karsen for one last hug goodbye.

"See you in a month."

"You still want me to come?" Karsen whispered. Perhaps she'd change her mind with Russell back in the picture.

"See you in a month," Addison repeated.

Karsen smiled, climbed the steps, turned one last time and waved as the door closed. She watched from the window as Russell and Addison walked hand and hand back to the terminal.

Epilogue

Karsen lifted her hand to knock on the door. The porch she stood on was painted white and a fall colored wreath hung from the evergreen door. She glanced back at Addison, who sat waiting in the car. She took a deep breath, closed her eyes and felt the wood against her knuckles as she tapped against it. Anxiously she waited.

The door opened and he stood before her. His face seemed to have aged since the first time they met. A combination of stress and guilt had taken its toll. He knew who she was, but did not know why she was there standing in front of him.

"Hello," he said tentatively.

"Matt?"

"Yes."

"I'm Karsen Woods."

He stared at her a moment. "I know." He waited in anticipation. There had been no formal punishment as texting was not yet banned in Indiana, but he continued to punish himself.

"I just wanted to say...," Karsen started. She felt it in her heart, but still the words did not come easily, "...that I forgive you."

His lower lip trembled and his eyes welled with tears. He stood speechless.

"If my mom were here, she'd forgive you, too."

"Thank you." he mustered, blotting his eye with the back of his hand. He didn't smile, he simply cried. "Thank you." His voice rasped.

She nodded and returned to the car. There was nothing left to say.

Karsen slid into the passenger side seat, buckled her seat belt and turned to look into the back seat. She reached across the console and tugged at the car seat straps, making sure they were secure.

"Next stop, Grandma," she spoke to the tiny infant sleeping contently.

"Ready?" Addison asked before putting the car in gear. Karsen nodded.

⌒

Addison pulled the car onto the shoulder of the narrow road and parked so that other vehicles had room to pass. There was a faint dusting of snow on the ground and the remaining leaves on the trees were hues of orange and red. She opened the trunk to retrieve the floral arrangements they'd purchased while Karsen crawled in the backseat to take out the infant carrier. They walked together across the grass. Karsen directed her to the gravesite. Addison's arms overflowed with flowers for the vases secured on both its sides.

Karsen set the car seat facing the headstone.

"Hi, Mom." She knelt next to her daughter and adjusted her blanket to keep her bundled. "I'd like you to meet your granddaughter. Her name is Katherine Addison Woods after the two women who've influenced me the most. We call her Kaddy for short."

Addison listened as she arranged the flowers.

"She smiled for the first time this week and it looked just like yours," continued Karsen. "Addison's here, too. You know, Lily. We both understand you had your reasons for keeping your secret. Maybe this was the way it was supposed to be. We miss you though."

She glanced at Addison.

"And we both love you."

She stood back up, kissed her hand and touched it lovingly to the headstone.

"We should get going," she said to Addison. "Dad will have a conniption if we're late for Thanksgiving dinner."

"It's never good to keep men waiting," agreed Addison. She had learned that lesson well. She adjusted one last flower then touched the headstone herself. "I wish we could have met," she whispered. "Karsen." Addison reached into her pocket. "Maybe this is an awkward place to give a gift, but I wanted to do it where Mom could be here, too."

She pressed a small, jewelry box into Karsen's palm. Karsen tucked the box under her arm and removed her gloves to open it. She pulled out a petite silver chain. On the end dangled a puzzle piece charm.

"I had it made by the same jeweler, so it should match up," Addison said. "Mr. Milton was amazed to say the least. So, what do you think?"

Karsen held the charm up to hers then focused on Addison through teary eyes.

"It's perfect."

www.ingramcontent.com/pod-product-compliance
Lightning Source LLC
Chambersburg PA
CBHW071456170626
46811CB00007B/2601